MORE THAN FAMILY

WATCHDOG SECURITY SERIES: BOOK 2

OLIVIA MICHAELS

Olivia Michaels

FALCON IN HAND PUBLISHING

Created with Vellum

ONE

So far, so good. But one false move and she's going to die, Camden Bains thought as he watched the teenaged pop star totter on her six-inch platforms through the gamut of fans, photographers—and one as-yet-unidentified killer.

Has Kyle spotted him yet? Camden studied every move the rookie bodyguard made as he escorted Caley from the awards ceremony to the black Tahoe belonging to Watchdog Security. The cameras flashed like blinding strobe lights in a nightclub, the fans screamed and reached for Caley like a multi-armed monster as Kyle blocked the vulnerable teenager from their reach. He'd been smart enough to wear shades that would help with the flashes and keep anyone from seeing his eyes scan the crowd.

They only had twenty feet to go but the crowd was hungry and aggressive, blocking their way and Caley was not helping. She did everything she could to give them the smiles, autographs, and attention they craved and that she thrived on. Kyle had little patience for it, putting his hand on the small of her back to push her along. Caley looked up at him with the supreme annoyance only a teen can pull off.

Come on, Kyle. Spot him. Stop him. And stop pissing off the principal while you're doing it.

A burly photographer pushed his way past a couple of skinny teens in hoodies and thrust his camera at Caley's face. *The killer?* Kyle started to shove Caley behind him and then his attention snapped immediately to one of the teens who'd gone strangely still.

"Get down, you idiot, don't make me say it again!" Kyle shouted as he pushed Caley to the ground.

"No!" Camden shouted as everything went sideways. He jumped down from his observation post and set off at a sprint.

Kyle elbowed the cameraman in the gut as he reached for the young man's hand, which had just disappeared into the front pocket of his hoodie. "I love you forever, Caley!" the kid shouted, but Kyle was faster as he twisted the gun out of the would-be assassin's grip.

Kyle held the gun aloft as the crowd went quiet. "Did it," he shouted when he spotted Camden making his way through the sea of people.

"Yeah, you did it all right," Camden said, his blood boiling with anger and frustration. "You okay, Caley?" he asked as he pulled the stand-in principal up from the hard pavement.

"Yeah, yeah, but I coulda done without the attitude." Caley shook her head at her would-be bodyguard as she pulled off her long wig, revealing herself as a twenty-something woman. "That won't win you any points," she added as she brushed dust off her skirt.

"How 'bout you, Freddie?" Camden looked down at his co-worker in the hoodie as Kyle gave him a hand up.

"I'm fine. This dude is *fast*," Freddie said as he took the plastic, orange-tipped gun back from a dejected-looking Kyle. "Gotta give him that."

"Camden, what'd I do wrong?" the rookie pleaded as the rest of the crowd of actors dispersed, some off to vape, others back into Watchdog Security's headquarters. "I neutralized the threat and protected the principal."

Camden sighed. "Meet me and Lachlan in the briefing room in five."

***

F *ive whole weeks.*

That's how long it had been since Jake and Rachael's wedding, but for their best man Camden Bains, it felt more like five years since he'd seen Elena Martinez in her little black maid of honor dress. Danced with her at the reception. Smelled the sweet vanilla and peppermint scent of her hair as he held her close.

Camden shook his head, trying to clear his mind and focus on the task at hand, which was helping his boss, Lachlan, straighten out Kyle.

Lachlan had the kid seated in the conference room. To Kyle's credit, he didn't look or act petulant, not something Camden necessarily expected, considering the kid was former military like most of Watchdog Security's staff, but it wasn't out of the realm of possibilities given the crap job he'd just done. The kid sat ramrod straight, kept a neutral expression, didn't fidget or clench his jaw while their boss paced back and forth lecturing him.

"Look," Lachlan said, "We've all been there, Kyle. Civilians can be a real pain in the ass. Unpredictable. Especially under a threat."

"Sir—"

Lachlan raised a hand and that was enough to stop him. "You'll get your chance to talk. This isn't a court-martial." He glanced at Camden, "It's a teachable moment."

Leaning against the wall in the corner, Camden rubbed his mouth to hide his smile. He wasn't there so much to intimidate Kyle but to remind Lachlan that, yes, it really wasn't a court-martial. The way Lachlan had snorted earlier when Camden used the phrase 'teachable moment' compared to the way the words rolled so naturally off his boss's tongue just now, struck Camden as hilarious. *Old dogs can learn new tricks*, he thought.

"Watchdog has a reputation to build. We're new as a company, but we're not wet behind the ears individually. Each of us has the training and the experience to pick out a threat and neutralize it, keeping our clients safe, and without collateral damage. That's what they expect. That's what they hire us for, why they trust us military guys over some civ asshole who watched *The Bodyguard* as a young-dumb-and-full-of-come teenager and thinks he knows what he's doing."

"I love that movie," Camden interjected.

"So do I, actually," Kyle said, his face momentarily brightening before he remembered where he was. "Sir."

Lachlan stopped pacing and shot Camden a look that said, *whose side are you on?* He turned back to Kyle. "Yeah, Whitney Houston was a tragic goddess. So, why would you yell at a tragic goddess, Kyle?"

"To keep her safe, sir." The look in the kid's eye told Camden he knew he was headed into a minefield.

Lachlan clasped his hands behind his back as he paced again. "To keep her safe," he echoed. At forty-four, with silver just creeping into the dark auburn hair over his ears, Lachlan reminded Camden of a college professor giving a lecture, though most professors Camden had known didn't have the ready-for-active-duty physique his boss possessed, but more of a ready-for-active-Netflix-watching dad-bod.

Lachlan got to the end of the room and turned on his heel. "Don't you think a simple command of, 'get down' would suffice?"

"It depends?" Kyle's voice held the slightest questioning tone.

Not good, kid, Camden thought. *You're giving my man fresh meat.*

"So you think a six-foot-four marine bodyguard telling a five-foot-two teen megastar in six-inch heels who's surrounded by crazed fans to 'get down' isn't enough to make her comply?"

"Well—"

"You think he needs to shout, and I quote, 'Get down, you idiot, don't make me say it again,' to get through to her?"

"Sir, I—"

"I've had principals ask for a different bodyguard just because the one assigned to them didn't match their outfit that day. You think one's gonna put up with being called a fucking idiot?"

"Teenagers can be defiant, sir, so I was just—"

Lachlan stopped pacing right in front of Kyle. Camden watched the blood rise in his boss's neck to his face.

Now we're getting to it, Camden thought. He practically beamed the words 'teachable moment' at his boss's cranium. As if Lachlan had caught the thought, he took a deep breath and his color faded back to normal.

"Did she show you defiance right then?"

"No, sir."

"What about before, when you met her and discussed and defined the parameters of the job?"

"Not then, either, sir." Kyle couldn't hold Lachlan's gaze so he looked at the polished surface of the table instead.

"This isn't the sandbox, Kyle. These aren't people whose town's been overrun by insurgents who were then beaten back and held at bay by us. We didn't needlessly push those civilians around, either, once we'd cleared their town. We won hearts and minds. Our clients are used to a high level of respect and deference from everyone around them at all times. Often, their biggest worry is that they got soy instead of oat milk in their twenty-dollar smoothie. But not always. They don't appreciate being reminded that they aren't always in control, and that very bad things can happen to them. A death threat is a death threat, no matter who you are and what you've been through. When you yell at them as you did with our actress today, it disrespects them. It panics them and it makes you look panicky, too. Worst of all, it makes Watchdog look like a joke."

"That was not my intent, sir. I apologize."

"I don't need a fucking apology, kid. I need you to get it right next time. Think you can do that?"

Dude thought he was about to get shitcanned, Camden thought as Kyle's face brightened. "Sir, yes, sir."

"Enough with the sir, yes, sir. You're dismissed. But I want you to review the video on talking to clients. The web address is in your handbook. You're gonna run through this scenario until you get it right. Win hearts and minds, just the same as Iraq and Afghanistan."

"Got it. Thanks." Kyle practically burned a trail behind him as he set a land speed record exiting the conference room.

Lachlan rubbed his face. "Damn kids these days. I feel more like a school principal than anything else."

Camden laughed at his boss.

"What?" Lachlan glared at him.

Camden pushed off from the wall and walked to the conference table. "I was just thinking you looked like an old-fart professor."

"Fuck you. I'm not getting older, they're getting younger."

"If you say so. He's not *that* young, just looks it." The men took a seat across from each other as Camden continued. "The Pup did good otherwise. Fast reflexes and good instincts. And he's exceptional with our K9 unit and service training. I like him."

"Yeah, he did all right," Lachlan growled. "Killer reflexes and cool except for his mouth. I like him, too. But the truth is, he's better with the dogs than with our clients in need of bodyguards so I'd like to keep him training the dogs. It's why I hired him, that's his wheelhouse, he was a dog handler in the military. Don't know why he thinks he needs to prove himself as a bodyguard. I think you can still shape him into what I want. Keep him training the dogs. Gonna take a while till I trust him out there, if ever."

"What about me?" Camden asked.

"What about you?" Lachlan smiled, cat-toying-with-a-mouse style.

"When do I get to play out there?" Camden stretched and cracked his neck.

"I kinda like you where you are. You're good at training the FNGs. You know the clientele—how they think, how they act, what they expect—so you know how to act around them. And except for Kyle, that training's sunk into the new hires." Lachlan smirked. "And you're good with keeping this old dog in line, dammit."

"Thanks, boss. But, Lach, I've been here the better part of a year, brother. I'm thankful for the job, don't get me wrong, and for you hiring Jake right outta the FBI along with me."

"I should be thanking you for him, brother. He's a damn good profiler, just like you're a damn good trainer."

Camden leaned forward. "And there's the difference. Jake fucking loves where he's at. Me, I wanna get back out there."

"Really? I had no idea." Lachlan reached down to his briefcase under the table.

"Come on, Lach, stop yanking my dick."

"How's this then?" Lachlan dropped a folder on the table and pushed it toward Camden. "That gonna yank it all better?"

Camden opened the folder. On top was an eight-by-ten photo of Roger Bennett, TV actor and now an up-and-coming politician since he turned his platform toward promoting various social causes near and dear to Californians. Thing was, he appealed to people from all walks of life, something so very needed at such a politicized time. Bennett was damn near a miracle-worker in Camden's opinion. Even though he was looking at a run at the House of Representatives, he had the support of California's favorite senator, Rock Higley.

Camden looked up at his boss as he broke into a grin. "You saying I get to watch this dude?"

"You and the team you pick." Lachlan tilted his chair back. "If you choose to accept."

"I choose to accept."

Lachlan lifted his hand, palm out. "Don't be so quick. Keep reading. There's a wrinkle."

"What's that? Somebody threaten him already? The guy's universally loved."

"Just read."

Camden flipped over the photo to read the first page of the profile—compiled, he noticed, by Jake. It even resembled the reports they used to get with the Bureau. The profile started with the usual background info on Bennett. Current address, age, and physical characteristics—forty-eight, Caucasian, six-foot-one, blue eyes, light brown hair, scar on his left shoulder—where he was born, his education, and his career, both in acting and now in politics. The political career section listed his voting status as an independent, his stint as an alderman, and his potential rise through the ranks to presidential hopeful. *Behold the power of the grassroots and the cult of personality, thanks be to social media.*

"Nothing I didn't already know, except for the scar," Camden said.

Lachlan templed his fingers. "You ever meet him?"

"Been at the same parties a couple of times. Friendly, good with crowds, a natural. Puts people at ease because he comes across as one of them."

Lachlan nodded. "Jake says the same in the motivation and behavioral section. Says Bennett can talk to anyone about anything."

"Not seeing a wrinkle yet, boss."

"Turn the page."

Camden did. The next page included a background check that showed a parking ticket (paid) and a couple of paragraphs about what motivated Bennett—a desire to listen to and empower people, strengthen relationships with allies, create jobs that didn't fuck up the environment, root out corruption in damaged systems all over the board. *Everyone's wet dream of a politician,* Camden thought. His behavior mirrored what he and Jake had personally observed, backed by other accounts and anecdotes.

And then there it was, the wrinkle—chatter both the FBI and the CIA picked up concerning Bennett.

"Oh." As Camden read the details, Lachlan spoke.

"They believe an unidentified foreign agent has infiltrated certain circles in our community."

Camden smiled. "Only one?"

Lachlan returned the smile before continuing. "Said spy will be approaching Bennett soon. We think they want to influence or gain kompromat on our young hopeful before he gets too big. Certainly before he throws his hat into the next election."

"So, I'm not only guarding him...." Camden let his words hang until Lachlan picked them up.

"You're observing the man himself and his interactions with everyone around him, yes."

"With an eye toward finding the spy."

"Of course. Using whatever means necessary, with the blessing of our friends who picked up on the chatter. Think of it as cultivating a source."

Fuck, yes! Camden broke into a huge smile.

Lachlan smirked. "So, how's that for getting out there?"

"Spec-ops to break my cherry? I'll fucking take it."

"Good. Thought you would. I said you could pick your team, but there are caveats. Right now, you, me, and Jake are the only ones who know the full extent of this assignment. To anyone else you pick, this is just a routine bodyguard gig for now. It's strictly need-to-know as the situation develops. Got it?"

That could be a wrinkle, too. Teammates didn't like being left out of the loop, but Camden answered, "I hear you."

"So, I want you to include Jake for the social engagements, including Bennett's public declaration for his political run coming up in a few weeks. *If* you can tear Jake away from his new bride."

Camden laughed.

Lachlan continued. "He knows the terrain even better than you and he'll blend in like you will. That level of guests won't blink an eye if they see Jake Collins swanning around."

Thanks to his family, Camden thought. Jake's mom, Bette Collins, was one of Hollywood's biggest stars. Camden had fallen under her halo of influence ever since Jake befriended him in the marines, which allowed him to mix and mingle with California's social elite. Not that he was any more comfortable with that scene today than he had been over a decade ago, but at least now he knew how to fake it. "I wouldn't do this assignment without Jake."

Lachlan nodded, satisfied. "You'll meet Bennett on Monday. Learn everything you can about him this weekend."

"Does Bennett know he's a target for foreign agents?"

"By all accounts, no. We want him acting normally. Don't wanna spook Boris and Natasha before we can flush them out." Lachlan stood up and Camden followed.

"Thanks, brother. I won't let you down."

"I know you won't."

As Camden walked back to his office, he thought about his upcoming weekend, which inevitably brought him back to Elena and the last time he spoke to her. Five weeks since he went from thinking he'd never see her again after the wedding, to discovering that she and her daughter Tina were moving from Nebraska to Los Angeles, to learning she wasn't interested in seeing him romantically once she got there, all in the span of a few unforgettable minutes on the dancefloor at the wedding reception.

True, he had talked her into at least considering seeing him as a friend, but knowing Elena and her devotion to her five-year-old—which came with the belief that she couldn't afford to divert her attention to someone else—she probably wouldn't budge him out of the friend zone. He respected her decision, as much as he hated it. In the short time he'd known her, Camden had never seen a braver, more devoted mom, and he wasn't stupid or arrogant enough to try and get between a mamma and her cub. But, he couldn't forget about how gorgeous she'd looked in her little black dress and how right she'd felt dancing in his arms.

Tomorrow was moving-in day. Jake insisted Camden and a couple other guys from work help out with lugging Elena's furniture up the stairs to her new apartment. Camden had played in the sandbox twice, once in Afghanistan and once in Iraq, and he'd faced gunfire stateside as an FBI agent, but he had no idea how he'd get through Saturday in one piece. Just thinking about seeing Elena made his heart race to ER-visit levels. As for Tina, that little girl melted what was left of his racing heart.

Doubt crept into his gut. What if Elena really didn't want anything to do with him and was just being polite at the wedding? Worse—what made him think he deserved a second chance at happiness considering how badly he'd fucked up his life the first time around?

Could he use his new assignment as an excuse to get out of seeing Elena and Tina?

Did he *want* to avoid them?

Both answers were resounding no's.

Damn. I've got it bad. No way forward but straight through. He'd move some furniture, crack some jokes, then he'd be on his way.

Unless Elena still smelled as good as he remembered. Vanilla and sweet peppermint. In that case, he'd try and convince her one more time that he was worth a shot.

TWO

I'll never get over wearing shorts outside of summer or the sight of palm trees, Elena thought as she drove the moving van down the broad avenue lined with palms that must have been thirty feet tall. "Look at those, Pepita. We didn't have anything like that in Nebraska, did we?"

"Do they have coconuts?" Tina asked. The five-year-old was under the impression that California coconuts were full of chocolate milk, so she asked about them incessantly. And who planted that crazy idea in her head five weeks ago? None other than Camden Bains.

Elena groaned. She'd wring Camden's neck if she ever saw him again. "No, baby, they aren't coconut trees. And even if they were, we couldn't climb that high."

"I could," Tina protested.

"You could?" Elena stopped at a red light. Her phone told her to take a left at the next light. Their new apartment was only a couple blocks away after that. "Are you a monkey?" She reached over to tickle her daughter before the light changed.

Tina rewarded her with a sweet giggle. "No! But I could climb that high for chocolate milk."

"You're gonna turn into chocolate milk, you keep talking about it." She took a left and kept an eye out for the apartment building that matched the photo online. She hadn't seen it yet in person, but her best friend Rachael made a video tour of the apartment for her and assured Elena that she'd love it, especially the peek-a-boo view of the Pacific from the balcony.

Elena saw the building and her heart sped up. *This is it. I'm really here. No turning back.* She glanced at Tina and wondered what Antonio would have to say if he could see his wife and daughter now. She felt the familiar pang, sad and sweet, that hit her every time she thought of her deceased husband. His wedding ring hung on its chain around her neck, a constant reminder.

Elena hoped Rachael and Jake were on their way to the apartment. She still wasn't sure how the three of them could get all her stuff upstairs by themselves, but she was thankful for the help. She would have done it on her own, hired a crew, but Rachael insisted she had it covered. The street was lined with cars but the parking gods had smiled and left her a big space right in front of the apartment, more than enough for the van and the trailer loaded up with her car behind it. Then Elena saw the truth.

Rachael and Jake came jogging down the walkway from the covered entrance, each holding up an orange traffic cone, which explained her parking luck—they'd blocked off the spot right up until they saw her truck, then grabbed the cones and quickly hid. Four of the biggest guys she'd ever seen followed Rachael and Jake out of the shade under the covered entry. One of them carried a potted palm with a ribbon tied around it, but it was guy number four, holding a traffic cone like Rachael and Jake's, who caught her eye.

Camden.

Oh, crap, Elena thought, even as she took in his friendly wave and the way his amber eyes locked onto hers. *And there goes my heart rate through the roof.*

"Surprise!" Rachael shouted. She ran to the driver's side as Elena opened the door and she embraced Elena almost before she set foot on the pavement. "I brought reinforcements."

"I can see that. Wow." Elena tried not to show her discomfort at Camden's presence, especially when she heard Tina shout his name. Her daughter adored the big guy who had saved her life back in Nebraska.

It wasn't that Elena wasn't grateful beyond belief, or that she didn't like Camden. She did. A lot. Too much. But the last thing she needed was a distraction in the shape of a gorgeous six-foot-something former SEAL who offered to show her around L.A. She needed to concentrate on her daughter and their new life, the same as she always had since Antonio died. Tina may like Camden, and with good reason, but it hurt Elena's heart to see Tina throw her arms around Camden's neck and kiss his cheek. Elena never wanted another man to replace her daughter's scant but happy memories of her Papa.

Elena barely heard Rachael ask her how the drive was as she concentrated on her daughter's chatter. She rapid-fired questions at Camden as he carried her up the walkway and they followed. Most involved coconuts (of course) but she ended her interrogation with, "Did you bring Toby?"

"Toby? Who's that?" Camden teased. He knew Tina adored the German Shepherd, probably more than she adored him. *And possibly more than she loves her own mama at this point,* Elena thought.

"*You* know!" Tina laughed, tagging Camden on the arm.

Camden opened the glass door and one of the other guys

grabbed the handle to keep it open for everyone else to enter. "You don't mean *that* guy, do you?"

Sitting there in the center of the lobby, his former-military training going head-to-head with his desire to race to the little girl who loved him, Toby's whole body wiggled and his tail thumped an impatient beat against the tile floor while he waited for the command that would set him free.

Camden took that moment to look back at Elena. His face —the mix of wonder and a hint of sadness in his eyes—took her right back to the first time she'd run to him as he held her half-conscious daughter in his arms. But this time, instead of walking fearfully into a safehouse, they were about to see their new home. And here Camden was again, ready to do anything he could to make sure they were safe, comfortable, and happy.

Elena nodded and Camden set Tina down while she squealed. She hit the ground running and Camden gave the command that freed Toby. The dog jumped to his feet and met the girl halfway across the lobby. He covered her face with slobbery kisses, two old friends reunited.

Elena smiled at Camden. "Thanks for bringing him."

His amber eyes lit with amusement. "Are you kidding? Toby would have driven here himself if I hadn't hidden the keys from him."

Elena grinned. She'd missed Camden's humor. "Toby can drive now, huh?"

Camden nodded. "He tends to tailgate. And occasionally go off-roading when he sees a squirrel. But he's still better than most people-drivers."

She laughed. "Yeah, after driving the moving van around here, I can believe it. He's welcome to drive the van back to the rental place for me."

Then she saw it. That look he gave her whenever she

joked back with him, the one that chased away any lingering sadness in his eyes. The one that made her feel like she was in a spotlight and filled her stomach with giddy butterflies. She looked away relieved when Rachael started introductions.

"So, you know Jake and Camden, obviously. This is Costello, Nashville, and Kyle," Rachael said. Costello carried the potted palm, Nashville wore a flashy cowboy hat that looked more country music than cowboy, and Kyle gave her a charmingly boyish grin.

"They work with me at Watchdog and have graciously offered to help out today," Jake added.

"I can pay you," Elena said. Before the words were even halfway out of her mouth, the guys were shaking their heads.

"No need, ma'am." "It's our pleasure," Costello and Nash said at the same time, just as Kyle said, "Camden says you make amazing cookies."

"Oh, did he?" Elena turned back to Camden, who was busy staring at Kyle with a frown that said, *Dude, you're seriously shaking her down for cookies?* He glanced at Elena, quickly put a smile back on, shrugged, and said, "Well, it's true. And that goes for everything else you cook, too. But," he went back to glaring at Kyle, "cookies won't be necessary. Right, Kyle?"

"Yes, sir." Kyle turned twenty shades of red and Elena immediately felt sorry for the guy who was obviously the newbie in this group.

A woman with graying chestnut hair and dangly plastic earrings that matched her brightly printed dress and fuzzy flip-flops stepped out of an office and approached Elena. "Hi, I'm Brenda," she said, extending her hand. "I'm the property manager. We talked on the phone? I showed Rachael around?"

"Brenda, hi, yes, thank you," Elena said, shaking her hand. "Sorry about the circus in the lobby."

Brenda's smile warmed the room. "No problem." She blatantly looked the guys up and down, then said, "Nice to have some big strong help," and Elena liked her immediately. "Why don't I give your friend Rachael the apartment key while you and I go over the rental agreement in my office?"

By the time Elena finished reading and signing everything, slowed down by Brenda—the woman could talk paint off a wall—the guys had moved most of her belongings into the apartment. Not that she'd brought much. The ramshackle little house she'd rented from Earnest Deal's real estate company back in Ross held bad memories and she didn't want to pack those up and cart them into her new life. So, she'd held a garage sale and sold off the recliner where Deal had sat threatening her and her daughter's lives, along with the kitchen chairs and table where he and his fellow bullies later planted their asses and ate her food. The majority of boxes in the van held Tina's things and everything from Elena's bedroom, which thankfully, hadn't been violated.

When Elena walked into her apartment, the first thing she saw was Tina directing the guys as they carried in each box clearly labeled kitchen or bathroom or one of their bedrooms. Elena loved the way they humored her daughter so seriously. Toby stayed glued to Tina's side and watched the others as if to say, *don't mess with my girl*. Not that any of them would—Elena could tell by the way Jake and Camden joked around with them that they were good guys, even if Kyle seemed a touch clueless. And Elena thought it was very sweet of Costello to bring her a housewarming plant. She totally planned on making them all cookies at the very least, especially since they'd spent their Saturday off helping her.

"Elena," Rachael called when she spotted her through the pass-thru between the front room to the kitchen, "come show me where you want everything."

"Go ahead, Mom," Tina said with the voice of an imperial princess, "I've got this part under control."

"Thanks, Pepita. Don't know what I'd do without your help."

When she got to the kitchen, Rachael was practically doubled-over trying not to laugh. "I. Adore. Your daughter," she whispered.

"Yeah, I think I'll keep her. If she stops begging for coconuts." Elena unwrapped a soup bowl.

"Speaking of, I'm not the only one here who adores her." Rachael kept her voice low as she set a stack of dishes in a cupboard Elena pointed to. "And you."

Elena set the bowl down and sighed. She did not want to have this conversation, especially with Camden within potential earshot. "Rachael. I know you mean well."

"Which is why I'm telling you to give him a chance. I've gotten to know Cam better these past months and he's amazing. Funny as hell, smart, loyal to a fault. And Tina's already got him wrapped around her pinky finger."

That's part of the problem, Elena thought. She unwrapped the next bowl as she said, "He's great, I'll agree. But he's not Tina's papa." She absently touched the wedding ring on its chain. "You remember Antonio. How good he was."

Rachael stopped arranging water glasses in the cupboard and came over to Elena. She put her arms around her. "I do remember him. He was one of the few at the meatpacking plant who always respected me. As quiet as he was, he defended me a couple of times from the other guys." She pulled back and looked Elena in the eye. "I was devastated over his death." Rachael's cheeks reddened and she dropped her gaze from Elena's as both women teared up. Rachael's voice dropped to a whisper. "And I felt even worse when I discovered the truth at my father's trial."

Elena tipped her friend's chin back up. "That's not on you, that's on Earnest Deal. I won't even call that man your father. He's the devil and you're an angel. Time and again, you've made up for his sins tenfold. Tina and I wouldn't be here without your help. The settlement—"

"Everything okay in here?" Jake asked as he stood in the kitchen door. His concerned look touched Elena to her soul, and for the millionth time, she thanked God for the man who loved and saved her best friend.

"Yeah," Rachael said as both women wiped their eyes. "Just catching up. Big day, lots of feels."

Jake nodded, knowing most, but not all, of the women's complicated pasts together. "We've got the van unloaded, the beds are almost put back together, and pizza's on the way." He grinned. "Tina told us exactly what to order."

"Of course she did," Elena laughed, grateful for the change in topic. "Why wouldn't she boss around a bunch of gigantic SEALs?"

Jake grinned. "We're not *all* SEALs, but close enough. She'll make a fine general one day. She's pure iron will wrapped in charm."

Elena put a hand on her hip. "Has she ordered any of her troops to bring her a California coconut yet?"

Jake cracked up. "Nope, but chocolate milk's on the way with the pizza. If that's not good enough, it's on Cam to get the coconuts." Jake ducked back out to the living room.

"I hope I get one just like her," Rachael said as she went back to arranging glasses in the cupboard.

Elena stacked the unwrapped bowls. "Be careful what you wish for," she said without thinking. She stopped midway to putting the bowls on a shelf. "Oh, shit, Rachael! Are you telling me...?"

Rachael's eyes got big and round. "Oh, no, no. I'm not pregnant. Not yet, at least. We're putting that off for a while, until Jake's totally settled in at Watchdog and I've toured on my first album."

Elena smiled and shook her head. "We really did it, didn't we, Chica? We got out of Ross, Nebraska. Out from under Earnest Deal and his company town."

Rachael's look was equal parts wonder and gratitude. "We promised each other we would, that we'd go to a warm place by the ocean. And here we are. I am so glad you decided to come out here to start your new life."

"We need to toast to that."

With a mischievous smile she only mastered after meeting Jake, Rachael said, "I can arrange that." She opened the fridge, revealing a shelf full of beer bottles.

Elena covered her mouth and laughed. "Where'd all that come from?"

Rachael's shrug said, *duh*. "The guys, of course. First thing they carried up from one of their trucks. Priorities, right?" Rachael pulled a bottle of champagne from the door. "But this is from me. And I just happened to have unpacked the glasses already."

The doorbell rang. Pizza had arrived. Everyone protested when Elena got out her wallet, Camden the loudest. Since she hadn't bought a new kitchen table and chairs yet—Rachael promised to go furniture shopping with her once she moved in —everyone gathered around the coffee table. Elena and Rachael bookended Tina on the couch, with Toby lying at her feet hoping for a stray crumb, while the guys sat on the floor around the low table, Jake at Rachael's end and Camden closest to Elena.

"Surprised you aren't picking off half the toppings, brother," Jake joked with Camden. He turned to Kyle. "Camden's a fussy eater."

"George Carlin said 'fussy eater' was a euphemism for big pain in the ass," Nashville said.

"Naw. Pizza's a perfect food," Camden said, then took another big bite. "Mmm."

Elena, a little tipsy from the glass of champagne Rachael poured for her, toed him with her foot. "You never picked anything off the plate when I fed you back in Ross."

"Your food's perfect, too," Camden answered. "You guys have no idea how amazing this woman is."

Elena felt the blood go straight to her cheeks, warming them, and when he scooted closer and his arm brushed her bare leg, she tried to ignore the other place that decided to heat up.

Your daughter's sitting right next to you, she silently scolded herself. *Focus on her, not some guy. Sweet and hot though he may be.* Elena moved ever so slightly away from Camden. She immediately missed the warmth coming off his sun-kissed skin. "Tina, that's it for the chocolate milk. You're still getting used to your new insulin pump."

"If she can get you to eat your vegetables, Cam, she's a miracle-worker," Nash said.

"She does and she is," Camden assured him.

"I'm no miracle-worker," Elena said.

"Don't let her fool you. She bakes like a dream, too," Rachael said.

"Oh, stop it, Chica." Elena shot her friend a warning look. "But, once I finish getting set up here, I insist on bringing you guys cookies at work. It's the least I can do to say thanks. I can't believe how much you guys did. I am so grateful."

"Our pleasure. Welcome to Cali," Kyle said, raising his beer to toast her. His smile carried a hint of interest that went beyond Elena's culinary skills.

From out of the corner of her eye, Elena saw Camden lean toward her. He could've given Toby a run for his money with the protective look he shot Kyle. Elena's pulse quickened the way it used to when she knew Antonio was on his way home from work. *Calm down, girl. It's just nerves catching up with you. And the champagne.*

The guys stayed a couple more hours, moving the bigger furniture around until Elena—but more to the point, Tina—was happy with where everything was. When Costello, Nash, and Kyle said their goodbyes, Elena hugged each of them, thanking them profusely. "You're like my brothers now," she said, noting the slight disappointment in Kyle's eyes despite his smile. *Kid, you're a bit too young for me anyway,* she thought, though she did feel flattered. At thirty, she wasn't ready to become invisible just yet.

After she closed the door, Jake laughed behind her.

She turned. "What?"

"Triple friend-zoned. Impressive."

"Jake!" Rachael tagged her husband on the arm. "Rude." She rolled her eyes and huffed. "We'll get out of your hair now, Elena. Let me know what time you want to go furniture shopping tomorrow. We'll use the moving van before you return it."

"I'm out the door right behind you," Camden called from the balcony. He'd gone out there at Tina's insistence that he put her on his shoulders so she could see the ocean. She wasn't quite tall enough to enjoy the peek-a-boo view without a boost, or at least that was her story. Toby shadowed them, of course.

Rachael hugged Elena and kissed her cheek. "Just give him a chance," she whispered.

"We'll see," Elena whispered back. Giving Camden a chance felt more and more like a possibility. *We can at least be friends, right?* she thought. *Good friends help each other move. That's practically the definition of true friendship.*

Though still on the small side, the apartment looked bigger without five huge guys crowding it. Elena smiled. Rachael had found a nice place. It was the tip-top of Elena's budget, but after years of living in a horrible house that wasn't much cheaper, she craved a little luxury. She walked out to the balcony to enjoy the view.

And maybe Camden, too. *Just a little. Just as friends.*

"Hi," she said as she came up behind him.

"Mama, can we go down to the beach now?" Tina said from atop his shoulders. "Toby needs a walk."

"I'm sure he does, Pepita, but I need you to go and unpack your clothes, especially your PJs. You've been bossing people around all day, now it's time for you to do some work."

"Mom," she protested as Camden set her down. "Camden, tell Mom Toby needs a walk."

Appalled, Elena's mouth dropped open. "I don't know where your attitude is coming from, but that's enough. You will go unpack right now."

"Mom—"

Elena pointed to the sliding doors. "Not another word."

Tina shot her a death-ray stare. Then she turned and hugged Camden and motioned for Toby to follow her as she trudged to her room.

Elena covered her face. This was not how she wanted her day to end. "I am so sorry about that."

Camden took her hand and gently pulled it from her face. "Hey, don't apologize. She's had the run of the place all day and now she's tired and wired. It's partly my fault. Me and the guys spent the day obeying her every whim."

He looked down as if he just realized he was still holding her hand and let it go. Elena immediately missed his touch. On impulse, she grabbed his hand and gave it a quick squeeze to let him know she didn't mind before letting go again.

"It was sweet the way you guys did that, actually. She didn't have the best male role models in her life for some time, and I can't imagine better ones."

To her surprise, Camden took in a sharp breath as if she'd just sucker-punched him. He regained his composure quickly, though he couldn't hide the trace of pain in his eyes. "Thank you," he said, and Elena got the impression that there were other words hiding behind those.

"Did I say something?" She took his hand in hers and held it.

Camden's eyes warmed, the amber in them almost glowing in the last light of day. "You said a very kind thing. And I do thank you." He raised her hand to his lips and brushed a soft kiss against her knuckles, sending shivers down her arm. "Elena, I don't want to overstep my bounds here, but I have to tell you, I like spending time with you, and with Tina. Today reminded me how much I've missed you. My offer to show you around L.A. still stands. On your terms, of course."

She was unused to being treated with such gentleness and respect, and by a man she knew firsthand could take down any enemy when he needed to. Elena covered her heart. Her thumb brushed the chain holding Antonio's wedding ring. He'd been the only other gentle man she'd known in her life, and yet he and Camden were so different from each other in almost every other way. For the first time, she wondered what Antonio would have thought of Camden. She thought he might have liked him once he saw past their differences.

"You know, I would like that. Tina and I can use all the friends we can get."

She expected to see disappointment in Camden's eyes at the word 'friend.' Instead, he beamed. "Then I look forward to it." His eyes filled with mischief. "And to a cookie. Dunked in chocolate milk from a coconut."

Elena laughed. "Okay, that's my first condition—that you cease and desist with the coconuts."

THREE

Monday morning couldn't come fast enough for Camden. Now that he'd seen Elena and Tina—with the promise of spending more time with them—he was ready to meet Roger Bennett and assess the man. He was eager to start this job and prove himself to Lachlan. Sure, he liked training the FNGs, but he was ready for some real action. If he could find and stop the foreign agent from corrupting Roger, he'd be doing a service to his country—something he missed from his SEAL days. As far as he was concerned, this was an attack on the nation. He couldn't afford to fail.

On Sunday, he'd done a deep-dive on the actor-turned-politician and learned a few more things about him. He'd married his college sweetheart and after some infertility issues, they'd had twins, one boy and one girl, now in grade school. Cici Bennett seemed on board with her husband's aspiring political career. They had no overwhelming debts or unexplained bank account deposits that might indicate either a weak spot to exploit or a bribe paid for a future favor.

"He's a choir boy," Camden said to Toby on the drive in to

Watchdog, "But there's got to be something there, don't, you think?" he added, as if the critter could understand Camden and give sage advice. Instead, the curled-up ball of dog just thumped his tail.

If Camden could find the man's weak spot—before the bad guys did—he'd know what threats to look for and what countermeasures to take. If they didn't have dirt on Bennett already they might try to cook some up. Maybe compromise Bennett through an extramarital affair, though by all accounts, his marriage sounded like a happy one. He'd never shown up high or drunk to a set, never made a spectacle of himself in a bar or nightclub, so they'd have a hard time tempting him with cocaine or pills and catching him doing something unsavory under the influence.

While Bennett wasn't the tip-top of the Hollywood scene —though that was changing, the more he soft-campaigned—he seemed to have plenty of money according to the financial information Jake probably shouldn't have had access to. He'd even made friends in the tech sector, guys with small start-ups that had gone on to become multi-billion-dollar corporations. He had his pick of big campaign contributors to go with his grass-roots donations.

I'll just have to judge the man for myself this afternoon. Camden had an appointment to meet Bennett at his house at two, which gave him time for the Monday morning briefing and to check on his FNGs—short for Fucking New Guys. He also needed to think about who to recruit for the rest of his team. He'd know after the brief who might be available. After talking to Bennett to assess his security needs, he'd make his final decisions.

Camden pulled into his spot at Watchdog, parking his black Tahoe in a line with six others just like it. Each bumper, front and back, had a small decal of a stylized watchdog and a number one through ten. Lachlan added the decals after the last Oscars. They'd been hired to guard three actors, which required their entire fleet. Thing was, every other security company was there supporting other celebrities too, and when it came time to escort everybody out after the show, no one could figure out which black Tahoe belonged to which company. Car alarms sounded and headlights flashed as everyone kept hitting their buttons trying to find their own vehicle. The small decals solved that problem for Watchdog at least.

Gladys the receptionist greeted Camden and Toby. The two made their way to the courtyard dominated by two obstacle courses, one for dogs and one for humans. Kyle was busy running two other dogs through their course—Reggie and Fleur. Those two dogs meant that Nashville and Gina were here already.

"Got room for one more?" Camden unsnapped Toby's leash and he joined the other dogs.

"Sure, no problem." Without pausing his work with Fleur, Kyle directed Toby into the mix. The Pup didn't know his way around a celebrity, but he had a knack with the canines.

Back inside, Camden grabbed a coffee and headed for the conference room. The Monday briefs were for upper management only. Camden took a seat next to Jake, who was engrossed in a conversation with Nash about music, so what else was new? Lachlan was punching at his phone like it had just insulted his mother. A cut-down, chewed-up plastic pen missing its cartridge and nib poked out of his mouth. Gina casually leaned against the wall, arms crossed, studying the rest of the group. Camden wasn't sure if her knees were capable of bending because she almost never sat during a meeting. Her gaze made a circuit of the men, the room, the door, then started over again, endlessly patrolling.

Costello came in a few minutes later with his usual apology and Lachlan mumbled his usual 'whatever' around his substitute cigarette.

"Okay, now that we're all here, let's get started." Lachlan tossed his phone aside and Nash started with his report, his smooth Southern accent making an account of a thwarted attack on a principal sound like a bedtime story. Camden pretended to listen politely and jot down notes—meetings were not his thing. They weren't Gina's either, he'd noticed. She never took notes, tapping the side of her head and saying 'Got it all in here' instead. And she did—Gina could rattle off verbatim anything she'd heard. She would neither confirm nor deny her time with the CIA, which was all the answer anyone really needed. That earned her the handle Spooky—which again, she'd neither confirm nor deny that she liked.

When Camden's turn came, he stuck to status reports on the rookies' training. He didn't mention the Bennett assignment per Lachlan's instructions, though Jake knew and had plans to go with him that afternoon. The meeting was mercifully brief and Camden was the first out the conference door, eager to get on with his day.

So when he walked into his office, he nearly jumped out of his skin when he looked up and saw Gina already standing beside the window.

"I want on the team," she said, arms crossed as she casually leaned against the wall.

Camden closed the door. "What the hell, Spooky? Lachlan told you?"

"He didn't have to." Her brief Greta Garbo smile said, *silly man.*

"You're the one who provided the chatter, aren't you?"

"I can neither confirm—"

"Nor deny that, yeah, okay, I hear you." Camden grinned. "I'd be an idiot not to let you on the team."

"Glad you see it that way. And thank you."

"Do you want to tag along this afternoon to meet Bennett?"

"No need." Gina tucked a lock of her dark brown bob behind her ear then walked to the door. Before leaving, she added, "Just for the record, if I thought you were an idiot, I'd be leading the team myself. I told Lachlan you were the man for the job and he couldn't agree more."

Wow. Camden had never known Gina to be so transparent. Or complimentary. "Thanks."

Gina's smile returned. "Thank *you*. It's one of the few things about this company he and I can agree on."

"She really said that?" Jake asked as Camden drove them to Bennett's house.

"I can neither confirm nor deny that Spooky thinks I don't suck."

Jake laughed. "You know, I can't find *anything* about her online outside her cover. It's deep."

"And I doubt she's ever going to break it."

"So, you think she's moonlighting at Watchdog and still with the CIA?"

"Who knows? Could be the other way around, seeing as she's part-owner." Camden pulled up to the guardhouse for Bennett's neighborhood. "But I still wouldn't give her Elena's secret barbeque sauce recipe."

"Spooky probably already has it. And...wait, when did Elena give you a secret recipe?"

Camden just smiled, remembering the safehouse back in

Nebraska, and rolled down his window. Before he could speak, the guard in the booth slid open the window and said, "IDs please." They handed their licenses over and the guard took extra-long to examine them, then Camden's and Jake's faces, then back to the licenses.

Finally, he said, "You're cleared to meet Mr. Bennett. Take an immediate right, then go left on Palm and it's the second house on the right. Have a nice day." The window snapped closed again, but not before Camden saw a bank of screens with various shots of the neighborhood's streets.

"Well. Friendly, open neighborhood." Camden said as he pulled forward.

"Yeah. Unless the agent already knows Bennett, they're not getting in here easily."

"So we'll keep an eye on any new friends the man makes."

Bennett's house was a typical Mediterranean-style with tall palm trees and neatly-clipped hedges. They walked up the brick path and one of the double doors opened just as they got to the porch. Bennett himself greeted them with a warm smile and stockinged feet.

"Howdy, glad you could make it. Hey, if you don't mind, could I ask you to take off your shoes? Cici's pretty protective of the floors." He pointed to a small Persian rug with several pairs of shoes lined up on it to the side of the door.

"No problem," Camden said as he eyed the white and gray marble covering the entryway and leading into the next room. Cold, stark, not to his taste—which ran to casual and comfortable—but typical of some actors who liked to show off a bit.

Shoes removed, Bennett led them past the kitchen which put Camden in the mind of a marble vault complete with a huge sarcophagus in the center with an offering of fruit in a cut-glass bowl that probably cost a month's paycheck. He'd seen dozens of kitchens like this and always wondered how much cooking actually went on in them. He couldn't see Elena working in a space like this, even though her food deserved a palatial kitchen.

Bennett ushered them into a den off the kitchen that at least had warm wood floors and paneling, with a view of the pool in the manicured backyard.

"Have a seat. Can I offer you guys something to drink?" He gestured at a glass-doored mini-fridge. "I've got sports drinks, bottled water, beer if you're so inclined. Coffee's in the kitchen and still hot."

Camden glanced at Jake. "Coffee'd be great."

"Same," Jake said.

"Cream and sugar if you've got 'em," Camden added to give them extra time alone.

"Can do." Bennett left and Camden waited until he was out of earshot before leaning toward Jake.

"I checked, but...Bennett's bank account really covers the monthly nut on this place?"

"This, plus the kids' private school makes it tight, but yeah, it does. His wife's some sort of trust fund baby, but her money goes for her stuff only."

"Doesn't leave much margin of error does it?"

Jake shook his head. "Nope. He totally relies on contributions for his campaign because he doesn't have a penny of his own money to spare for it."

Bennett returned, carrying a tray with three coffee cups, a pitcher, and a bowl of sugar cubes. "Jake, it's good to see you again. How's your mom?"

"Real good, thanks for asking. She's a fan of your work."

"That's great, as long as she's a bigger fan of my campaign than my acting."

Jake laughed. "She likes what you're proposing about healthcare."

Bennett took a seat across from Camden and Jake. "I'd love to get her input, actually."

"I'll let her know." Jake sipped his coffee. "There's a Bette's Backyard Bash coming up, maybe I can wrangle you an invite."

Bennett smiled wide. "I'd love one. I've never been to one of her parties."

Excellent, Camden thought, glad that he'd thought to bring Jake along. Though he'd never used his friend for his connections, he saw how handy they were coming in at Watchdog.

"Nice place you got here," Camden said as he grabbed a mug, dropped in a sugar cube, and splashed in a drop of half and half after it.

"Thanks. It's Cici's house, she just lets me live in it," Bennett joked, though good-naturedly. His tone and the light in his eyes told Camden the man adored his wife. Camden had seen Cici at a few events but hadn't talked to her. She seemed to be in love with her husband, supportive and good-natured.

"I'll have to compliment *her* on the house, then," Camden took a sip of his coffee.

"She's in and out all day today, but we might see her when she drops off the kids before she goes to her next meeting. This afternoon's the one on free daycare for all, I think." Bennett chuckled.

"Actually, it's affordable housing," Jake said, and Bennett raised his eyebrows.

"When you hired Watchdog and gave us your family's schedules, we memorized them," Camden explained. "We like to know where everyone is at all times, especially since we don't have guards on them yet, and it slows us down if we have to constantly check a calendar."

Bennett grinned. "You've got the job as my personal assistant too if you want it."

Camden smiled. "Think I'll stick with personal body-guard for now. So, can you tell us more about what you need from us?"

Bennett's grin faded and the man became serious for the first time since they walked in. "I never thought I'd need something like this, back when I was acting. I didn't have a rabid fan base like some of my co-stars. Never felt like I was being stalked or anything like that. When I got recognized, people were always cool about it. But now that I've decided to run—and yes, I do want to go for the presidency eventually, but that doesn't leave this room—I'm feeling uneasy."

Camden and Jake exchanged looks. "Why is that? Has someone approached you in a threatening manner? Any emails or phone calls?"

Bennett shook his head and put his hands up. "No, nothing like that. I mean, not yet. And I'm hiring you guys to ensure that not yet stays never."

Camden leaned forward. "But something is bothering you, obviously."

Bennett looked like someone had just elbowed him in the ribs. He changed his expression quickly, the lines in his fore-head smoothing over. "Just a feeling, probably nothing. But every now and then, I feel watched. Which sounds crazy, because of course I'm being watched—that's the whole idea, to get people's attention so you can get their votes. This feels different though. I think I know how a rabbit feels when a hawk's shadow passes overhead. It's like I'm waiting for some-thing to strike, know what I'm saying?"

Another look passed between Camden and Jake. They

knew exactly how that felt—how in spite of no indicators, the air could crystalize, sounds and colors and smells intensify right before a barrage of gunfire came from a roof, or a roadside bomb detonated—and that vague unease became the shadow of death.

Sometimes it was the ring of your phone at an unexpected hour when you're lying in your bunk sweating your balls off and wishing you were stateside instead of in the sandbox—just the tone of it, the way it slices through the silence—that lets you know things have changed forever back home.

Camden suppressed a shudder at the sudden unwelcome memory. He nodded at Bennett. "We hear you, brother. And it's good you don't discount that feeling. It's almost always correct."

"How well do you trust the people around you?" Jake asked as he set his empty mug on the coffee table.

"Depends. My wife, my family, without hesitation. I've hired Lawrence Franklin to run the campaign team, on Rock Higley's advice. He's the best campaign manager in California, heck, the best anywhere, and he and my wife went to college together so he's thrilled to be helping us out. He's vetted everyone on my campaign team. We wouldn't knowingly hire anyone sketchy but we're a new crew, so it's still trust but verify." He smirked. "But I'm sure you've checked them all out as well."

"Sure," Camden said. "And you're right, no one's raised any red flags or we'd let you know." If anything, Bennett's team was almost slavishly devoted to him and his ideals, judging by their social media, even before they got their jobs. It was a young group, the oldest being Lawrence Franklin, but he was the same age as Roger. Jake had researched him extra deeply. On the trail of corruption, it was always safe to follow the money. But even Lawrence checked out.

"Do you feel safe at home?"

"I do. This neighborhood is tight. What I want is security for the night I announce that I'm running. That's going to be a big shindig up at the Sol Villa Museum in Beverly Hills."

Camden took the last swig of his coffee. "You sure you don't want a team before that?"

"I'm sure. I don't want to spook Cici and the kids."

"Let me know if you change your mind about that. So, here's what we'll do. I'm assembling a team for security at the villa. Someone will ride with you to and from, and there'll be a second vehicle tailing you, watching for anyone who might be following. At the event, besides the obvious security, there'll be personnel in the crowd who you won't be able to spot. I'll be at your side, the obvious target. We'll evaluate from there. If someone is watching you, we'll spot them pretty quick. I'll assign additional people to watch your wife and kids at the villa. Sure you don't want to make that security round the clock?"

Bennett blanched. "I don't think all that's necessary. I mean, I want them safe, but I don't want to scare them."

"If you're serious about this run," Jake said, "they're going to have to get used to it."

Bennett sighed. "Can I ask you a personal question?"

Jake's eyebrows raised. "Sure."

"What was it like for you as a kid? Did you have bodyguards? Especially after what happened with your mother?" His tone said he didn't want to stir up bad memories.

Jake gave him his easiest smile. "We did, after that. You actually get used to having bodyguards around pretty quick, especially if the team is good. And I've got to say, Watchdog is good. We all have military backgrounds and we go through extra training on how to make our clients as comfortable as possible. Cici, Brittany, and Brice will forget we're even there."

Bennett looked out at his pool as if it held the answers. "All right."

The rest of the meeting was taken up with getting the names of all the guards and groundskeepers for the neighborhood. By the time they finished up, Camden heard the front door open. Two kids' excited voices along with their mom's laughter echoed in the foyer. Bennett's face immediately lit up like any good dad's, and Camden felt an old ache turn over in his heart. He decided then and there he'd drop by Elena's place and take her and Tina out for dinner that night.

"Sounds like the troops are home." Bennett stood up and Camden and Jake followed. "Let me introduce you."

They made their way to the kitchen where Cici was pouring glasses of milk and setting out two plates with sandwiches. The twins sat at the island, engaged in a fierce game of thumb war. The ten-year-olds inherited their mom's light blond hair and Brittany wore hers long and straight like her mother's. They barely looked up when the three men entered, probably used to people coming and going as their dad's political ambitions revved up. Such innocence, such trust in their parents, in the safety of their home. Absolutely Camden was assigning them a protector. He'd be damned if something happened to them on his watch.

While Bennett wrapped his arms around the twins in a double-hug, Cici smiled at Camden and Jake and extended her hand. "Nice to meet you. I didn't think you'd still be here when I got home, but can I offer either of you a peanut butter and jelly sandwich?" Her eyes sparkled with mirth.

"I'm sure they're the best peanut butter and jelly sandwiches in the world, but I won't put you to the trouble,"

Camden said, gripping her hand. "Jake and I have to get going, but it was a pleasure. You have a beautiful home."

"Thank you," she said, glancing around the kitchen. She leaned forward and mock-whispered, "We're hoping to trade up. A nice white house on the East Coast, if you know what I mean."

"Cici," Bennett warned, though without any malice. She winked at him.

Bennett saw them to the front door. "Thanks again."

"Our pleasure." Camden pulled his boot on. "You have a beautiful family. I look forward to keeping them safe."

Back in the SUV, Jake commandeered the stereo and streamed his favorite Laurel Canyon playlist from Spotify. Through the speakers, Stephen Stills advised them to love the one they were with. "So, current impressions, Cam?"

"Bennett's too fucking naïve to be playing with politics, though Cici seems ambitious. Heart's in the right place, though. Nice family, like I said." His heart clenched. So many memories stirring up lately. Seeing Bennett's reaction to his family coming home, the twins and their mom just doing normal shit, with no clue how lucky they were to have that chance. Meeting Elena and Tina started it, resurrected pieces of his heart he'd buried five years before.

On the day he put his wife and daughter in the ground.

"You okay, brother?" Jake's voice held the weight he'd started using on that same day whenever he suspected Camden of thinking about the past.

"Never better, brother."

Jake side-eyed him but dropped it. "I'm going to ask Mom to invite them to her Bash, like I said. It'll be a dry run for Roger's upcoming announcement event at the villa. You picked out anyone else for the team I should invite, too? Well, besides Spooky."

"Gina picked herself out." Camden slowed as he hit a wall of traffic. "I'm thinking Costello for starters. It'll be good to have Psychic watching our backs."

"Spooky and Psychic. Is this a team or are we on a Netflix show?"

Camden grinned. "Your lady's gonna be the first one on Netflix, brother."

"Truth." Jake grinned proudly just as "California Dreamin'" started playing. Camden knew that was one of their songs and that Rachael's new version was taking over social media.

Having the Bennetts at Bette's party could also be a liability. Camden wondered who else had been invited. "Anyone gonna be at the Bash we need to keep an eye on?"

Jake shrugged. "Mom keeps the invite list tight. Well, tight for her, which still means north of fifty people. Most are old friends, no one I'm worried about. The newest guests'll be Bennett and fam. And Elena and Tina."

Camden kept his expression neutral even as Jake watched him. What was the man expecting, for Camden to bounce in his seat like a girl at her first boyband concert? So what if his heart sped up? *Stupid heart.* "Figured that."

"You gonna be able to focus on the job with her there?"

"I could ask you the same, with Rachael."

Jake chuckled. "Fair enough, brother."

FOUR

"So, this is your station," Elena's new boss, Julia Wittington, said as she led Elena back to the receptionist's desk at Brant and Phillips Promotions. The desk looked clunky after seeing Julia's spare Scandinavian furniture in her sunny office. "You can set up your little self right here. Feel free to personalize, but not where anyone can see it, okay? We want to keep everything looking professional, and nothing says 'not professional' like a picture of a kid with food all over its face."

"Right. Got it, Ms. Wittington." *Well, there goes at least three photos of Tina I was planning to pin up,* she thought as she sat down.

"Oh, and speaking of food, it was really, totally sweet of you to bring in your little homemade cookies," Julia said as she leaned against the desk.

"Oh, my pleasure. I—"

Julia's voice lowered as she cut Elena off. "But in another way, it's kind of passive-aggressive considering how everyone here is either gluten-intolerant, or vegan, or fasting, or cleansing. You're not in steak-and-potatoes country anymore, Elena.

People are health-conscious here and you have to be aware of that."

Seriously? Elena fought to keep her tone civil. She'd spent time and good money on making her 'everything but the kitchen sink' cookies and she'd meant them as a goodwill gesture to warm up her new co-workers.

"I didn't mean to offend anyone. I made them to break the ice. You know, first day and everything. Wanted to make a good impression..." The more Elena talked, the colder Julia's eyes turned, despite the smile plastered on her face. "They're organic?" Elena finished, sounding totally lame to her own ears.

"So you might want to consider thinking about taking them out of the lounge and keeping them to yourself, okay? I mean," she gave Elena a once-over, "obviously you eat them with abandon, and that's fine, but it's just a temptation that the rest of us don't need."

Oh my God, did she just fat-shame me? How much do I need this job? Too much—the healthcare benefits were by far the best out of the job offers she'd received, and that decided everything. Tina's new insulin pump was a game-changer neither of them wanted to give up, but it was not cheap.

Swallowing her pride, Elena said, "I understand, Ms. Wittington. My daughter has type I diabetes, so I know all about special diets. I'll get them—"

The ringing phone on her new desk cut her off. Julia pointed to it and said, "You'll get that, first. Remember to be polite and professional." Then she turned on her stilettos and marched back to her office.

Between the phone and a steady stream of clients coming in, Elena didn't get to the lounge until well past noon. When she saw the plate, she smiled. Every cookie had vanished down someone's supposedly gluten-intolerant, vegan, fasting, cleansing throat. When she got back to her desk, a yellow sticky note on her chair seat said:

Thanks for the amaze cookies! P.S. Julia ate three.

Elena suppressed a laugh as she surreptitiously glanced around hoping to identify her new friend. No luck—everyone ignored her, busy with their own tasks. She tucked the note into her purse with plans to stick it to her bathroom mirror when she got home.

"So, how was your first day on the job?" Camden asked over the phone later. Elena had just walked in the door with Tina after picking her up from the after-school program. She tucked the phone between her ear and her neck as she sliced an apple for Tina's snack while considering what to make for dinner.

"Mixed, at best. My new boss hates me and the feeling's pretty mutual, but I think I have a friend there already."

"Uh-oh. You wanna tell me about it?"

"Julia didn't approve of the cookies I brought in—"

"So she's a monster," Camden interrupted.

Elena laughed. "But they disappeared completely, and somebody left me a note thanking me and said that Julia ate three."

Camden chuckled, the deep growl of his voice up close and personal in her ear sending pleasant tingles up and down Elena's spine. "Bet she ate four. So none left, huh? That makes me sad. I wanted one."

Elena grinned as she plated up the apple slices and set them on the table, then called to Tina who was playing in her room after a very successful day at her new school. "No worries, I always make extra. I promised I'd stop by Watchdog with a batch to thank you guys, and I thought I'd bring extra for everyone else to say thanks for loaning you Toby when you came to Nebraska."

Tina heard the dog's name as she ran into the kitchen and her face brightened. "Are we gonna see Toby today?"

At the same time, Camden said, "What do I have to do to get my very own?" and this time, that growl made Elena's toes curl. She quickly turned away from her daughter before she could see the blush rising in her mom's cheeks. "I'll go straight to your office and make sure you get first pick."

"Mom, are we gonna see Toby?"

"Not today, Pepita," she answered as Camden spoke again and she missed what he said. "Sorry, I was talking to Tina. What did you say?"

"I said I have a better idea." *Could his voice get any sexier?* Elena doubted it.

"Yeah, what's that? Wait, are you driving?"

"Not anymore. I parked a couple minutes ago."

"Are you just now getting home from work?" Elena opened a cupboard and grabbed a pot to make rice. She still didn't know exactly what to cook for dinner, but she could do a dozen different things with rice. "I should let you go, Cam, so you can make yourself something to eat."

Someone knocked at the door and Tina said, "I'll get it!" as she jumped up, adding to Elena's distractions.

"Tina, wait." Elena rushed after her. She put a hand on her daughter's shoulder before she could turn the knob and Elena gently stepped in front of her. "Camden, sorry, I've gotta let you go, there's someone at—" Elena opened the door.

"—the door. Oh, hi."

Camden stood in the doorway, and God did he look good in cowboy boots and a white button-down shirt tucked into the waist of his tight jeans. *Oh, mercy.*

He fixed her with a smile but his eyebrows pulled down. "You shouldn't ever open the door without checking first. It's a safe enough neighborhood, but you and Tina are on your own."

The scolding was enough to cool Elena off. *How dare he assume I'm so stupid, when it's just that I have twenty different distractions going on.*

"Good thing it was you, then, huh?" she said. "Come on in."

Tina was already pushing past Elena to hug Camden as he dropped to his knees to catch her. A pang of sadness squeezed Elena's heart while she watched. Tina forgot a little more about her father every day that passed, but some things didn't change. Her little girl used to toddle to the door squealing 'Papa' every time Antonio came home, and Camden reacted the same way her husband had, every single time.

Her heart broke a little more remembering Tina going to the door every night for months after Antonio had been killed. She'd pat the wood and whisper 'No more Papa.'

Elena cleared her throat and blinked back tears as Camden carried Tina in. "So, this was your idea how to get a cookie?"

"Did it work?" Camden smiled at Elena over his shoulder as he set a giggling Tina down on the couch.

"Well, I have cookies but no dinner yet."

"Perfect, because I'm taking the two of you out."

"Cookies!" Tina said.

"You need to finish your apple. Your blood sugar's a tad low but I don't want to spike it with cookies." Elena pointed to the kitchen table. "Go eat."

Camden went from smiling to looking worried as he watched Tina walk to the kitchen.

"She's okay," Elena answered his unasked question. "She's

still adjusting to her new schedule and to the insulin pump, so we're having some little dips and spikes here and there. The pump helps so much though. Normally, I'd be mentally readjusting insulin doses while waiting to retest her blood sugar after she eats."

Camden's lips curled up into a sweet smile that made Elena go a little weak in the knees. "You're a wonderful mom."

Elena shrugged. "It's what any mom would do, right? She's my world." *And I need to keep that in mind, especially with you standing there looking so damn good,* she thought. "So, I'll give you a cookie, but you don't have to take us to dinner. We're good."

Camden crossed his arms. "What? You want to make me a lawbreaker?"

It took Elena a second to remember what he was talking about. "Oh, right, what you said at Jake and Rachael's wedding about native Californians showing the newbies around." She laughed. "How did you put it? It's the law so us noobs don't hurt ourselves on all the awesomeness?"

He winked at her. "Good memory. So, you see, it's not up to me." He dropped his arms to his sides and took a couple steps toward her.

Elena folded her arms and nodded. "Yeah, I see how you are. You'll do anything for a cookie."

He stopped inches from her. He smelled as good as he looked, a light, citrusy scent floating over salty skin. "Not just *any* cookie."

"No?" Elena released her arms. Her heart sped up. "What kind of cookie, then?"

He traced down her bare arm with one finger, bringing her awareness right to the surface of her skin. He leaned down until his mouth was right next to her ear and Elena thought she'd faint from the way her heart pounded. *If he growls anything even remotely sexy, I'm a goner. I need to shut this down right now. This is not going to happen.*

Instead, she stilled as Camden opened his mouth and growled, "Pounds of butter. Extra gluten. All the processed sugar. I'm a feaster, not a faster."

Elena's eyes looked heavenward as she pushed him away. "You're terrible, you know that?"

Camden grinned down at her. "How so?"

"Oh, I think you know."

If he did, he didn't say. "So, how about dinner?"

"I can make something for us here."

Camden shook his head. "Not tonight. You've had a rough day—"

"It wasn't that bad."

Camden frowned. "You've had a rough day and I want to make it better. Let me treat you. We'll get something to eat and then take a walk on the beach. It'll be fun."

Elena sighed. *Maybe just this once,* she thought. *But I can't make it a habit.* "Okay, you win. But nothing fancy, all right?"

"First," Camden said, counting off on his fingers, "this is not a competition, it's dinner. Second, you don't have to go fancy to eat good in L.A. Let me introduce you to the concept of food trucks."

"Camden, I lived in Nebraska, not on the moon. I know what a food truck is."

"Yeah, but have you ever been to one?"

Elena's gut clenched. She hadn't—Ross, Nebraska was not known for haute cuisine or low cuisine. What they had was Betty's Diner, Taco Hut, and a McDonald's off the interstate that mostly served people hurrying off to someplace better. When she and Antonio first moved there from New Mexico, she'd worked the kitchen at Betty's and enjoyed it. When Tina came along, she needed a job with better hours so she worked the day shift at the meatpacking plant while Antonio worked nights.

Camden frowned. "Did I say something?"

"No." Elena shook her head to clear it of bad memories. "But you'll probably think I'm a total hick because no, I haven't ever eaten at a food truck."

"I never implied you were," he said as his voice softened. "I think you're one sophisticated lady. Now, why don't you go change while I keep an eye on Tina? Just don't count the cookies after that." He grinned.

Elena rolled her eyes. "Make sure you leave some for the other guys." She turned to head for her bedroom.

Behind her, she heard Camden mumble as he walked to the kitchen, "'Other guys' are the last two words I wanna hear you say." Before she could think of a response, Tina asked Camden where Toby was, and he was telling her the dog was spending the night with Kyle.

E lena shut the bedroom door behind her and scrubbed her face with her hands. When she stopped, her gaze landed on the photo on her bedside table. She, Tina, and Antonio posed together under a cottonwood tree dominating a small park. Baby Tina had just turned her face up to her dad when the photographer took the picture. What sat outside the frame was the children's hospital adjacent to the park, where they'd just spent the better part of a month first trying to determine why their shaky, feverish little girl couldn't keep anything down, then coming to terms with her diagnosis of type I diabetes. The hospital volunteer taking the photo captured both the bone-deep fatigue she and her husband felt, and their relief at Tina's release. Not for the first time, everything in Elena's life changed after that day, but she had one constant—Antonio's love and devotion. Right up to the day of the accident.

Elena blinked back tears. How could any man ever compare to her Antonio? Ever love her and Tina as much and as fiercely as he had?

She turned to her closet and picked out fresh clothes. Growing up, Antonio had been soft-spoken, a pacifist shaped by long hours alone riding horses and herding cattle on the New Mexico ranch where his father worked as a third-generation cowboy. She'd first seen him on horseback when she was sixteen years old during an overnight field trip with the rest of her group home. He was only seventeen but looked older from the way he carried himself with quiet dignity, and the muscular body he'd developed working the ranch. Elena couldn't look away, and when she caught the first shy glance he sent her direction over supper, she felt the earth move.

Elena stripped off her office clothes and carried a red tank dress with yellow flowers into the adjacent bathroom as she remembered how she'd spent that night lying awake in the bunkhouse, acutely aware she was sharing the same roof with her future husband—there was no doubt in her mind she was going to marry the handsome, stoic cowboy. *Mrs. Elena Martinez*, she'd whispered to herself, *wife of Antonio Martinez*. She'd pictured herself working in the ranch house kitchen beside the other women, laughing and joking as they prepared the big mid-day meal for the hands. How Antonio would come in dusty and sweaty—yet still smelling good, of course—from herding steers or breaking horses. The jingle of his spurs as he crossed the room and took her in his arms for a quick kiss before their meal. With these fantasies still filling her head at breakfast, she'd slipped Antonio the number to her contraband burner phone before piling into the van that would take her back to the drab group home in Albuquerque where she'd lived for six years.

Texts followed. Each time her secret phone vibrated in her pocket, Elena's heart buzzed with it. Antonio wouldn't call her, wouldn't answer when she called him, texting that he'd just get tongue-tied and waste her minutes.

Elena smiled into her apartment's bathroom mirror as she plugged in her iron and freshened her make-up, remembering how frustrated she'd been that he didn't even record his name on his generic voicemail message, leaving her to try and remember what his voice had sounded like from the half-dozen words he'd spoken at supper. But he did text her several times a day. She'd sneak a peek during class or at her food service job and let his words sink in. He told her little things about his day, about how the clouds looked as they gathered on the horizon, the smell of rain in the distance. To her, his texts read like poetry.

He surprised her on her seventeenth birthday by driving to Albuquerque and showing up at the group home. She called in sick to work for the first time ever and they walked hand-in-hand to a nearby park. He stayed quiet until they sat on a park bench and he slipped down to one knee, opened a black velvet box, and asked her to marry him when she turned eighteen.

Their wedding night—two virgins sweetly fumbling. But they'd still given each other what they needed, and as time went on, they perfected the ways of pleasure. Elena was happy down to her bones for the first time in her chaotic life, living on the ranch away from the city. They planned on staying there forever.

Life had other plans.

Elena took a deep breath as she came back to the present. She appraised herself in the mirror and realized she'd put on a little extra makeup, done her hair fancier than she normally wore it. Was it because she was thinking of Antonio, wishing they were going out one last time? Or did she want to impress Camden? Guilt stabbed at her heart with the last thought.

Too late to undo it. Elena fluffed her hair one more time and headed for the kitchen.

FIVE

"So, what do you think?" Camden asked Elena as she took another bite of her vampiro taco. They sat at a picnic bench beside the food truck in a parking lot on a hill, the early evening sun still hanging over the Pacific. The rose-colored light flamed the gold highlights in Elena's dark brown curls. Camden tried not to stare but lost that battle pretty quickly.

Elena fanned her hand in front of her mouth as she chewed and then stuck her index finger up—*one second.* "Steaming hot. Spicy. Amazing." She pointed to Tina. "And I think I know why they call them vampiros." Two lines of red juice streaked from the corners of Tina's mouth down to her chin and dripped onto her plate.

Camden laughed and handed the grinning little girl a napkin. "Mystery solved. Once we're done, we can walk down to the beach to watch the sunset." He bit into his taco, which he'd asked for with double the carne asada and minus the finely chopped cabbage.

"Really? The view from here's spectacular." Elena gazed

out at the shining water past the buildings clinging to the steep hill.

"Sure is," Camden said, gazing at her face.

She looked away from the view to him. "You're not even looking at...oh." She stared down at her plate while her cheeks turned pink. *Damn, she's just so charming and sweet,* Camden thought.

"So, yeah," he continued. "View's great here, but there's a neat little magic trick I want to show Tina, and it only works on the beach."

"What is it?" Tina wiped her chin and took another bite.

"Nope. You'll just have to see when we get there. And you have to do exactly as I say or it doesn't work."

Tina's eyes went to her mom. *As they should,* Camden thought. *I'm still a bit of a stranger.* When Elena nodded, the little girl looked back at Camden with a smile that opened his heart right up. "Okay. Can we go now?"

"Let the grown-ups finish their meal first," Elena said, running her hand over her daughter's hair.

Tina looked squarely at Camden. "Eat faster."

"Pepita!" Elena exclaimed. "Don't be rude. Say sorry."

"Sorry."

Camden moved his taco toward his mouth in slow-motion just to make Tina and Elena giggle. He wanted to ask about Tina's nickname, Pepita, the Spanish word for little pumpkin seed. It was cute and he'd never heard anyone else use it before. Maybe when they got to the beach—after the trick, of course. He remembered his own dad showing him the trick when he was even younger than Tina, and his amazement when he thought, just for a second before his father explained the trick, that his dad could move the universe.

The pain in his heart caught up to him the next moment.

He remembered the second time he'd seen the trick—at sunset riding up the glass elevator of Burj Khalifa, the tallest building in the world, in Dubai while on a short leave from his post in Afghanistan. Watching it then sparked his memory of the first time. He'd wanted to show the trick to his own little girl when she was old enough and never got the chance. He pushed down the guilt. That was years ago. A different life. He needed to live in the present, with an eye toward the future. One he wasn't sure he deserved, but desperately wanted anyway.

Elena touched his hand, sending electric tingles up his arm that definitely grounded him in the here-and-now. "Are you okay?" Concern filled her warm brown eyes.

"Fine, fine. Just thinking about my job." Not a lie—it was a man's job to spoil the sweet little girl and the beautiful woman who held his heart. He devoured the rest of his vampiro in two huge bites. "Let's get down to the beach. It's magic time."

After their walk down the hill, with Tina imploring them to hurry the entire way, the three of them stood on the beach and faced the Pacific. When they got there, Tina surprised them both by pulling her dress off over her head and revealing the swimsuit underneath.

"Did you wear that to school?" Elena asked, looking totally flabbergasted.

"I wear it *everywhere*, Mama. Just in case."

Elena looked at Camden and shook her head. "My daughter, the mermaid. Thing is, I can't actually argue with her logic right now," she waved her hand toward the ocean, "because this."

She held her hand out to Tina. "At least give me your

pump so that it doesn't get all sandy or wet." The little girl expertly undid her insulin pump and turned it over to Elena.

"Will she be okay without it?" Camden asked, hating the pit he felt in his stomach. He upbraided himself for not educating himself more on diabetes.

"Sure, for a while. I always have extra glucose and some fast-acting insulin on hand, just in case. But I see we're gonna have to upgrade her pump to a waterproof one." She smiled up at Camden. "It's sweet of you to be concerned."

The sun was a red sliver slipping down into the water. *Perfect timing*, Camden thought. "Now, don't stare straight into the sun," he warned. "But lay down flat on the sand and tell me the *exact second* when the sun totally disappears, and be ready."

Tina immediately went belly-flat, but Elena shook her head. "No way, not in this dress."

Camden winked. "That's okay. This magic only works for one person at a time." *As opposed to the magic I want to show you, which always works for two*, he silently added. But his thoughts must have shown in his eyes, because Elena quickly looked away, back at the horizon.

He crouched down, waiting for Tina.

When she said "Gone," he quickly grabbed and lifted her as high as he could.

"It's back!" she shouted. "Now it's gone again. You made the sun set twice." She beamed down at him, her eyes twice as bright as the actual sun.

"Nope. That's the magic of science. The earth curves, so when you're down flat and then up high suddenly, your eyes 'catch up' with the sun. It's even cooler when you're in a tall building. I saw it once at Burj Khalifa, in Dubai."

Camden set Tina on the sand. "You should do that to Mom next time."

Elena laughed. "I don't think he can lift me like he can you, Pepita. Not with these." She gave her luscious, rounded hip a slap, sending Camden's brain straight to his dick. *Lord, give me strength if she does that again,* he pleaded silently, *or I will pick her up and do things that will make her beg me to never put her back down.*

Oh, hell with it.

Camden drove at Elena like a linebacker and swooped her into his arms. He ran down the beach behind other sunset-watchers, carrying Elena while she shrieked and laughed. Tina ran alongside, mingling her laughter with her mom's. He set Elena back down gently, resisting the urge to plant a kiss on her forehead before traveling to her lips. He loved seeing the mirth in her eyes, proud that he put it there. *We are going to kiss tonight, Elena Martinez, fucking count on it.*

"You weigh nothing," he told her. "I wish I could have carried you instead of Old Misery during BUD/S."

Elena blinked rapidly. "I think I know all the words you just said, but strung together that way they make no sense. So, um, thanks, I think?"

Camden laughed. "BUD/S is SEAL school. Old Misery is the telephone pole-sized log we had to carry over our heads during beach training."

Tina gazed up at Camden. "You went to school with seals on the beach? I wanna do that, Mama."

Camden cracked up. "Not real seals, you little mermaid. SEALS are elite teams with the Navy."

"Oh." Tina immediately lost interest and went chasing after a plover running in and out of the surf.

"Well. Glad I could impress her." Camden thumped his chest and Elena held her stomach laughing. "I can tell you're just as impressed. My job here is done."

But just as Elena straightened, a beach bunny strolled

past and casually said, "*I'm* impressed." She sauntered on a few steps before smiling back over her shoulder and continuing down the beach.

Does she actually think I'm gonna follow her? Camden thought. *Clearly, the Frog Hogs have migrated north from San Diego and are out in force tonight.*

He rolled his eyes before he caught the briefly devastated look on Elena's face. She covered it with a smile that came and went whiplash-quick. "I'm sure you get a lot of that." She glanced down the beach toward the woman. Her hand wandered to the chain around her neck with its unmistakable wedding band looped through it. "Look, if you want to go after her or anything," she shrugged as her words trailed off.

What the actual hell? "You think I'm into all the toothpicks running around here?"

Elena's eyebrows arched and her eyes widened. "That's mean."

Camden held his palms out. "Hey, I'm not disrespecting skinny women. I'm just saying, that's one thing I hate about L.A., about Hollywood. It takes a perfectly confident, beautiful woman, and whittles her down into a toothpick body—with a soul to match if she's not careful. If she's too hungry going after what she wants, it starves her even more."

Elena nodded, but her frown stayed in place. "Even so, if you want, Tina and I can call a ride home. I don't mind."

"Why would I *ever* do that?" Camden ran the back of his finger down Elena's bare shoulder to her elbow, enjoying her silky skin and the little shivers that ran behind his touch. "I just told you, I'm not attracted to women like her. Not just her body, but her attitude. We are clearly on a date and she—"

"We're not on a date." Elena turned and started walking toward Tina who had gotten a little too far ahead of them for comfort. She'd taken at least five steps before Camden snapped out of his shock and caught up.

"We aren't? Why? Just because Tina's along? I don't—"

"We aren't because we aren't dating. We're friends." She shrugged. "That's why I offered to find a ride home for Tina and me, if you wanted..." she gestured behind her and left the rest unsaid.

"First of all, I don't want any of that." Camden waved his hand dismissively. "Second, I want..." He trailed off before his words about wanting to pull her to him, kiss her until her toes curled and she begged for more got him into trouble. *Damn it. I did tell her we'd do this under her terms, didn't I?* But, he'd expected or at least hoped that her terms would quickly change to his, which included getting naked together as soon as humanly possible.

"You want what?" Elena looked up at him, her hair softly glowing in the last light of the sunset.

Why lie? "Elena, I'd hoped that I've shown you I'd like to move on past friends sooner rather than later. This," he swept his arm out, indicating her and Tina, "feels really good."

Tina took that opportunity to look back at them and hold up something she'd found. "Mom! Camden! Look!" She sprinted back.

"We just got to California, Cam. I'm..." Elena's hand found the chain with the ring again, and as she tugged on it, Camden felt as if she were pulling his heart out of his chest instead. "Give me time, okay?"

Tina showed off the sand dollar she'd found and Camden told her the myth of the star etched on its surface and the dove-shaped pieces rattling inside. He kept his voice happy, but he felt hollow as he spoke and he couldn't help glancing time and again at the wedding band on the chain around Elena's neck.

I'm fighting a ghost. That's a tough job, even for the strongest SEAL.

Camden took Elena and Tina home. He lifted Tina up for one last hug and loved the way the little girl wrapped her arms around his neck as she thanked him for dinner and the magic trick. When Elena hugged him, he couldn't help but feel the metal of the ring press into his solar plexus like an accusing finger.

Camden had a hell of a time falling asleep that night. When he did, he fell deeply, then sat bolt upright in bed when he heard a cell phone ringtone he hadn't used in five years. He flailed around for the phone as cold sweat trickled down the back of his neck, thinking he was back in the dry desert heat on the night he got the call telling him his wife and baby were gone from the world.

Only a nightmare.

But his phone had dinged—an alert for new email from one of his teammates. He grabbed his secured laptop from his bedside table and opened it, wondering who the hell was up and working in the middle of the night. Smart money said Gina.

And the smart money was correct. Gina had forwarded a pic of a heavily-redacted page. From what wasn't blacked out, Camden put together the message that one of the agents maybe wasn't so foreign, was actually a US citizen, and that Roger already knew this person.

Camden smacked the back of his head against the headboard. Bennett knew roughly a bazillion people. Was it someone close to him, or a new acquaintance? How could they ever narrow it down?

He closed his laptop, punched his pillow, and lay back down. As Camden tossed and turned the rest of the night, images of his wife Susan's face flashed through his mind. And then the tiny scrunched-up face of his newborn daughter Chloe as he held her in his arms just before his last deployment. If he'd known then it would be the last time he'd ever see her, he would've never put her down, would have gone AWOL instead, anything to stay and prevent the tragedy that he carried squarely on his shoulders. Guilt seized Camden and shook him in its teeth.

He realized he wasn't fighting just one ghost, but three.

SIX

Elena spent the next couple days settling into her job with the firm. Well, at least she tried her best to settle in. While the job in no way, shape, or form came close to being as terrible as the day to day she endured working at Earnest Deal's meatpacking plant, it was difficult in completely different ways. Back at the plant, she knew who she was and where she stood. She'd had a scorecard and knew what to expect from whom and exactly how much she could dish back without running afoul of Deal or his thugs.

Brant and Phillips Promotions was a different story. New, complex social rules sometimes left her confused as to whether she'd been complimented or insulted. Part of the problem was that everyone acted as though they didn't want to offend, and yet sometimes their gleaming, toothy smiles reminded her of kitchen knives lined up and waiting to be used. Even when she took her boss's advice and baked a new batch of gluten-free, maple-sweetened blondies—which turned out as delicious as the 'guilty' cookies and disappeared twice as fast—she still felt like she'd done something wrong, even if no one came out and told her directly. Except, she'd gotten another anonymous note saying how great they were.

Elena mastered the details of her job quickly. She'd been born to organize and design systems that hummed with efficiency even in the midst of chaos, which had served her well when she worked restaurant jobs, because nothing was more chaotic than a kitchen when the dishwasher didn't show and the line cook was too hungover and nauseous to grill onions without running for the bathroom, and the chef was on about how they'd never get out of the weeds and the patrons filled the dining room all at once. Elena walked into that kitchen like the Goddess of Calm and Tranquility gliding untouched through the fires of hell. She thrived on kitchen chaos, calming down the chef by sending him out to swan among the adoring patrons and buying them time, calling in a dependable backup dishwasher, and jumping onto the line to grill onions while the line cook chugged her homemade hangover remedy.

But those days were a long time ago and she missed them. To Elena, food meant comfort and safety and a way to show others she loved them.

Elena finished up sending out a batch of emails and realized it was almost time for lunch. She usually brought her own but decided to treat herself by going out as a way of learning both the literal landscape of her new home and the food landscape as well. Her thoughts wandered back to when Camden took her and Tina out for vampiros. Her mind went immediately to that moment on the beach when she impulsively told Camden they weren't on a date.

Even now, she cringed at the memory. She hadn't meant to be so harsh, but the skank who'd hit on Camden right in front of her rattled Elena. She'd felt so many things—embarrassment and anger mostly, even a touch of sadness related to a sense of loss. But the hot surge of jealousy took her by surprise. Jealousy was such a foreign sensation that she almost didn't recognize it, but no question, she hated it. Hated the way it made her heart race and her blood pound in her ears and her mouth dry out. Worst of all, she'd wanted to grab Camden and scream *Mine*!

Since she couldn't do that without looking like some insane cavewoman, to make the jealousy go away, Elena took the opposite tact and told herself it didn't matter, they weren't together. She'd had her chance at love and lost it too soon when Antonio died. Who was she to expect she could find that spark again, and that it would be returned in equal measure?

No. Even if it hurt him in the short run, it was better to push Camden away now than to develop feelings for a man who was the polar opposite of her quiet, stoic husband. Camden laughed with his head thrown back, he joked and flirted and had been in the military and seen and done God-knew-what in Afghanistan. Antonio had been a pacifist. He couldn't even kill the spiders that made Elena shriek whenever she saw them. He'd give her a sweet smile before cupping them gently and carrying them outside. Camden would probably tease her and then smash them as hard as he could. They'd never make it in the long run, could they?

Elena didn't dare think about what the two men had in common. How they would both protect her and Tina even if it meant risking their lives. Camden had already proven that.

Stop it right now, Elena thought as her chest filled with a gooey warmth like hot caramel.

She opened her bottom desk drawer and took out her purse—she never, ever let her purse touch the floor out of superstition that the money would 'drain' into the ground, a superstition her mother had taught her, and one of the only things Elena retained of the woman who abandoned her. She turned her phone on to see if she'd missed any calls or texts—she wasn't allowed to have her phone on during working hours, which bothered her since she wouldn't know right away if anything was wrong with Tina. It buzzed with incoming messages.

The first was a text from Rachael reminding her that she'd stop by the apartment before Bette's Bash the weekend after next:

And bring a dish to pass!

So weird how normal that sounded, considering Jake's parents lived in Beverly Hills and Bette was a household name. *I wonder who all will be there and how many I'll know from movies or the top forty music charts?* She remembered Rachael and Jake's wedding, how tongue-tied she'd been among the glitterati.

How did I end up in this crowd? And worse, how will I ever fit in? Then she shrugged. She'd fit in the way she always did—by making irresistible food. And if worse came to worst, she'd hide out in the kitchen while the stars all lounged by the pool.

The second text was from Camden:

Hope to see you at the party. If you're uncomfortable about what to expect at a Bette's Backyard Bash (that's trade-marked BTW) don't be. She's the best and she already thinks of you and the little mermaid as family. That's a good thing.

Elena smiled at Camden's thoughtfulness. He must have remembered how awkward she'd felt at the celebrity-studded wedding. He'd admitted while they danced that he still got star-struck at times, too.

His second text read:

If you need a breather I can hang out w/ you in the

kitchen. As a friend. Ok, and selfishly hoping you might spontaneously cook something while we're there... ;-)

And damn if that melty, caramel feeling didn't flood her chest again.

"Knock, knock," a quiet voice said and Elena looked up quickly.

"Sorry! I was trying not to startle you." A tiny woman with sun-streaked hair tied up in a messy bun held her hands up as she stood by Elena's desk. "I'm a big fan of your work." Her smile revealed deep dimples on either side of her mouth.

Elena frowned and looked around her desk. "My...work?"

The woman laughed. "Not your receptionist skills, though you do kick serious butt in that department. I'm talking about the cookies and blondies. They totally rocked. They've kept me going this week. I think I'm on like hour eighty-five."

"You work here?" Sitting at the front, Elena thought she knew everyone by sight, but this woman was completely unfamiliar.

"Yeah. I'm back in IT. I've been getting in before everybody else and leaving late all damn week. We had a breach and it's all hands on deck. I'm Elissa. Lissa for short." She stuck her hand out.

Elena shook it. Lissa looked too tan to be stuck in IT all day. Then she noticed the dark circles under her eyes that contrasted with the woman's peppy energy.

"I'm Elena, but you probably knew that. Wait, are you the one who left me the notes?"

"Yup, that's me." Lissa beamed. "I didn't have time to give you a proper thank you until today. So thank you officially. Are you getting ready to go to lunch? Do you want to come with me? I'm starving and this is the first break I've had all week." She leaned in close and lowered her voice. "Julia's out today. Maybe you and me can go a little longer than usual."

Elena felt a guilty pleasure at being a co-conspirator. "Let's do it."

Lissa's dimples reappeared. "I bet you're a foodie like me. I know just where to go."

"Lead the way, fellow foodie," Elena said, happily leaving her receptionist's desk behind.

They went to a nearby restaurant called Delia's. The second Elena walked in, she knew it was exactly the sort of place she wanted someday. It was small and pretty and smelled divine. The air had a relaxed vibe the way it does in a restaurant when everyone is working in flow. That usually only happened when the manager knew exactly what she was doing. Elena could practically hear the gears turning efficiently in the kitchen, even with a full house out front.

"Do you think it's gonna be a long wait?" she asked Lissa.

"Not for us." She caught the maître d's eye and he winked at her past eight other people ahead of them. He held up his hand, beckoning.

Everyone turned and looked at Elena and Lissa. The tiny woman parted the crowd like the Red Sea as she said *excuse me* over and over, and Elena followed in her wake.

"Table in the back?" the maître d asked, though he looked like he already knew the answer before Lissa confirmed it.

"As always, Pete," she said as they wove between the tables, and to Elena's astonishment, through the kitchen doors and to a little table set and ready for them off to the side and out of the way of the kitchen's hustle and bustle.

"Pete, this is my new friend, Elena. I think she likes food as much as I do."

"Impossible," Pete said, smiling at Elena. "But I'm willing to give you the benefit of the doubt for now." He grinned and bowed and added, "Welcome to Delia's and enjoy your meal."

The table was set up so that both women could watch the kitchen. As Elena sat down, she realized Pete had not left them menus. She looked at the door leading back to the dining room. "Oh, I think he forgot—"

"Nope, no menu for us." Lissa patted the tabletop. "We are at the tender mercies of Delia now."

Elena smiled. "I am so glad I met you."

Lissa beamed. "Same."

"So, how do you rank the VIP treatment?"

Lissa looked toward the kitchen and gave a chin lift toward a woman Elena assumed must be Delia, watching over a line cook's shoulder. Her hair was hidden under a navy-and-white calico bandana that matched the full apron over her chef's whites. As soon as Lissa caught her eye, Delia nodded, patted the cook on the arm, and headed for their table.

"Dee and I went to culinary school together. I dropped out when I realized I was way more skilled at appreciating food than actually making it. Dee graduated and worked her way up to the restaurant goddess she is today. But she never forgot her bumbling little friend."

"I heard that," Delia said when she reached their table. "Half my recipes wouldn't exist without your refined palate, girl, so shut the hell up."

Lissa introduced Elena to Delia. "I am in awe of your kitchen even before I've taken a bite," Elena said.

Delia raised an eyebrow. "Really? Why's that?"

"I worked in kitchens for years. Yours is a well-oiled food-making machine." Elena pointed to the line. "Look at how they're working in-sync. That doesn't just happen. It's so easy to get in each other's way. You've even got the lefty on the far end where he won't bump into the righties."

Delia looked at Lissa. "Bring her back anytime," she said as she returned to her domain. After that, plate after delectable plate found its way to their table. Elena leaned into the buzz good food always brought her. And Delia's dishes were exceptional. Elena's mind went to work on deconstructing the food—especially the meat dishes—so that she could recreate them for Camden. Only if the opportunity arose, of course.

Delia briefly stopped back at their table to ask their opinions at the end of the meal, and Elena was happy to give hers. Delia only nodded, holding her cards close to her vest, but Elena got the feeling she took her suggestions to heart.

Back at her desk, Elena patted her stomach. "Thank you so much for taking me out to lunch, Chica. Next one's on me, I insist."

"It's a date, fellow foodie." Elissa waved before disappearing back into the bowels of the IT department. She'd told Elena over lunch she hoped to wrap things up tonight because tomorrow, the pipe promised to be killer at Malibu and she didn't want to miss it. Surfing was an even bigger passion than food for her new friend.

Just before tucking her phone away, Elena answered Camden's text:

I appreciate you wanting to hang in the kitchen with me at the party, friend! Hope you feel like being my food Guinea pig cuz I wanna experiment.

Each time she went to hit send, Elena stopped and read the message over one more time. On the fifth attempt, she bit her lower lip, blew out her breath, deleted the word friend, and sent it before she could change her mind again.

SEVEN

"Not gonna lie, Jake," Camden said between sips of beer as they leaned against the half-wall on Bette's back patio, "my week sucked bright green monkey balls."

"Not gonna lie, Cam," Jake answered, "but that was obvious to everyone at Watchdog." He took a swig of the hoppy, fancy-ass beer Camden brought as his 'dish to pass' per usual for Bette's Backyard Bashes. Camden would set up his Tequila Sour station at the bar later when more guests arrived and those in the know clamored for it. He wouldn't be drinking one himself—the minute the Bennetts walked through the door, he was unofficially on the job. Gina and Costello were already there, Costello mingling and Gina standing statuesque in the shadows, though immediately friendly when approached.

Camden shook his head, angry at himself for letting his emotions get in the way of his work. Granted, he was frustrated with the chatter—or lack thereof, nothing new came through about this American agent—but his not-a-date with Elena must have soured him more than he realized. But looking back, he saw what Jake meant. He'd been short with the FNGs and the dogs steered around him whenever he entered the courtyard—all except Toby, though even he'd given Camden the doggy side-eye a few times. *Guess dogs can smell a total prick just as well as they can smell fear.* Good thing he'd already met with Bennett and family beforehand or he was sure he would've come across as a complete asshole.

The only bright spot was receiving a text back from Elena last week about the party. He'd half-expected her to blow him off, but instead, she'd offered to make him her foodie Guinea pig. Hard to tell though if she was serious or just being nice. Still, he'd jumped at the chance to spend more time with her, texting back that he looked forward to any torture she wanted to dish out. *Ha-ha, dish out, get it?* he'd added lamely. But maybe the more she saw how much he could be there for her and Tina, just like her first husband, the more she'd let him in.

And the more he could attempt to put his past behind him.

"Anything I can help with, brother?" Jake's question brought Camden out of his thoughts.

"Not unless you know how many vampiros it takes to conquer a ghost."

Jake blinked at him. "Okay, one shrink coming right up, unless you care to elaborate on what the hell that even means."

"It means my date—no, my *attempted* date—with Elena snafued."

"Dude, how? You guys are perfect for each other."

The rich, salty smell of grilled kobe beef wafted across the porch, making Camden's stomach grumble. Jake's dad, Grant, was already at it, grilling more food than anyone needed, though Camden would give it his best shot. "I guess I'm not as perfect for her as her first husband was."

"Ohhh. Damn, brother, cockblocked by a memory?"

"That about sums it up."

Jake balanced his beer on the top of the patio wall and studied Camden like a piece of complicated sheet music.

"What?"

"You haven't told her, have you?"

Shit. I do not want this conversation, Camden thought. "Told her what?"

Jake pointed at him. "Do not be a dick to me by insulting my intelligence. You know exactly what I'm talking about. She's not the only one with ghosts that need conquering." He folded his arms and added, "See? Not dumb. I figured it out."

"I don't want to talk about that. About them. Not with her." Even the thought of bringing up Susan—let alone Chloe, God fucking forbid—sent his heart racing at deathmetal speed. The last thing he wanted was Elena to know how badly he'd fucked up with his own family. How he'd let them down. The two people most precious to him in the universe, and he failed them.

Oh, fuck no. He wasn't talking about that with Elena. *Ever.*

Jake's phone buzzed. "Well," he said, checking the text, "you'd better think of something to talk about, because she just pulled up with Rachael."

"Shit." Camden slammed the last of his beer and a server appeared out of nowhere to take his empty bottle. He followed Jake back through the house to the front doors. Bette beat them there. Her motorized wheelchair glided almost silently across the foyer. She looked regal, like the Hollywood queen she was, with her platinum blond hair bobbed just under her jawline and a sporty but classy pink outfit. Camden wondered for a second if Rachael had texted her too, but then realized Bette's security team had probably alerted her before the women even pulled onto the property, or possibly their driver sent a quick message. Which meant she was really looking forward to greeting Elena and Tina.

"Oh, sure, Mom," Jake said. "Cam and I've been here an hour and we see neither hide nor hair of you, but you're skirting like NASCAR to the door for Rachael and Elena."

"*And* Tina," Bette said. "How dare you forget the little lady who upstaged you at your wedding reception."

"I'll get the door, Mom." Jake jogged past his mother.

"Thank you, sweetheart." She fell in next to Camden, who bent and gave the woman he loved like his own mother a quick kiss on the cheek. "At least he's picking up *some* good manners from you," she said, patting his arm.

"Only by accident, Ms. C.," Camden answered, winking. "I think Rachael gets the real credit."

Bette smiled fondly at her daughter-in-law's name. Jake had told him the two women had bonded hard over their past tragedies—and their shared path forward. Camden hoped Bette would do the same with Elena. She deserved all the people she could get in her corner.

Jake opened the door and insta-hugged Rachael. She'd gone to Elena's that morning to help her get ready for the party. No doubt Elena was internally shaking in her boots, but the woman standing in the doorway stealing Camden's breath away appeared confident and capable on the outside. Goddamn, she looked gorgeous, from the tips of her iridescent-painted toenails peeking out from her wedge sandals, up her tan legs to the hem of her rose-colored dress which caressed her delectable curves tapering to her waist, only to bloom again into a teasingly sexy peek at her cleavage. She or Rachael had pinned her long hair up, leaving only a few curling strands to brush her bare shoulders. Her lips matched her dress and Camden wondered if they tasted as good as they looked. He imagined fresh strawberries and his mouth watered.

Good God in heaven, he wanted her.

"Thank you so much for inviting us, Mrs. Collins," Elena said as she stepped forward to give Bette a bouquet of purple irises tied with a green bow. Her voice held the slightest quiver.

"Oh, my dear, no. Never call me Mrs. Collins. Only Bette, please, unless you're Camden who insists on formalities." She gave him a quick grin. "We barely had time to talk at the wedding, so I'm glad you're here, Elena." Bette took the irises and clutched them to her chest. "Thank you. These are my favorite flowers." Her gaze went to Tina, holding an identical bouquet. "And there's the flower girl who stole the show at the reception."

At Elena's touch to her back, Tina solemnly held out her bouquet to Bette. "These are for you, too. Thank you for inviting me."

"How could I not invite such a charming scene-stealer? You'll have to tell me how you do it. I could use some new pointers." The Oscar-winning actress shared a smile with Elena, who appeared to relax just a little.

Tina tilted her head. "Why are you in a wheeling chair? No one will tell me."

Bette's attention snapped back to the little girl. Her chin tilted up and her eyes narrowed in an expression Camden recognized from one of her roles—as a powerful and brilliant killer. She used the same look on Camden when she wanted the truth out of him whenever Jake went undercover and she got worried. It seldom failed.

Elena's eyes widened, her cheeks flushed, and her smile disappeared. "Tina, that's—"

"A perfectly reasonable question," Bette said, studying

Tina. "A bad man did this to me because I wouldn't do what he wanted. He thought he could destroy me but he just made me stronger."

"What happened to him?" Tina asked.

"He's staying in prison for a long time. I was one of many who helped put him there."

Tina nodded, a thoughtful look in her eyes. "He's a loser."

"The biggest. So, that's how I ended up in a 'wheeling' chair. How about you? I understand you have some sort of pump? What's that thing for?"

"Diabetes." Then Tina grinned. "It thought it could destroy me when I was a baby."

Bette pursed her lips as she considered the girl. "Yeah, you look pretty strong to me, kid."

"Yup. I'm hungry and something smells good. Is it time to eat?"

Bette's eyes crinkled when she smiled. "That's the whole point of today. Eat, drink, and be merry. For tomorrow, we'll... recover from today."

Bette turned her chair around and started through the house. "Follow me to the grub. *Allons-y*," she said, raising her hand in the air like a matador. "That's French for let's go."

"*Allons-y*," Tina echoed as she skipped to catch up with Bette while Elena blinked rapidly and mock-collapsed into Camden's arms. He happily folded her to his chest.

"What just happened?" Her big brown eyes met Camden's, melting his heart.

He squeezed her around the waist, pleased that she squeezed him back. "Two things. Bette just gained her billionth fan. And so did Tina."

Jake and Rachael came up behind Elena. Jake squeezed her shoulder. "On behalf of the band," he said in his worst Liverpool accent, "you've passed the audition."

Rachael smiled and shook her head. "Ringo Starr."

"Got it in one per usual, Angel. Now, let's go see what my dad hasn't burned to a crisp before everyone else gets here. As Mom says, *Allons-y*."

Much to Camden's continued pleasure, Elena kept her arm around his waist as they followed Jake and Rachael, along with Bette's driver as he carried in the dishes Elena made and a tote bag full of toys to keep Tina busy. Right before they got to the kitchen, Elena stopped him.

"Camden, I just want to apologize for my behavior on Monday."

His heart lifted. "What do you mean? You didn't do a damn thing wrong."

Elena shook her head and touched her fingers to his lips to quiet him. Her fingers smelled like cinnamon and spice and everything nice and he fought not to lick them. "But, I did, Cam. I acted like a freaked-out teenager, and..." Her eyes went a little unfocused and her strawberry lips parted as she seemed to realize just where her fingers were.

But to his delight, she didn't remove them. He raised his eyebrows and parted his lips ever so slightly as he exhaled.

She swallowed hard. "And, um." She blinked and laughed lightly as she shook her head. "If it isn't obvious, I'm not used to dating. Which, yes, that was a date, despite what I said." She lowered her hand and grew serious. "I'm afraid of messing this up. Okay, messing it up more than I already have."

Camden took her hand and rubbed his thumb across her palm, delighting in the shivers he felt run through her body. "Hey, I'm in this with you. I don't want to fuck anything up, either. Not with you, and not with Tina. I haven't had a significant relationship in, well, a long time."

She must have seen something in Camden's eyes

because she squeezed his hand as a little worry line crept in just above the bridge of her nose. "Do you want to talk about it?"

Oh, hell no.

His stomach, champion of champions, saved him with a loud rumble. "What I want to do is eat. My lord and master stomach has spoken."

The worry line stayed long enough to alarm Camden before disappearing as she smiled. Elena laid her hand on his belly, this time giving him the shivers. "What stomach? All I see is a washboard." And then, God help him, she ran her fingers up his abdomen. "All I feel, too."

He grabbed her hand out of self-defense. If she kept touching him that way, he'd throw her down right there in the hall, and that would just be rude toward Bette. *And it'd be just my luck that the Bennetts would come in right now.*

Camden brought Elena's fingers and their sweet, spicy scent back up to his lips and this time he didn't hesitate to taste them. *Yes.* Cinnamon, sugar, cardamom, and a spicy little kick at the end.

Elena shut her eyes. She leaned forward and stretched up to meet his lips with hers. The softest brush, the lightest tease, before Tina's laughter in the kitchen mere feet away reminded them they were at a party.

Elena bit her luscious lower lip and looked down, grinning. He licked his lips. *I was right—her mouth tastes like strawberries.* His jeans suddenly became way too tight and thoughts of all the empty bedrooms upstairs and the fun they could have in one of them filled his mind. He shifted his hips, hoping Elena hadn't noticed.

"It is like being a teenager again, isn't it?" he asked her. "Only, instead of sneaking around your parents, you gotta dodge a kiddo, am I right?"

Instead of laughing and agreeing, Elena looked away. *Ouch.* Not the reaction he'd hoped for.

"Fine," Camden said. "I'll make sure Tina doesn't see me kissing her mama."

Just as quickly, Elena looked back up at him. "It's not that. I think she'd be overjoyed."

That flipped his heart right over, but he couldn't bask in the warm feeling more than a second as long as something still bothered Elena. "Then what is it? What'd I say?"

Her mouth wavered and she gave a little head shake. "Nothing. It's not you. Dodging parents was never much of a concern for me." She looked past him. "I'm hungry, too, and I need to pop something in the oven to warm it up." One last little smile, just enough to assure Camden he wasn't in trouble, and Elena slipped past him and through the kitchen doorway.

It's ghosts all the way down for both of us, isn't it? Camden thought.

Just as he was about to follow Elena into the kitchen, his phone buzzed. Gina texted that the other guests Camden was waiting for had just arrived. He trotted back to the front door to greet the Bennetts. Talk about your All-American-apple-pie-looking family. Their clothing, while not being identical, coordinated enough to make them look like a team. Camden suspected Cici dressed everyone that morning. Well, Bennett would be marketing himself as the 'family's candidate' so it made sense to project that image hard.

"Good to see you again, Camden," Roger said. "Where's Jake? I have to tell him thank you for the invitation."

Cici held up a gift bag tied with a ribbon. "And I have something for the hostess." She looked past Camden as if Bette would suddenly materialize in the foyer. "I'm afraid I don't cook, so I didn't bring a dish to pass. I hope this will do instead."

"Ms. C. will love it, I'm sure. I think she's in the kitchen. I'll show you on the way to the backyard, where Jake's probably giving his dad a hard time over the grill."

Cici's eyes widened at the word kitchen. "I'm amazed Bette Collins even knows she has a kitchen. I assumed she'd have people for that."

"You don't know Ms. C." Camden motioned for them to follow him. "She had to hire outside staff for today. She likes things small and personal otherwise." He paused at the kitchen door. "The backyard is straight on through this hall if you want to join us out there after you give her your gift." Camden didn't need to break out his crystal ball to guess Cici wouldn't stay in there long, unless she was truly star-struck.

Roger and the twins followed Camden to the back patio, where Jake was grilling his dad harder than Grant was grilling the meat. Toby, Fleur, and Anubis the dog assigned to Costello, were chasing each other in the yard, a cloud of kids trying to keep up in their wake. The twins watched, obvious longing on their faces.

"Go ahead, kids," Roger said. "Just don't get dirty or your mom will kill me." He gave Camden a *know what I mean?* smile as Brittney and Brice practically launched themselves off the patio after the dogs.

Jake turned and greeted Roger. Then he asked, "Have you met my dad?"

"Sir, I haven't had the pleasure." He stuck his hand out for Grant Collins to shake. "I love your work."

Grant laughed. "I'm surprised you're familiar. Nobody

knows stuntmen, and I haven't been in a movie since 1995. Or was it 1998?"

Roger laughed. "Ah, but I'm familiar. The twins love the *Double-O Trouble* series. I've watched it with them a gazillion times. I don't know how you survived those stunts."

Grant laughed and waved him off. "I've got the scars to prove I almost didn't. They're rebooting the series, only now they're making the secret agent's kid a girl instead of a boy. They asked if I'd do a walk-on part. I said sure, but I don't do explosions anymore."

True to Camden's prediction, Cici had already joined them, taking Roger's arm in hers. She smiled at Grant's story, until she spotted the twins running in the yard, then frowned with concern. "I hope they don't fall. Grass stains are impossible."

Camden was suddenly concerned too, but for an entirely different reason than grass stains. Something about one of the servers down there seemed out of place. He didn't have a tray and he wasn't heading to or from the kitchen. He was just standing there, watching the kids through thick-framed glasses.

Shit.

Camden nudged Jake and motioned with his chin. "See?" he said even as he started jogging toward the man.

"Shit. On it." Jake followed.

Behind them, Camden heard Cici ask, "What?" But he was too focused on his target to answer. This wouldn't be the first time a Bash got compromised.

"Hey there, can you get me a Shirley Temple?" Camden said as he and Jake approached the man, standing between him and the house. He turned and Camden was close enough to confirm it—the asshole was wearing camera glasses. His eyes went round as he looked back and forth between

Camden and Jake, then looked past them to Gina and
Costello coming to join the party.

"We can do this easy or we can do this hard. Which is it?"

"I don't know what you're talking about." The guy took a
step back.

"Easy is, you give me the glasses and your ID and I escort
you out quietly to a waiting security vehicle. Maybe Mrs.
Collins files trespassing charges, maybe not, but either way,
you get questioned by me. Hard is—"

The idiot turned and bolted across the lawn toward the
far wall behind the hedgerow.

Camden sighed. "Hard it is. Toby!" The dog's attention
immediately went to Camden, who gave him the signal to
apprehend. The dog took off like a shot after the dude, who'd
made it behind the hedge—a bit of a blessing, since it meant
no one would have to see Toby at work.

Camden and Jake ran after the dog, who by then had
taken down the man, judging by the guy's shouts. Sure
enough, Toby had a hold of the man's leg as he still tried to
crawl to the wall. Camden pulled Toby off him while Jake
zip-tied his hands behind his back. He found his wallet and
flipped through it. Two of Bette's security guards came
jogging up, embarrassment all over their faces.

Jake tore the guy's glasses off. "Yeah, I thought that was
you, Anderson."

"You know him?" Camden asked.

"Paparazzi scum."

Anderson pointed to his glasses even as the guards pulled
him up. "That's private property."

"No," Jake said, pointing to the ground. "*This* is private
property. And these are mine now." He slipped them on and
Camden braced for the inevitable Elvis impression.

Gina sidled up to the guards and smiled. "I'd like to have a talk with him." She pointed back toward the hidden guard-house at the back of the property.

"I'll come with you," Camden said.

Gina held up a hand. "I've got this."

"I can—"

She fixed him with her golden eyes. "No. I've *got* this." She held out her hand to Jake. "Glasses. Please."

EIGHT

As the commotion in the back yard died down and Bette's house filled with new guests either unaware of the breach or laughing it off once they heard Ron Anderson's name, Elena successfully stayed in the kitchen for almost an hour, but Rachael wouldn't let her keep hiding and neither would Bette.

"Are you sure everything is all right?" Elena asked Bette.

Bette waved her off. "It's nothing. It happens. Usually, they ignore the law and send a drone over our heads. Ron Anderson just likes to be a pain-in-the-ass daredevil."

But—"

"No, my dear," she said as she led Elena to a room just off the patio full of women lounging on chairs and couches. "You're new to town and I won't have you hiding during my party. You need to mix and mingle. Make friends. Take advantage of the free babysitting." Bette winked at her, then went off to see what her new bestie Tina was up to. The kids had been brought inside for obvious reasons.

Elena's head swam from all the introductions. Or it could've been the Tequila Sour Camden pressed into her hands with a smile and a wink before he returned to the back terrace to talk to the guys. Or maybe, it was from the kiss that she still felt tingling on her lips like the last trace of a ghost pepper.

That kiss. The first brush of a man's lips against hers since Antonio died, leaving her wanting so much more. And judging from the hungry look in Camden's eyes and the unmistakable bulge he tried unsuccessfully to hide, he wanted a second helping as well.

"Really, Elena, I'd ask for the recipe but I'd never cook it."

Elena blinked as she felt her cheeks redden. She'd completely lost track of the conversation going on around her, and now Cici Bennett had just...what? Insulted or complimented her spicy peanut Thai dip?

"It's absolutely delicious!" Cici went on, her voice slightly slurred. She'd acted especially upset by the incident and evidently decided to self-medicate. "But, I'd probably turn it into a hot mess even one of the dogs running around here wouldn't eat." She gestured to the floor-to-ceiling windows looking out at the patio and backyard where Toby and Anubis continued to patrol.

The other women sitting and standing around the—Elena didn't even know what exactly to call this room full of chairs, couches, and low tables but no TV or dining set—laughed at Cici's comment. But Elena smiled and shook her head. She gently touched the other woman's arm. "It's so simple to put together and you barely even have to turn the stove on. I promise you'd have no trouble at all."

Cici rolled her eyes. "You have no idea. How about I just have you over some time to make it? I can't cook, but I can open a mean bottle of wine." She raised her own Tequila Sour. "Or I'll just have you over when Camden's there and he can make up another batch of these."

When Camden's there? Elena wondered at that. Had she just met Camden because of the man in the back yard, or were the Bennetts using Watchdog Security? Made sense, since Roger Bennett was talking about running for office. It made Elena sad to think the family had received any threats. She liked Cici, who'd started up a conversation with her right away in the kitchen earlier. And the twins seemed like nice kids, the girl even offering to play with Tina once they all came in. As for Mr. Bennett, it was odd to see someone in real life who played so many different characters on TV. She half-expected him to behave like one of them, but of course he was a real person and seemed genuinely friendly when Cici introduced them.

Cici leaned in. "Judging by the way he watches you every time he walks by, I'd say Camden wouldn't mind. Do you know him already?"

Elena broke into a grin even as she felt her cheeks heat. "Yes, actually. He saved my daughter's life."

Cici's eyes widened to the size of dinner plates as she gripped Elena's arm and leaned back. A few women looked over. "Saved her *life?* Oh, my God, after what I just witnessed, you have to tell me that story!"

Heads swiveled. Whoever wasn't already looking at the two of them immediately snapped to attention, much to Elena's embarrassment.

She fidgeted with the hem of her dress. "Well, I was living in a horrible little town in Nebraska called Ross. And I worked for this monster named—"

"Wait, wait, let me go grab Roger. I want him to hear this." Before Elena could stop her, Cici jumped up and jogged out to the patio where a small group of people had gathered around Roger in the outdoor kitchen. One of them was Camden. Elena watched through the windows, mortified as

Cici approached her husband. Her drink sloshed around as she gestured wildly and pointed back inside. Camden first looked curious, then alert, then pissed. To Elena's dread, he followed the Bennetts back inside. Jake stared hard after Camden.

Oh, shit. What did I do? Elena's stomach flip-flopped and she regretted the tequila as it threatened to make a reappearance. She lost sight of them as they came in. When they reappeared in the wide arch of the doorway, Camden had regained his composure. He looked right at Elena, his expression unreadable but definitely not pleased. Roger had his arm around his wife, steadying her as she walked. His mood was just as unreadable as Camden's but in the opposite way—his smile looked forced.

"Okay, okay, start over, Elena." Cici dropped onto the couch next to her. Roger and Camden stood behind them. Elena felt Camden's hand land on her shoulder. She flinched and waited for a painful squeeze, something to let her know she'd fucked up royally. Instead, she was surprised by a gentle caress, his fingers stroking down her shoulder to her upper arm then back, over and over, and she relaxed under his touch. *Maybe I'm misreading everything,* she thought. She glanced up at him. His eyes softened, then turned wary as he looked at Cici.

The room went silent. All eyes were on Elena. "I'm sorry, I don't know how much I can actually say." She touched her new friend's arm. "There's an ongoing trial and I don't want to ruin Rachael's chances at justice by revealing something I shouldn't. But the important thing is, Camden was there when Tina and I needed him, and he literally saved my daughter's life."

Camden's hand froze on her shoulder. Elena glanced up to see his expression hadn't changed, and yet he held his breath. When their eyes met, something flashed deep in those amber-colored depths.

Cici gripped Roger's hand. Elena watched as sudden tears sprang to the woman's eyes. "He saved a little girl, Roger. We might be okay after all."

Roger laughed without any real humor behind it. When she started to say something, he interrupted her with, "That had nothing to do with us earlier. You look hungry. Why don't we see if there are any burgers left, huh?" He pulled his wife up and practically carried her out of the room.

Camden whispered, "Excuse me," and left the room, heading deeper into the house.

The other women, some Elena had only seen on the big screen, returned to their quiet conversations. Confused and mortified, Elena excused herself to no one in particular and went off to find Camden.

———

She found him in a room lined with full bookshelves and worn leather chairs. He stood with his back to the door, head bowed, gripping the back of a chair like a drowning man.

"Camden?" she called tentatively.

He straightened and turned. Anguish burned in his eyes. He closed the gap between them in three strides and pulled Elena to his chest. He nuzzled his face in her hair and took a deep, ragged breath. "Those words," he whispered.

"What words?" Elena pressed her cheek against his chest and felt his heart pounding. "I'm sorry if I said something I shouldn't have about what happened in Nebraska."

He shook his head. "No, baby, not that. What you said... that I was there when you and Tina needed me. You have no idea." He pulled back and looked down into her eyes. He searched her, sought to look inside, to know all of her. The passion she saw in his eyes was almost too much. And yet, she wanted it. Wanted to be seen like that, to be known. Desired.

"It's true," she said. "You saved her. Saved us. If anything had happened to Tina, it would've killed me. But it didn't because you were there when we needed you."

While she spoke, Elena watched the storm raging in Camden's eyes. He was fighting what she said and at the same time, clinging to it. He took her face in his hands and gently stroked her cheeks with his thumbs. Heat built up inside her. She wanted another kiss. But Camden just studied her face, his gaze roaming from her eyes to her cheeks to her lips where he paused. Elena sucked in her lower lip and bit it, watching as Camden's lips parted and his eyes softened, some of the storm abating. She gripped the nape of his neck and he groaned. Elena stood on her tiptoes as she pulled his face down to hers.

He paused just as their lips touched. "Elena," he whispered. "Thank you." The brush of his lips, the soft vibration of her name, and then he took her mouth. Rough, hot, demanding. Their arms tightened around each other. She wanted to crawl inside him, to take him inside of her. Her whimper drew another groan from him.

Camden slid his hands down her back, gripped her bottom, and lifted her. Her legs automatically went around his waist and he carried her back to the chair. He sat down and positioned her on his lap. His erection pressed against her panties and found the wet heat there. Elena glided against him, acutely aware they could be found at any moment but past caring. It had been years since she'd been held and kissed, and never like this—with so much raw hunger and need. Years since she'd wanted any sort of attention from a man, but here she was, throwing herself at a man who was the polar opposite of her husband. And all she wanted was more.

Camden's lips never left hers as he undid her hair, then buried his fingers in it. He pressed back against Elena, grinding and growling, his tongue teasing hers, thrusting into her mouth then pulling back so she could explore his mouth with her tongue. Then he abruptly cupped her cheeks and gently pulled her face away. He dropped his head back against the seat and rolled his eyes as he groaned. "I can't be doing this right now."

Elena's heart plummeted into her stomach. Camden was pissed at her after all. "I'm sorry. I said the wrong thing to Cici and I messed everything up."

Camden's head snapped back up. Concern filled his eyes. "You said nothing wrong, baby. Cici was drunk and talking out of turn. She was upset, but she shouldn't have put you on the spot like that."

So, if it wasn't what Elena said that had Camden in knots, then it must be something else. "Are you working for them? Are they okay? Was that Anderson guy trying to get pictures of them?"

He stroked her hair and gave her a smile that was almost a grimace. "I...am working for them."

"But you can't talk about it. I get it."

Camden's eyes widened slightly as if he were surprised at her response. He kissed her forehead. "It's not that I don't trust you."

"I know. Your job, sometimes it requires secrecy."

He tilted his head. "Are you okay with that?"

No, she wasn't. Elena hated secrets. She'd escaped a town full of toxic secrets that nearly destroyed her and Tina and Rachael. Secrets that had destroyed Antonio.

"I can tell you aren't." A little bit of light went out of Camden's eyes.

"I...it's not that. Okay, yeah, I hate secrets. But I know that they're necessary sometimes. To keep people safe. I get that."

"But can you live with it? Or is this a deal-breaker for us?"

"It's not a deal-breaker. As long as these are the only secrets you'll keep from me."

Camden swallowed and glanced down. *Not good.* He quickly looked up again and gazed deeply into her eyes. "I promise I will never keep any secrets from you that will hurt you. Or Tina. Anything I can't tell you is because I'm doing my job, trying to keep someone safe." He paused and Elena watched him fight with himself. "Sometimes, the person I'm keeping safe is gonna be me."

She touched his face. "Camden. You can trust me with your secrets. I know there's something you can't tell me because it hurts you. Something from your past that's still haunting you. That's what chased you from the room just now, isn't it? I'm guessing there was a time when you weren't there for someone. Somebody important to you."

The devastation on his face made her regret her words immediately. She'd hit more than a nerve—she'd bludgeoned his entire nervous system.

"Camden, God, I'm sorry." One hand covered her heart while the other cupped his cheek. "You don't have to tell me anything."

Camden's hand covered the one over her heart. "Don't apologize. It kills me that you always think you're saying or doing the wrong thing. You aren't. It's not your fault that I'm a minefield sometimes." He took a deep breath and blew it out. "No, that's on me. And it's on me to dig out some of those landmines so that you aren't always feeling like you need to walk on eggshells.

When we're together, I want you to be happy and relaxed. I want to have fun with you." His gaze drifted to her lips. "So many ways I want to have fun with you." He ran a finger down her arm, raising goosebumps. He nodded as if coming to a decision. "There is something I need to tell you, and it will hurt me to do it. It'll hurt because I'm afraid I'll lose your respect. And it'll hurt because it's a wound I've carried around for a long time now, something that I didn't think could ever begin to heal. I didn't think I *deserved* to heal." His eyes clouded. "And maybe I don't, but you make me want to get past it."

"Camden," Elena made her voice stern. "Everyone deserves to heal. Especially you. You're a good man. Brave, strong, sweet, funny as hell. Sexy." She felt the blush creep into her cheeks. "So sexy, I can't even believe you look at me twice."

"Have you *looked* in a mirror? Do I need to take you to get your eyes tested?" He dipped his head to her throat and kissed her while she laughed. "And it's not just that you are drop-dead gorgeous. You are so warm and caring and funny, too," he said against her skin. "And have I mentioned your cooking?"

"It's all about the cooking, isn't it? You love me for my cookies." Her heart clenched. *Did I just say love? Do I want him to love me?*

He looked at her, humor in his eyes replacing the earlier pain. "I can't believe you think...yeah, no, okay, I'm not gonna deny that it's partly about the cookies." The corners of his eyes crinkled. "But even if you never—God forbid—made me another cookie or any of the other billion wonderful things you cook, I'd still want to be a better man for you. I'd still want to make you laugh. Make you feel safe."

Elena's heart melted like warm butter. "I am honored that you feel that way. And I want you to know, I'm here for you. I want to help you heal. You can tell me anything—anything, Camden—and I'll never think less of you."

The hurt crept back into his eyes, but it seemed diminished, belied by a gentle smile. "Tell you what. It's too much to talk about right here, right now. But I will when we have some alone time. Is that acceptable?"

She couldn't say no. Not to those amber eyes. Not to the man who made her feel this alive and happy. "Absolutely. When you're ready. But make it soon."

He nodded. "I will, Gorgeous. For you, I will." His smile faded.

"Now what?"

"You read me too well. It's about the things I need to keep from you. I can't talk to you about the work I'm doing for the Bennetts."

"I understand. He's in politics. He needs a bodyguard, I'm sure."

"Yeah. And babe, I don't want to tell you who you can and cannot associate with. But, if you and Cici are friends now, well, it might complicate things."

Elena did not like that. "You're right, you can't tell me who's my friend and who isn't."

"I'm not saying for always. But just for now, can you just," he growled in frustration, "it's not about controlling you, it's about keeping you safe."

Elena pulled back. "I can keep myself safe."

Camden sighed. "Then do it for them, all right?"

For them? "I don't know how being friends with Cici is a security problem."

"Please, just trust me?" His eyes pleaded with her.

"I won't do anything stupid like open my mouth and share state secrets or whatever, if that's what you're worried about."

"That's not what I'm worried about. It's not you." He

stroked her cheek. "You know what? I'm doing it again. I'm putting things on you that I shouldn't. I'm sorry."

This was going to be hard. No, at times, it might be impossible. Elena had to accept that there were parts of Camden's life that would be closed to her. Not by his choice, but that's how it was. Maybe she needed to stop putting her guard up every time she felt uncomfortable. Maybe she did need to trust him more.

Elena smiled and stroked his cheek. "I forgive you, as long as you trust me."

"I do."

She kissed him. "Then I'll trust you. Now, let's go find out what sort of trouble my daughter's gotten into."

Camden lifted her to her feet. He lightly slapped his cheeks and blew out a breath. "Probably not as much as we've gotten ourselves into. Jake's gonna wonder where I've been and I need to talk to Gina." Then he turned Elena around and helped her pin her hair back up. "But getting in trouble was totally worth it."

NINE

As they surreptitiously made their way out of the library and back to the party, Camden mentally kicked himself for being such a fuck-up. First, he should have stuck closer to Cici, not Roger. Gina was supposed to be on her, but of course that prick Anderson had messed everything up. From the moment they apprehended him, Roger and Cici acted on-edge, not the relaxed, happy couple he'd met a few days before. They should have brushed off the incident like the other guests used to the paparazzi's antics had. Instead, he watched Cici make a beeline for the bar. She'd had too much to drink and he should have seen it as a warning sign instead of assuming she was trying to relax. Camden needed to look deeper into Cici's life and how she really felt about her husband's political aspirations. Maybe she was the reason Roger turned down full-time security. If so, after today, she might change her mind.

He also worried that if Elena started a friendship with Cici, she'd be putting herself in danger without knowing it. Roger Bennett was being targeted by both foreign interests and an American who was close to him. Those interests wouldn't hesitate to look into any and all family, friends, and acquaintances for a weak link to be exploited. Was that link Cici, and would it spill over onto Elena? Camden wasn't willing to take that chance. But how to convince Elena that Cici was a person to avoid—at least for now—without compromising the job, and without coming across as a complete and utter control freak? He felt as though he'd skirted the edge already in the library.

"Oh my God, *Tina, no!*" Camden was pulled out of his head and his heart screeched to a stop as Elena left his side and dashed into another room. Had the little girl fainted? Was she hurt? Camden tore off after Elena only to see her standing in front of Tina who was sprawled out on the floor. Near-panic seized Camden, followed by a deadly calm, a feeling of inevitability. He'd missed some crucial clue and failed to protect the little girl as history repeated itself.

But if so, then why was Elena standing there with her hands on her hips if Tina was...

...Not anywhere near dying unless Elena chose to take her out herself. Which looked like a possibility. As Camden took in the entire situation, he stifled a laugh. Tina had decided to play with her dolls, but it looked like Wedding Barbie had ditched her fiancé Ken for a fourteen-carat upgrade.

One of Bette's Oscars was gone from its normal place on the mantel and stood proudly beside Barbie on the floor, complete with a toy top hat on its shiny bald head.

Elena stamped her foot. "Tina! I cannot even speak right now. Where did you get...you put that back before you break it."

"Mama, it's okay. And he's too heavy and it's too high for me to put him back up there, see?" Tina lifted the Oscar about a foot off the floor and then it slipped through her fingers and hit the hardwood with a healthy bang.

Elena shrieked. "Oh my God, stop. How did you even get that down off the mantel?"

"I didn't get him down. We were playing."

Elena squinted. "Oh, no. Is it scratched up?" She dropped to her knees. "Oh, God, it's scratched up."

Camden swept past Elena and picked up the statue. "You're not kidding, Mermaid, this thing has to weigh somewhere north of six or seven pounds."

"Eight pounds, eight ounces, actually," Bette said from behind them.

Elena jumped up and turned, her face beet-red and her eyes wild. "Mrs. Collins, I am so, so, unbelievably sorry."

Then her forehead scrunched up as her brain must have registered what lay in Bette's lap.

Oh, classic Bette, Camden thought as it registered with him, too. A worn vinyl case with a faded graphic of Barbie printed on the top.

"Call me Bette, remember? What are you sorry for, dear? I'm the culprit," Bette said. "When Tina told me she forgot her Ken doll, I improvised. Oscar's taller than Ken, anyway, and I think bald men are very handsome. And then I remembered that my daughter Samantha might still have some Barbie clothes packed away so I went to look for them." She patted the case. "I was right."

"So you," Elena looked from Bette to where the Oscar had been on the mantel, to Tina, and back to Bette, "*you* took him down? But, I'm so sorry, he's all scratched up now."

And he was, pretty badly, Camden noted, as he turned the statue in his hands.

Bette waved her hand dismissively. "Yes, Oscar could use some professional skincare. But that's not Tina's fault. Jake did that to old Oscar years and years ago, back when he tried to dress him in fatigues from his GI Joe doll and then pretend to blow him up."

Camden almost dropped the Oscar. *Oh, the sweet, sweet blackmail. Thank you, Bette.*

"Can I have him back now, please?" Tina asked Camden sweetly.

"Uh." Camden looked from Elena, who appeared gobsmacked, to Bette, whose smile and nod indicated that yes, Camden should give back the priceless award to the five-year-old so she could fit him for a tux. Barbie was waiting, after all.

Bette rolled up and took Elena's hand. "Elena, dear. It's all right. I have a couple more. But there is only one Tina in the world." Then she rolled forward beside the little girl as Camden placed the Oscar back—gently, he couldn't help it—onto the floor.

Bette opened the case and rummaged through the doll clothes. "Now, let's see if we can't find Barbie's mink stole. It used to be a collar from one of my old coats before I cut it off for Samantha's dolls to use..."

Bette's Bash wound down earlier than usual. By eleven o'clock, the party had dwindled to family, and friends who might as well have been family. The Bennetts had decamped not long after Cici's outburst, Roger making excuses about the kids needing to get to some activity or another. Gina had finished questioning Anderson and offered to tail them to make sure they got home safely and to see if they'd by chance picked up a second tail at the party. It was a longshot—Bette was careful who she invited into her life and home—but after Anderson slipped through, they took no chances.

Gina had reported back that the family made no detours and looked like they were home for the day. She'd also thanked Camden for the excuse to leave. Parties weren't Gina's thing. He had to disagree—he'd watched his usually tight-lipped co-worker schmooze like she was the one running for office, all while picking up intel and keeping a close eye on everything the Bennetts did.

So with his principals gone and the dry-run over, Camden could spend the rest of the party relaxing before he debriefed with Jake and Costello, with Gina on the phone—hopefully with more information she could actually divulge.

Right now, Camden shared a loveseat with Elena. Jake and Rachael sat together in another while Costello and Jake's sister, Samantha, both pulled up chairs, with Sam sitting next to Elena. Tina was off watching a movie with Bette and Grant, probably one of those old Eighties or Nineties kids' action films where he was a stuntman. Camden's guess was *Double-o Trouble: The Spy Who Played with Me*. Most of Bette's movies were a little too mature for a five-year-old, to say the least. Camden imagined Toby was lying exhausted at Tina's feet. That little girl could wear out a SEAL team.

Samantha bent forward and covered her face as she convulsed with laughter. Jake was covering his face, too, but out of sheer embarrassment. Rachael rubbed his back while laughing as hard as Sam. Costello had a huge smile on his face and Elena was blushing and shaking her head. Camden had just finished sharing the Oscar story.

"What?" Jake said. "Mom always told me that Oscar was part-mine. She was pregnant with me the last few weeks of shooting."

Rachael rolled her eyes. "A star before you were born."

"God, I remember your GI Joe dolls," Samantha said.

"You were too old to play with them but you kept them in your room. I thought you'd take one along to boot camp."

Camden snickered. "My only question is, how hard was it to slip GI Joe fatigues onto an Oscar over that great big sword, Jake?"

"Easier than what I do every morning in real life," Jake answered.

Elena's eyes went wide as her lips parted in shock. "You guys are *terrible*." And then her face contorted as she tried not to burst out laughing. "Just terr—terrible." She failed and bent over, face beet-red, shoulders shaking. "I think I'm laughing mostly because I'm so relieved I don't have to hock everything I own for the rest of my life to pay for a new Oscar. Can you even *buy* a new one? Jeez!" She wiped a tear from the corner of her eye.

"Mom would never make you do that," Jake said.

"I don't know," she said. "This is the last time I'm bringing Tina over here."

Samantha grabbed her arm. "*No*. Elena. I'm begging you. Please, please, please bring Tina back as often as possible so Mom gets off my case about finding a nice man and popping out grandbabies now that I've graduated college." She gave Rachael and Jake a mock-glare, her pretty green eyes dancing with mischief. "Especially since these two are putting it off."

Rachael put up her hands. "Only putting it off, not counting it out. We want a family, but I've got to navigate this insane music world first before it eats me alive."

"Jake, are you playing on any of Rachael's songs?" Elena asked. Her voice was light, but Camden caught Elena's frown at her best friend's words about the music industry. He wondered if today had sunk in for her, that Rachael was now part of this world. He'd have to reassure her that Rachael was well-protected—Jake and Bette would never let anything hurt her.

Jake shook his head while Rachael answered, "I wish he would play on the album. He's no slouch."

"I'm no session musician, either," Jake said. "Any producer would drum me right out of the recording studio."

Rachael looked heavenward. "Would not." But she dropped it after that. Camden could tell this was already an old, well-worn argument.

"You sing my heart," Jake said simply. "I just want to listen."

"Aw!" Sam said, beaming at her big brother. "I think I'm gonna puke."

Jake picked up a pillow and threw it at her. She ducked and it almost took out a vase on a nearby table. Their eyes went round as they looked at each other like a couple of kids in trouble.

Camden squeezed Elena's knee. "See? You have nothing to worry about bringing Tina over here. She's the most mature of the bunch."

"Ha-ha, Joker," Sam said. She looked at Elena. "Do you call him that yet?"

Elena looked perplexed. "No, why would I?"

"It's my old SEAL nickname," he told her. "And no, you really don't need to call me that." He narrowed his eyes at Samantha, though good-naturedly. He'd known her since she was in grade school and she'd only become more like a little sister in the intervening years. A few times, Jake had called on him to help chase off an asshole who wouldn't leave the gorgeous young woman alone, which always infuriated her. Sam would rather toy with a jerk herself than have someone step in and fight her battles.

"Oh, I had no idea," Elena said. "Do you guys have nick-names, too?" She looked at Jake and Costello.

Jake placed his fingertips on his chest, "I'm Crooner." He pointed at Costello. "And he's Psychic."

Elena leaned forward. "Crooner makes sense for you. You have a really good voice."

Camden laughed. "His voice didn't sound so great when he got the name."

Jake raised an eyebrow. "Must we?"

"Fuck, yeah, we must." Camden leaned back. "Hell Week in BUD/S, the first night. We're camping on the beach and our instructors wake us around midnight, yelling, shooting guns with blanks, throwing smoke grenades, it's complete chaos, right? But what does our guy notice? Not the bombs, not the men screaming in our faces. He's listening to the sound system they've got cranked to eleven playing, "Welcome to the Jungle." And he's singing along to it at the top of his lungs. The rest of us are just trying to find our asses and Axl over here's putting on a concert. One of the instructors named him Crooner, so for the rest of the week, Jake would spontaneously shout out a line and the rest of us were like, shut the ever-lovin' fuck up, Crooner. He finally went hoarse."

"That song got me through Hell Week. Every time I wanted to ring the bell and quit, I sang instead. And now I never want to hear that song, or that story, again."

Elena grinned at Jake before turning her attention to Costello. Before she could open her mouth, he held up his palm and said, "No, I'm not psychic."

"Which means you're psychic, because that's what I was going to ask."

Costello smiled and brushed back the dirty-blond hair falling over his forehead. "Nope, just means I've been asked that about a thousand times by everyone outside the military."

"Why *outside* the military?"

Camden jumped in. "Because anyone who's served or worked with Psychic knows he's got a sixth sense for danger. What was it, a week after we started working together? I witnessed this man stop a dude from holding up a convenience store before I even knew what the hell was happening. It was downright supernatural. I don't care what he says, he's psychic."

Costello shook his head. "There is no supernatural and there are no psychics. If you hadn't been so focused on picking out potato chips, you would have noticed that guy's flannel shirt was way too hot for the weather, but was perfect for concealing his .38. And you would've seen the way the dumb redneck scoped out the guy behind the counter and then us and reached for his piece."

Camden scoffed. "Psychic here noticed all this within the first half-second the guy walked in the door. Didn't even make it all the way in before Costello was on him, had him down on the ground and disarmed."

"That's impressive," Elena said. "Oh, and before I forget again, Tina loves that little palm tree you gave us. She strung it with fairy lights. Thank you."

Camden noticed Costello's cheeks take on some color. He was normally so cool and detached, his other nickname could have been Mr. Logic. "You're welcome. Plants make a house a home." His brief, faraway look contrasted his usual sharp-as-a-falcon gaze.

The faint whir of Bette's wheelchair announced her approach. Elena and Samantha stood, Elena still looking nervous, as Bette entered the room.

"Oh my God, Mom, where did you find my old doll clothes?" Sam asked.

Bette rolled her eyes at her daughter. "At the back of your

closet where you've always stashed all your good stuff." Then she smiled at Elena. "I wanted to let you know Tina's nodding off and that you're welcome to stay the night."

Elena covered her heart and smiled back. "Oh, that's very generous of you, but I think we'll head home." Her eyes widened. "I forgot, we didn't drive ourselves, you sent a car."

Camden immediately recognized Elena's look of confusion. *I bet she's wondering what would be easier for Bette.* His assumption was confirmed when Elena said, "I mean, if it would be easier to stay, or..."

"I can take them home, Ms. C.," Camden interjected.

"Really, it's no trouble either way," Bette started, then he caught the twinkle in her eye as she looked from Elena to Camden. "But, don't let me stand in the way of you being a gentleman."

"I just need a minute to talk to the guys here, and then we can get going." Camden was eager to hear what Gina had to say about Ron Anderson and get Jake and Costello's impressions of the Bennetts, especially Cici.

Rachael stood and joined the other women. "I've come to know that means business." She linked her arms through Elena's and Samantha's. "Let's go check on Tina and get her ready to go." Bette led the way, presumably to the home theater.

Camden pulled out his phone and called Gina, who answered immediately. He put her on speaker. "Whatcha got, Spooky?"

"Here's what I can tell you. I plugged Anderson's glasses into a laptop. One-hundred and twenty photos and three videos."

"Our boy's a shutterbug," Jake said. "Always has been."

"Most of the photos are crap. Blurry, as if he were in motion, a few close-ups of the guests when he was serving them, and not very flattering. Several of Bette from a distance. And Rachael too, sorry, Jake."

"Forewarned is forearmed," Jake said. "Not like we didn't know this was coming."

"A few stills of the interior of the house."

Camden leaned forward. "Like he's scoping the security?"

"More like for a house and home mag." Gina paused, blowing her breath out in a quick huff. "The videos are a little more concerning. Not that every shot isn't, when you see the whole picture through a, shall we say, skeptical brain like mine."

"So what's got you paranoid, Spooky?" Camden asked.

He heard her chuckle, then her tone turned serious again. "He didn't run video until after the Bennetts arrived, which you could chalk up to coincidence, except that they were the main subjects of the videos. The kids especially, though he got some footage of Roger and Cici up on the patio by the grill when she first came out. That's the last video. It starts with the twins running around with the dogs, pans up to the patio and zooms in on Roger and Cici, then back to the kids, until some doof comes up behind and orders a Shirley Temple. From there it's an action movie starring Anderson as a scared shitless photog and the dog who can't get enough of him."

"Heh. So, what's your overall impression, and what did he say during your friendly chat?"

"My overall impression is that he got here early and took some throwaway shots, some decent ones for extra cash, but that his main objective was to get footage of the Bennetts. The photos he took of them are crystal. I think the other photos are meant as a cover—which is the story he stuck to, that he saw an opportunity to infiltrate a Bash and took photos like a kid grabs candy in a candy store. I think if you hadn't spotted him, he would have eventually taken a video or two of someone else to add to the cover, but that he didn't want to fill his battery before he got the Bennetts."

"But he denies all that?" Camden asked.

"He does. Still looks fishy to me. But again, it could be nothing and I'm just biased. Either way, My friends are keeping an eye on him now. He'll sue to get the glasses back, but it's funny how footage just gets corrupted sometimes."

Camden could practically hear her shrug over the phone. "Thanks, Gina." He looked at Jake and Costello. "Thoughts?"

Costello spoke first. "Cici Bennett is not happy about her husband's aspirations. As soon as her kids were out of sight inside, I watched her slam three of your Tequila Sours while keeping an eye on you, Camden. She appraised you like you were a pit bulls she was thinking of buying for home security. After she exchanged pleasantries with Millie Ellington and Bree Croft and moved on, I listened to them discuss how Cici's become so overprotective of the twins lately. Later inside, she hovered around them with her arms slightly out like she was ready to catch them, and kept her body between them and the rest of the party. Her shoulders didn't drop from around her ears until they left."

"She was not the same woman Cam and I met the other day," Jake said. "That woman was calm and in control, excited about moving to a white house on the East Coast, her words. The woman I watched today was fighting to keep her shit together. Roger, too, was different. Closed off, even when he smiled and made small-talk. And when Cici came out to get Bennett to hear about Camden, there was more desperation in her eyes than anything else. Roger mirrored it."

"That was easy to see," Camden said. Since Costello wasn't yet in on the CIA and FBI chatter, and they weren't in the office, he didn't want to give it away, so he said, "Do you think they've been threatened, or is she only anticipating trouble?"

Costello scratched his ear. "I thought it was anticipatory. She's definitely anxious, but it seemed generalized. But now that you've given me a baseline of their behavior, I'd say something's happened between your meeting and now."

"I agree," Gina said.

"Make that three," Jake added.

Goddamnit, Camden thought. *Barely started the job and we've already missed something.* "It's late. Let's talk more at the office on Monday. You okay being on our principals tomorrow, Gina?"

"Absolutely. It's a cakewalk. They don't have anything scheduled beyond Sunday services. If Cici leaves the house otherwise, I'll let you know immediately so you can replace me while I'm on her tail."

Camden let out a breath. "Thanks, Gina. Maybe today will convince her they need round-the-clock protection for the time being. That'd make our jobs easier."

"Surprised she or Roger didn't ask today," Jake said.

"Me too," Camden said. "Great work, team. We'll talk Monday." Even as he smiled at the other two men his stomach plummeted. What did he miss and why did it have Cici tied up in knots? What was her resistance to bodyguards all about? Now more than ever, he needed to make sure Elena stayed out of harm's way. He'd pay attention to the danger signs this time, and protect the woman he was quickly falling for, and falling for hard.

TEN

Monday morning at work, Elena could barely concentrate on her tasks. Her mind kept drifting back to the party, to the scene with Cici followed by making out with Camden in the library. She'd wanted to talk to him on the way home about the Bennetts and whatever Camden had started to tell her, but Tina was overtired, swinging between chattering excitedly about staying up later than she ever had, asking Camden questions, and begging to keep Toby overnight. By the time they pulled up to the apartment building, Elena was too exhausted to form any coherent thoughts.

Camden had walked them to their door where he hugged Tina and gave Elena a chaste peck on the cheek, though his gaze was full of heat. Enough that Elena impulsively invited him to dinner Sunday night. Disappointment replaced the heat as Camden turned down her offer, saying he had a prior commitment, but that he wanted to see her this week. It was just as well—Tina spent Sunday acting more like a crab than a sweet little mermaid.

Elena was putting together a PowerPoint presentation for

the next staff meeting and trying not to think about the reasons why Camden could have turned down her invitation. Maybe it was his job getting in the way, but she couldn't help wondering, was it Tina's behavior after the party? Was it the scene with Cici? Was it something Elena herself had done or didn't do?

Speak of the devil, when she looked up at the person coming in the door, she realized it was Cici. Her hair was pulled back in a chic French braid, her makeup while not overdone was perfect, and her outfit was something Elena imagined Cici would wear to a country club for lunch and drinks with the girls. She'd learned that some of Cici's charities were clients of Brant and Phillips, and that the firm was hoping she'd tap them to market Roger's open-secret political aspirations, but she didn't see the woman's name on anyone's schedule today.

Elena smoothed down her pencil skirt, feeling self-conscious as the other woman's kitten heels clicked across the marble foyer. She took a deep breath and smiled, trying to remember how far she'd come in her life, and that she had nothing to be ashamed or embarrassed of. Cici had sought out her friendship at the party, not the other way around.

"Cici, hi," she said, standing. "Do you have an appointment? I'm sorry, I don't have you on the schedule with anyone."

Cici's smile reached all the way to her eyes as a faint blush spread across her cheeks. "That's because my meeting is with *you* today. If you'll agree to join me for lunch as a way to make up for my behavior on Saturday." Her blush deepened and she looked down. "I was acting inappropriately, and I want to apologize."

Elena reached across the receptionist's desk and touched Cici's arm. "Oh, Cici, no, you weren't at all. That photographer was the inappropriate one. You don't need to take me out." She sighed inwardly. Cici had just put her in an awkward spot with Camden. Why couldn't they have talked sometime over the weekend about why he thought she needed to stay away? Why couldn't Cici be self-absorbed enough not to care if she offended Elena or not? But the woman standing in front of her looked absolutely remorseful.

"I did behave badly, and I like to take responsibility for my actions and make up for them when I'm in the wrong. My kids call it adulting." She grinned, though her eyes still looked troubled. "Please, let me take you out to lunch. Your choice. Besides," her grin turned impish, "you never did give me the recipe for that dip, and I'm sure you have others that are just as amazing. I'd love to discuss them."

But you told me you don't cook, Elena thought but didn't dare say out loud. Was Cici just looking for any excuse that might appeal to Elena? Under her put-together façade, the poor woman looked like she might burst into tears at any moment. *It's just lunch,* Elena rationalized. *How bad could that be? Besides, the last thing I need is for her to break down here in the foyer.* The sound of Julia's office door opening and closing behind her decided things. She didn't need her boss coming up front and deciding Elena was somehow star-struck and behaving unprofessionally with a client.

"I didn't give you the recipe, did I? In that case, I'd love to go to lunch." She quickly forwarded the office phone to the answering service and grabbed her purse from a desk drawer. Cici rewarded her with a beaming smile and they made their way out before Julia was close enough to comment.

"What a charming place," Cici said, looking around the dining room of Delia's restaurant. "And you know the owner?" Elena hadn't missed Cici's surprise when Pete the maître d greeted Elena by name before acknowledging Cici and asked if she'd prefer her usual table in the back or the one by the front window that miraculously opened without a reservation. Since her first visit a couple weeks ago, Elena had returned almost every day for lunch, usually with Lissa, and Delia had spent more and more time at their table, always asking for Elena's opinion on a dish. The last couple of times, Delia also asked questions related to Elena's management style back when she'd worked kitchens.

"I do know Delia. She's an amazing chef-owner, as you're about to find out."

"It smells incredible. I can't wait. Or decide," Cici said as she scanned the menu.

"If you're game, I always just let Delia feed me whatever new dish she's working on."

Cici looked up from her menu. "Oooh, that sounds fun, let's do that." She grinned and lifted her eyebrows. "So, she depends on your expert opinion? Smart lady."

Elena laughed and covered her mouth. "Oh, I wouldn't go that far."

"Well, I would, judging by the food you brought to Bette Collins' party. Delia would be a fool not to take your recommendations."

Elena's favorite server, Claudia, brought a silver water pitcher to the table. The young woman had an excellent sense of timing and really paid attention to her customers. "I see you've set the menus aside, are you ordering off them or is it Delia's choice?" Ice clinked against glass as she filled their goblets with lemon-cucumber water.

"Delia's choice as usual, Claudia, thank you."

"You're welcome, Elena. Good to see you." She smiled at Elena, then Cici, and returned to the kitchen.

Cici's smile looked genuine and her eyes widened. "I feel like I'm dining with a celebrity."

Elena started to demur again when she realized just how comfortable she was in Delia's restaurant. Everyone knew her and treated her respectfully. Delia looked for and valued her opinion. She even liked the people-watching, like the stylish woman in the oversized sunhat reading from a tablet on a bench right outside their window as she waited for a table. The restaurant had become Elena's happy place in L.A. She made a mental note to bake a batch of brownies for Lissa in gratitude for bringing her the first time.

"I'm far from a celebrity, but, yeah, I feel like one when I'm here."

Cici tilted her head. "Have you always been a foodie?"

"I...yes, I think so. I mean, I love food, obviously, and I used to work in the restaurant industry."

"So, why aren't you working in a restaurant now?" Cici took a sip of her water. "I mean, no offense, receptionist work is important, but from the minute you walked in here, your whole demeanor changed. You went from taking up as little space as possible to blossoming. There's no other way to put it." Cici pointed at her. "You, Elena, need to own a restaurant."

Elena nearly spit out the sip of water she'd just taken. "Oh, no, I could never." She looked around. "I can't imagine ever having a nice place like this."

Cici narrowed her eyes. "Don't ever put limits on yourself." She picked up her purse and rummaged through it until she found a business card case. She opened it and flipped through until she found the one she wanted, then handed it across the table. "One of the non-profits I volunteer for helps women own and run their small businesses. When you're tired of working for Brant and Phillips, give them a call. Give me your cell number, too, and we'll get you fast-tracked."

Elena tapped her cell against Cici's to transfer her number. She picked up the business card hesitantly. "I don't want to take out a loan, I—"

Cici waved her hands. "Oh, no, no, it's not like that, they offer grants. They help women figure out business plans, teach them networking skills, sometimes even introduce them to influential people and mentors in their field. Though," she gestured at the restaurant around them, "it looks like you've already got the networking and the mentorship down."

"Huh." Elena studied the card. *My own restaurant.* When she was much younger, before she'd met Antonio, she'd sometimes daydreamed about running a restaurant, a warm, welcoming place that made everyone feel as safe and comfortable as she did working in the kitchen at the group home. But those were naïve dreams, unrealistic, dreamed long before she grew up and realized all the blood, sweat, and tears—not to mention time and money—that went into owning a restaurant. No, it was too much, especially being a single mom.

"Thank you." She put the card into her purse. "I'll have to think about it."

"Please do, Elena. I think you sell yourself short. A lot of women do."

Claudia brought the starters—bright, paper-thin sliced watermelon and tomato drizzled with reduced balsamic and sprinkled with fresh basil. It tasted sweet and fresh and cool, perfect for the hot day outside.

"You like helping people, don't you?" Elena said, taking another bite.

"I do. Women, especially. Sometimes, we just need a little

boost and don't always know where to look or how to ask. I like to help with that." She took a bite of watermelon. "This is delicious."

Elena agreed. "So many politicians are out of touch or just don't seem to care past their own voters. You aren't like that. I wouldn't mind if *you* were the one running for office."

Cici's face fell. She looked at her plate. "I never would. And now I wish Roger weren't," she said to herself. She looked up suddenly, eyes round with shock. "I shouldn't have said—"

Elena reached across the table and touched Cici's forearm much as she had back at the office. "Hey, it's okay. We're just friends here, talking. You don't need to campaign in front of me or anything." She felt terrible for bringing up such a touchy topic. She should have known from the party that everything was not all right.

Cici dabbed at her mouth with a cloth napkin and blinked rapidly. "Thank you. You have no idea how hard it is to be 'on' all the time. I was raised to be perfect. There's so much..." She glanced around as if everyone in the restaurant had suddenly stopped to listen. No one paid them any attention, each table involved in their own small talk.

Cici grabbed Elena's hand. "I believe in what Roger is doing. He's a good man, the best man I know. He wants to make a difference, especially now that our country is so divided. But I worry, Elena. I worry so much. We're going under a microscope, and I just...."

"What?" Elena leaned closer.

Cici shook her head. "Nobody's perfect, right?" She gulped down some water. "We all make mistakes. We all have regrets." She blinked back tears. "Sometimes, the only choices you have are bad ones, and you're left trying to make the best bad choice." Cici looked her straight in the eye. "You must know what I'm talking about, right? After the story you told me at the party. We do what we have to do to keep our families safe. *Whatever* it takes."

Elena's stomach dropped. Her first thought was that she should have listened to Camden and stayed away from Cici. *Who does she think I am?* But then again, what did Elena know about politics and the intrigue surrounding them? Cici was obviously distraught and needed a friend right now. She deserved help as much as she loved to help others.

"Sure, we've all made mistakes, Cici. I can't imagine there's anything *you'd* need to worry about."

Cici leaned in closer. "You and Camden are dating, right? Do you know if Watchdog has done any...how can I put it? Have *they* looked into—"

"Cici, is that you?"

So engrossed in their conversation, Elena hadn't noticed the man now standing at their table. He was good-looking in a professional way, his chestnut hair neatly trimmed with a razor part and just beginning to whiten at the temples. His suit murmured success and his tie screamed power. He was all smiles, and the smiles were all for Cici.

"Larry, what a surprise," Cici's demeanor immediately brightened. "Elena, I'd love for you to meet Lawrence Franklin, Roger's campaign manager and a dear old friend of mine from college."

Lawrence touched the white hair over his ear. "I hope the latter is more important than the former, but did you have to say 'old' friend?" He winked at Elena, and she tried not to feel skeeved out. Strange men who winked like that always bothered her; they were right up there with the ones who told her she'd be prettier if she smiled more.

Cici laughed. "Nonsense. You look wonderful as always."

She stood and accepted a kiss on the cheek. "I've seen you around but we haven't talked in ages."

"Roger has me busy, busy, busy." Lawrence looked around as if a brilliant thought had just occurred to him. "I'm down here for a meeting that just got canceled. I was about to leave when I saw you. Mind if I pull up a chair?" Without waiting for an answer, he swiped an extra chair from the table next to them, winking at the two women sitting there instead of asking their permission.

Ugh. Really? Elena gave him a tight-lipped smile while he made himself comfortable. Her conversation with Cici was effectively over, since Lawrence drained the restaurant of oxygen while he talked almost non-stop about himself, his work with the campaign, himself, asked Cici and Elena a question or two, and then went back to talking about his favorite topic. Oh, but in the three minutes of asking Elena about herself, he did manage to get in some passive-aggressive remarks about Elena's job, her home state of New Mexico, and single moms. Subtle enough that they could be taken as compliments, but Elena knew that game by now—they weren't.

How did this asshole convince Roger he was the best man to run his campaign? Funny, but Cici seemed completely enraptured, though she did cringe at the single mom jab.

Elena breathed a sigh of relief when she got back to the office. Cici and Lawrence both walked her back, which she found a little odd. She didn't have time to think about it—Julia was waiting, actually *waiting* with her foot tapping, by Elena's desk. Her relief melted into a cold puddle of dread in her stomach when she realized she'd been gone an hour and a half.

"Sorry to have kidnapped your wonderful receptionist, Julia," Cici said, "but I owed her a nice lunch after my *faux pas* while we were at Bette Collins' party on Saturday. I trust she isn't in trouble?"

Julia blinked once, slowly. She looked at Elena like she'd never seen her before. "Not at all. Perfectly understandable. We certainly value Elena around here. Wonderful to see you, Mrs. Bennett. I hope we can offer your husband our services, should he ever need them."

"Well, Lawrence and Roger are shopping for a new ad firm and we'd love to set up a meeting with Mr. Brant, actually. Think you can make that happen?"

Elena opened her scheduling software. "Here, let me look at Mr. Brant's schedule real quick."

Julia laid a hand on her shoulder. "I've got it, Elena."

Cici went around the desk and kissed Elena on the cheek. Lawrence, thankfully, left with barely a wave. Julia marched back to her office without another word. *Thank God for small victories.* She did a mental happy dance.

Elena was relieved lunch was over, but she wished Cici had been able to confide in her. She seemed so worried. But, maybe it was for the best that Lawrence had come along and interrupted them. Her gut told her Cici's life was already complicated and on its way to becoming even more so, and Elena couldn't afford to get sucked into the drama. As relieved as she felt though, a little voice nagged at her, saying how nice Cici was in wanting to help her, so shouldn't she do the same?

Elena's phone buzzed. She quickly checked her texts before having to turn her phone off. She'd missed one from Camden:

Sorry I was busy the other night. I'd love to take you and the mermaid out for dinner tonight. Someplace maybe a bit fancier than a food truck? Then if it's ok, I'd like to talk.

. . .

The second text was from Cici.

Lunch was so nice! Let's get together again. And I have a favor to ask you. I think we'll both benefit!

Elena squeezed her eyes shut and groaned. *Why me?* Maybe she needed to learn how not to be so nice. She sent off a quick reply to Camden saying she'd love to see him, then turned off her phone without responding to Cici's message.

Why would Cici need a favor from her? She reflected on Cici asking her about dating Camden, and if she knew about Watchdog. *This is going to take some thought.* Should she tell Cici yes or no? And should she even mention her lunch date to Camden?

ELEVEN

C amden sat behind his desk smiling at his phone. Specifically, at the text Elena had just sent saying she'd love to have dinner with him, and now he couldn't stop thinking about how good she'd felt in his arms in the library. Even now, his cock stiffened at the memory of the spicy-sweet taste of her fingers and her lips, the vanilla-mint fragrance of her hair. He'd barely looked at another woman since losing Susan, and now he couldn't get Elena off his mind.

He'd put off going to her apartment for dinner Sunday night in case Gina had needed him for backup while watching the Bennetts, and now he couldn't wait for tonight. He was ready, or at least as ready as he'd ever be, to put the past behind him and have another serious relationship. God, she was so beautiful. So kind. She deserved the truth from him. Then, she could decide if she wanted to keep seeing him. Decide if he was worth it.

"So, when are we hiring your girlfriend, Camden?" Gina casually leaned against the doorframe, arms crossed. She was a few minutes early to the Bennett meeting.

"What are you talking about?" Could she somehow tell that Elena's text was the reason for his smile? Was this Spooky's sense of humor?

Gina walked in and sat down at the small conference table that dominated the rest of Camden's office. "Elena's got a real future in espionage. She managed to wrangle a lunch date with one of our principals, and it looked like Cici spilled her guts."

"The fuck?" Camden felt his world tilt and he didn't like it. After warning her to stay away, what was Elena doing? This had to be a misunderstanding.

"Yeah. After a totally uneventful day yesterday, I followed Cici Bennett to Brant and Phillips today at lunchtime. She and Elena walked to a restaurant called Delia's a couple blocks down. I sat outside their window hoping the glass wasn't too insulated. I got lucky and heard some of their conversation. It sounded like Cici's trying to help Elena, which I read as possible manipulation. But then things got too quiet, right before Bennett's campaign manager showed up and joined them."

"Lawrence Franklin?" He set his phone down. *Why would Elena be meeting with Bennett's campaign manager?*

Gina tilted her head, her gaze piercing Camden. "Didn't you say he and Cici went to the same college?"

"They did. Could be a coincidence he showed up."

Gina's eyebrow quirked up. "Whatever. They all went back to B&P, then Franklin and Cici came back out about ten minutes later and went their separate ways after a nice long hug. Lawrence looked like he was trying to buck up his old college buddy."

Camden scrubbed his face. "Shit. Shit shit *shit*. I told her to stay away from Cici Bennett."

"And you thought she'd listen? Have you *met* women?"

Gina grinned. "So, what's Elena's angle then? Is she trying to help you on her own? I thought maybe you'd decided to use her to get closer and you'd bring it up at our—whoa." Gina put her hands up and leaned back as Camden felt heat rising up his neck and flushing his face with red as his blood boiled. "Didn't realize I'd just pissed in your cornflakes."

Camden ground his teeth. "What makes you think I'd *ever* put a civilian, especially one I care for, in harm's way?"

"Of course you wouldn't. That is *not* what I said." Gina's voice had taken on the same cadence she used at Bette's party when gathering intel from unsuspecting guests—calm, deep, and slow. "I'm sorry you took it that way. You know I have the utmost respect for you. I thought maybe you were strategically deploying every possible resource, but I was wrong."

Camden's gut churned. "Don't try to handle me. I'm not CIA, Gina. I don't take advantage of people like you were trained to do." He regretted the words as they left his mouth.

Gina looked at her boots, her hair swinging down to frame her face. She inhaled like she'd been sucker-punched, which was exactly what he'd just done.

"Sorry. I didn't mean it like that." Camden pinched the bridge of his nose.

She looked up. "Don't be. You did mean it, and I prefer direct honesty. I'm sorry I assumed you'd use Elena as an asset." She furrowed her brow, and just like that, Camden watched Gina go from openly hurt back to completely professional. "So, if you didn't ask Elena to cultivate Cici Bennett, could she be trying to help without telling you? Or maybe Elena isn't actively cultivating her at all, and Cici is seeking her out."

Jake and Costello walked in and took their seats. Jake gave him a look that said *what's up, why so tense?* Camden wished he could tell his brother the reason was that Gina's first instinct about Elena was that she was going behind his back and inserting herself into his work, and that went down like a beer full of razor blades.

"Hey, guys, have a seat. I'll let Gina fill you in on today's fun." While she did that, Camden pondered his next move with Elena. He'd see her that night. Should he ask her straight-up what was going on? Maybe she'd tell him about her lunch before he needed to ask. Either way, he needed to push down his irritation with her for not listening to him and getting involved instead. For not staying safe. Damn it, he'd been so looking forward to seeing her, and now the thought of sitting across from her at dinner made his temples throb.

"So," Gina concluded, "considering how upset Cici was on Saturday, and the fact that she's normally like clockwork with her schedule but canceled two of her regular meetings today to go to lunch, I'm wondering about four things." She stuck out her index finger and tapped it with her other. "One, the full extent of Cici Bennett's relationship with Lawrence Franklin." She extended her second finger and tapped it next, counting off. "Two, her relationship with Elena Martinez." She tapped her ring finger. "Three, what she so desperately wanted to discuss with Elena." She tapped her pinkie. "Four, if there's some sort of connection between Elena and Franklin now."

Great. As much as I hate it, Elena's now part of the investigation. "I'm seeing Elena tonight," Camden said, crossing his arms. "I can look into points two and three. Other than the Bennetts' infertility issues, Cici seems to have led a charmed life—wealthy parents, graduated from a good college, married well, managed to overcome infertility and had two lovely children. No public scandals. So, maybe there's a private one." Gina quirked up an eyebrow at that.

Camden continued. "Jake, I want you to dig deeper on

Lawrence Franklin. Too bad social media wasn't really a thing yet when he and Cici were in college. I'd love to know more about their relationship back then, if it ever turned romantic, if it was unrequited love, whatever. Considering that Cici and Roger were dating at the time, but Roger went to a different college, things could get interesting."

Costello frowned as he looked between Gina and Camden. "Is there more going on here than just a routine bodyguard job? Why are we worried about Cici and Lawrence?"

"There is. I wanted to rope you in on Saturday night, but we weren't secure." Camden filled Costello in on the chatter. "Sorry to have kept you out of the loop thus far."

Costello shook his head. "I get the need-to-know. Thanks for looping me in this soon. Does Bennett provide dedicated cell phones to campaign members?"

Intrigued, Camden raised his eyebrows. "You thinking a wiretap?"

Costello nodded. "If the phones are campaign property and Bennett gives permission, that frees us up. Either way, I can always drop an IMSI-catcher into their office and at the Bennetts' home. I'd love to do a third one at Franklin's residence, but if it's his private cell, that complicates things legally."

"No, it doesn't." Gina gave Costello her best Garbo smile. "It's a matter of national security. My friends can provide you with something a little more tricked-out than a plain old IMSI."

Costello grinned and chuckled. "The girl with all the gifts. I like your style, Spooky."

"Yeah, that's me, a real giver." Her voice was flat as she tucked a lock of hair behind her ear.

Camden turned his attention to his best friend. "Jake,

what are Ms. C.'s impressions of Roger Bennett? I know they talked about healthcare policy at the party." Bette was about as good at reading people as the best FBI agent.

Jake cracked his neck from side to side. "Mom likes his politics but thinks he's way too optimistic. Even a tad naïve. He admitted to the pressure he's putting on his family, feels bad about it. He's got a lot of grassroots support but he's hoping to rope in some bigger supporters with deeper pockets after he makes his official announcement."

"He mention any donor in particular?" Camden asked.

Jake smacked his lips together. "Someone in Silicon Valley would be my first guess. With Senator Higley's support, they'll be crossover with his donors, I'd imagine, so that'd be safe to look at. Mom said Roger's leaving the details up to his campaign manager."

"So, we're back to Lawrence Franklin. Follow the money."

"When do we officially start the bodyguard work?" Costello asked Camden.

"At Bennett's announcement and fundraiser at the Sol Villa Museum in Beverly Hills, just over a month from now. Big venue, and they're expecting around three-hundred people. We'll survey the property, talk to the villa's security team, then set up the night before with the full Watchdog team. Keep it need-to-know, obviously."

Camden drummed his desk. "Okay, then. Gina, you keep on Cici. Sorry you're doing this alone for the time being, but even after the Bash, Roger insisted he didn't want regular bodyguards yet, which would have made our jobs easier. Jake, you're shoveling for dirt on Lawrence. Psychic, you do the tech voodoo you do so well."

"May I suggest we add Nashville to the need-to-know? My voodoo is good, but that man raises zombies."

Camden nodded. "I'll speak to him. And I'll talk to Elena

tonight, find out what's going on there. I'll also get Lachlan up to date. Class dismissed."

They all stood and Costello and Gina left. Jake lingered just inside the doorway.

"Anything you want to talk about, brother?" Jake asked.

Abso-fucking-lutely I want to. But will I? Of course not. "You're sounding like a broken record, brother."

"Well, I worry about your dumb ass getting in trouble. So, what's wrong? Lay it on me."

Not...yet," Camden said.

Jake blew out a breath. "If you say so. Just know I'm around."

"'Preciate it. Maybe after tonight."

C amden spent the rest of the afternoon catching up on new recruit reports and writing up a report on Bennett for Lachlan, hating that he had to add Elena as a person of interest. He sent it off and decided to clock out early since he was having a hard time concentrating on anything but the evening plans. Camden headed for the kennels to pick up Toby. He'd take the dog along to give Tina something to do while he and Elena talked after dinner. Besides, he hated to leave old Tobes alone at home or overnight in the kennels, and he loved watching the little girl and dog play together. Hard to believe Toby had been trained to track and hold an enemy combatant, when he was licking her face, his tail wagging hard enough Camden was surprised he didn't wag his entire ass right off.

Toby wasn't in the kennels so he went to the courtyard. Through the glass door, he saw Gina kneeling and pressing her forehead against her dog Fleur's forehead, her hands cupped behind the medium-sized, caramel-colored dog's head. Both had their eyes closed, as if silently communing. The moment seemed so intimate, Camden looked away, feeling embarrassed to have witnessed it. He knew even less about Fleur's history than he did about Gina, except that the two were a package deal. Judging by the small but deep scar between Fleur's eyes, the dog had seen some shit. *Just like her owner*, he thought.

Camden waited until Gina stood before he opened the door. She squinted and shaded her eyes, her posture stiffening as she realized who it was.

He approached her as Toby got up from a shady corner where he'd been napping and padded over. "Hey, again, I'm sorry about earlier," he said.

Gina waved him off. "It's fine." She scratched Fleur's head as the dog stared at him. He couldn't help but notice how similar Gina's eye color was to Fleur's—pale gold with a dark brown circle around the iris. Sharp intelligence shone in both sets of eyes.

Camden bent and slowly stretched out his hand below the level of Fleur's muzzle. She rewarded him with a lick. He scratched the dog's chest and looked up at Gina. "Tell me about this pretty girl. How long have you had her?"

Gina flashed the briefest—and warmest—of smiles, never taking her eyes off Fleur.

"Found her during a mission in Africa. Can't tell you which country, that's classified. I was there during some...civil unrest, we'll call it. Soldiers had just cleared out a streetful of protesters using tear gas and batons. Lots of arrests, protestors were rounded up and carted off by the truckload. I found her leashed to a pole in a back alley. Someone, probably her owner, had tied a rag over her muzzle, I guess to protect her from the tear gas." Gina shook her head. "Obviously, their first rodeo. Who the hell brings an untrained dog to a protest without any protective gear, anyway?"

"That's awful." Camden scratched Fleur's head.

"I brought her back to the room where I was staying. Cleaned her up. Fed her. She curled up into the tightest ball you can imagine next to me on the bed. Woke me up the next morning licking my face. I fell head over heels in love. I did try to find her owner, but I imagine he or she was carted off. Possibly killed." Gina grimaced. "So I moved heaven and earth to bring Fleur home with me. Been together ever since."

"You saved her life."

Gina pressed her lips together before answering. "Not as often as she's saved mine." She hooked a leash onto Fleur's collar—pink with silver studs. "Let's go home, girl."

TWELVE

Dreading whatever favor Cici wanted, Elena decided to just get it over with and call her before dinner with Camden. He'd texted again, promising her that the restaurant was kid-friendly and not too fancy, but the food was phenomenal, so Elena let Tina get herself ready while she made the call.

"Elena." Cici sounded a little out of breath like she'd been in a hurry but still pleased that she'd called. "Thanks so much for getting back to me so quickly. I have the worst dilemma. The caterers I was hoping to use for the villa went poof, and I'd planned on interviewing replacements the next few days. But, that's going to take too much time, and after that amazing lunch today, I got this great idea. So, I was wondering—could you maybe ask Delia if she'd be willing to cater an event for around three-hundred people?"

Elena breathed a sigh of relief. Was that all Cici wanted? She put the phone on speaker while she got ready. "Absolutely. I'd love to ask her, but no promises. I have no idea if she does catering, too."

"Tell her it's just an open bar and appetizers—you know,

small food, not a whole meal. I trust whatever she'd come up with. And we'll pay extra to make up for the short notice and if she needs to hire extra people—so long as they're carefully vetted because I don't want a repeat of Bette's party. I'm kinda desperate." Cici's laugh was full of nervous energy. "The publicity for her restaurant would be amazing."

"Sure, I'll tell her and give her your number." Elena checked her hair in the bathroom mirror and put on a pair of silver hoop earrings.

"Thank you! I mean it. Oh, and, you and Tina are welcome to come as my guests. The twins adore your daughter, and she'll have other kids to play with there—I'm hiring childcare for the night so no parents have to stay home. I'll text you the details, though I know Camden will be there and he can tell you, too." Cici paused. "Maybe you're already coming as his date?" Her voice had brightened.

Elena frowned at her reflection. *Is she serious? Camden can't bring me as a date, he'll be working.* Not to mention, he'd already warned her away from Cici. She tried to ignore the little voice in her head that chafed at that, as much as he might be right. "Well, we'll see. I hate to cut this short, Cici, but speaking of, I've got to check on Tina."

"Oh, right. Of course." Cici sounded disappointed, like she'd wanted to say more. Then she brightened again. "But, I'd love to have lunch again. Just you and me next time so we can really talk." That nervous laugh came back. "Larry sometimes has no boundaries."

Elena watched her reflection's eyes roll. *Got that right, Chica.* She glanced at the clock. Camden would be there any minute. "Yeah, sure, I'd love to. I'll get back to you about Delia as soon as I can."

"Thanks again. I'm so glad we met." The warmth and

palpable relief in her voice made Elena feel sorry for Cici. Did she really not have anyone else she could confide in?

While Elena was on the phone, Tina had put on a yellow sundress, her bathing suit obvious beneath it. Elena sat her daughter down at the kitchen table to do her hair. "Not sure we're going to the beach this time, Pepita," Elena told her as she arranged the little girl's long hair into two braids.

"Just in case, Mama." The doorbell rang and Tina jumped up just as Elena finished tying the second bow.

"Wait, let me get it, sweetie." She raced after Tina.

"But it's Camden and Toby." Tina was already reaching for the doorknob.

"Stop. Let me check." Tina pulled a face and Elena echoed her words back at her. "Just in case." The briefest image of Lawrence winking at her flashed through Elena's mind and she shivered.

She looked through the peephole. Even through the fisheye lens, Camden looked yummy in his fitted jeans. His shirt pulled across his chest with just the right amount of tightness to show off his physique without being gross about it. She undid the locks and opened the door.

"Thanks for humoring me and checking first." Camden rewarded her with a panty-melting smile, making her want to skip dinner and pick up where they'd left off in the library. She became acutely aware of her daughter hugging Toby. What would Tina think if she saw her mother kiss Camden beyond a peck on the cheek? She'd never seen Elena kiss any man except Antonio every time he came home, right before he'd sweep his daughter up into a bear hug. Did Tina even remember those hugs and kisses from her Papa? She'd been so young when they'd lost him. Could such old memories become so fragile they'd crumble to dust, replaced by the sight of Elena and Camden kissing?

And how would Tina feel if Camden just left? Disappeared from their lives like Antonio?

Suddenly, Elena wasn't sure she wanted to take that risk yet.

Camden must have read her reluctance as she watched Tina and Toby. He didn't try to kiss her, only brushed her upper arm, sending the most delicious shivers all the way down to her fingertips. This wouldn't be easy. She gave him her warmest smile, hoping he'd somehow understand. He'd told her they'd talk tonight, that he'd tell her about his past. It was only fair that she opened up to him as well. Then he could decide if she was worth pursuing. And, she needed to talk to Tina, to see how much she remembered of her father beyond the stories Elena told her and the photographs they had.

"You're far away tonight," Camden said softly. The look in his eyes asked her what she was thinking.

"Yeah. Maybe a little." She watched Tina lead Toby to her room, where Elena imagined the little girl had a cracker hidden away as a treat. The sound of crunching a moment later verified her hunch.

She turned to Camden, stood on her tiptoes—without her heels on, he was significantly taller—and kissed him. As he deepened their kiss, she felt like she wasn't just on tiptoes anymore but floating. Any contact with him left her feeling that way. His tongue carefully probed her mouth and she reciprocated, running the tip of her tongue along his lips until he groaned. She pulled back feeling light-headed, and smiled into his half-lidded gaze.

Hand on her upper arms, he steadied her. "Well, hello there. God, you look amazing." When she glanced at Tina's room, he touched her cheek and gently turned her face back to him. "I get it. No kissing in front of Tina."

"It's not you, it's—"

He touched her lips. "I know." A brief flash of pain shown in his eyes. "At least, I think I know because...well, it has to do with something I want to talk to you about tonight."

"Are we good?" Elena asked. She never wanted to be the cause of any pain, however brief, that took away his happiness.

"Solid." He bent and brushed his lips against her forehead. If he kept doing lovely things like that, he'd have to tie a string to her wrist so she could float above him like a balloon.

He laid his hand against the small of her back. "Let's go to dinner and then talk."

The restaurant was everything Camden had promised— family-friendly, relaxed, and the food was phenomenal, though Elena thought of ways she'd riff on each dish. They sat on the patio where Toby could join them, lying at Tina's feet the entire time, hoping for scraps. The dog was no fool. But while Elena admonished Tina when she 'accidentally' dropped a piece of bread, Camden just shook his head and laughed.

"Pepita, that's enough. You don't want to make poor Toby sick, do you?"

Tina stared at her mother with wide eyes and put the next piece of bread she'd hidden back on her plate.

Camden grinned at Tina. "My boss Lach said Toby's

eaten MREs, including part of the plastic package once. He'll be fine."

Elena glared at Camden. "You are *not* helping." And he really wasn't. Give Tina an inch and she'd take a mile. Her daughter loved pushing boundaries and needed to be reined in sometimes, and he obviously didn't get it.

Camden bowed his head, keeping his playful gaze on Elena. "I apologize. I'll stop encouraging her bad behavior. So, tell me about Tina's nickname. It's unusual."

"Pepita? Antonio named her that right after the first ultrasound. She was the little seed that turned my belly into a pumpkin." Elena grinned at the memory.

"Antonio was your husband."

Elena's hand absently went to the wedding ring on its chain. She quickly dropped her hand back into her lap, but to Camden's credit, he didn't look jealous or upset. "Yes. He was...is...Tina's Papa."

Camden reached across the table and took her hand in his. "It's a sweet nickname."

After dinner, they took a brief walk on the beach, which was only a block from the restaurant. Camden confessed it was one of the reasons why he chose the place, knowing Tina would want to go back. They didn't get to the beach in time for another magic trick, but Tina was still happy to play in the surf with Toby while Elena and Camden followed along behind in the pink and orange light. At one point, Tina ran back and asked, "Camden? Could you put two cameras somewhere on the earth so that you could see the sun rising and setting at the exact same time?"

Camden's eyebrows shot up as Elena's belly filled with warm pride for her bright daughter. "I guess you could."

"Where would you put them?"

He laughed. "I have no idea off the top of my head. They'd have to be really far apart though. Why do you ask?"

"I don't know. It'd be cool." She started after Toby, got three steps away, and turned back. "You could set one up at the top of Burj Khalifa in Dubai."

Camden stopped walking and his jaw dropped. "How did you...?" His eyes widened along with his smile. "Wait. I can't believe you remember me telling you that name the last time we were on the beach."

The little girl shrugged like it was no big deal. Then she raced away to scold Toby for barking at a flock of seagulls.

Camden gave Elena a look full of astonishment. "Wow. Just, wow. She is so smart and observant."

That took Elena's mood over the moon. The men she'd known back in Ross would've seen Tina as an obnoxious kid, but not Camden. "She's like a little tape recorder sometimes, I swear. She's thought non-stop about that sunset trick since you showed her and now she's obsessed with the sun." Elena gave Camden a soft and playful slug to the arm. "At least she's off the chocolate milk coconuts now."

He grabbed her hand. "Mea culpa."

"She does that with stuff, gets obsessed. You know how kids are. She likes science. Nature science, specifically. I don't know where she gets it. The only science I know is kitchen science."

Camden draped his arm around her shoulders, making her feel warm and sheltered against the wind picking up off the ocean. "She gets it from her mama, who needs to give herself more credit for her brains."

Heat infused Elena's cheeks. "Now you're spoiling *me*."

He kissed the top of her head. "Not nearly enough. Yet." He stopped her, turning her in his arms to face him. "You, Elena Martinez, are a wonder, in the kitchen...and out of it."

His gaze went from her eyes to her lips and back up, making Elena feel light-headed again. "Let's get these two settled in back at your place. And then we can talk."

Only talk? She found herself thinking, a little shocked by how much more she wanted.

THIRTEEN

Back at Elena's apartment, Camden did what he could to help her get Tina ready for bed and school the next day, much to Elena's protesting, insisting that he should just grab a beer and relax on the couch. But no way would he sit there on his ass while she did all the work. He did not want to fuck this up. He headed for the kitchen instead.

At one point when he was cutting the carrots he'd found in her fridge into sticks, she came out of the bathroom where Tina was in the tub, in search of a plastic boat the girl had left by the sink. She smiled sheepishly at Camden. "Sorry. Not the most romantic date you've even been on."

His heart flipped at the word 'date' considering the last time they'd been out together, she'd denied that's what they were doing, even if later she admitted that yes, she'd considered it a date.

"Hey." He set the knife on the cutting board and pulled her in for a hug. He nuzzled into the top of her head, inhaling the sweet mint and vanilla of her hair and her salty skin underneath. "There is no place on earth I'd rather be right now. You have no idea how good this feels."

"I think I do." She squeezed his waist and sighed into his neck. He hadn't realized how tense her body was until she relaxed into him. "It's been a long time since I've had someone helping me like this. Besides at the safe house in Nebraska, where you were amazing."

He tilted her chin up until he could gaze into her warm brown eyes. "You were the amazing one, keeping it together, taking care of Rachael. Of all of us. That was a lot of work and," he fought down an old ghost, "I want you to know I appreciated it." He ran his thumb across the smooth plane of her cheek and watched the color bloom in her rounded cheekbones. She closed her eyes, stood on her toes, and their lips met. God, how he'd wanted this.

"Mama! The boat!"

Elena stopped the kiss, groaned, and buried her face in his chest, her shoulders shaking with silent laughter. "So romantic."

Camden picked up the red and yellow toy. "The mermaid requires her ship."

"The mermaid requires some patience and manners." Elena took the boat and walked backwards a few steps, fixing Camden with a look that said they'd be picking up right where they left off, before she turned and headed for the bathroom. "Patience, Pepita. Patience, patience, patience."

Without warning, Camden found himself swallowing past a lump in his throat, his mood threatening to darken as it had so many times in the past five years. Years that should have played out just like tonight. When he'd told Elena this was what he wanted, he'd meant not just the kiss, but every damn thing. Cutting up carrots while he listened to a beautiful woman and her daughter singing in the bathroom. Packing a lunch for someone other than himself. Kissing Tina's forehead when they tucked her in for the night (he hoped they'd include him). And then sitting down with Elena curled up on his lap to hear about her day and to tell her about his. A normal, everyday, shared *life*. Something he'd never appreciated until it was too late.

Except, he didn't want to talk about today. He rubbed the tight spot on his forehead between his eyes. He didn't want to know how involved Elena was with Cici, and God forbid, Lawrence. And there was so much he couldn't tell her about the assignment. To keep Elena and Tina safe, he'd have to figure out a way to walk that fine line.

Or, he could spend the evening telling her about his past instead, which would be about as pleasant as a root canal without Novocaine. *Fuck.*

By the time Elena had Tina clean and dry and in her pajamas, Camden had made both mother and daughter lunches. Way too many vegetables for his taste, but thank God she didn't make anything with lentils—Camden's mom had served them at nearly every meal growing up and he couldn't even stand the smell of them now. But Elena's homemade dips that went with the veggies would taste pretty fucking fine slathered on a burger.

He put the insulated bags in the fridge and walked to the living room instead of Tina's bedroom where he heard the little girl's non-stop excited chatter and Elena's soothing tones. He didn't want to presume that they'd want him there. Tina ran out of the bedroom with Elena in tow. "Camden, can you tuck me in, too? And can Toby sleep in my room and keep the monsters away?"

The tiny smile and hopeful look in Elena's eyes, the nod of assent, lifted him right out of his darkening mood and made his heart pound.

"Whatever you want, Mermaid."

He scooped Tina up in one arm, and when Elena turned,

he placed his other hand on the small of her back as they walked to Tina's bedroom. Toby had already stationed himself on the foot of Tina's bed, just like he had at the safehouse. Nobody was gonna touch a hair on his girl's head, not on his watch. Camden gave the dog a scratch on the ears as Tina climbed into bed and Elena pulled up her covers.

"Goodnight, Pepita." Elena kissed Tina and then it was Camden's turn. He ran a hand over the top of the girl's head and kissed her forehead. "Night, Mermaid." He stood and gave Toby one last scratch. "Keep the monsters away, marine. That's an order."

Elena clicked on a nightlight and closed Tina's door behind her. They went to the couch and Camden pulled Elena into his lap, just as he'd wanted to do all evening.

"The new furniture looks nice," he told her.

"Thanks. It was fun shopping for it. Oh." She started to get up. "Can I get you a beer?"

He pulled her back down. "Nope. I have everything I need already."

Her gaze softened and he felt her body relax into his like it had in the kitchen. She smoothed her hand across the nape of his neck while he played with her silky hair. "You're always so busy taking care of everyone else, Gorgeous. Nothing needs doing right now. Relax and just let me hold you for a while." He rubbed up and down her back and she relaxed farther into him.

"You," she whispered.

"Me? Me what?" He kissed the top of her head.

"Just you." She kissed his jawline where it met his throat and he groaned, wanting nothing more than to carry her into her bedroom and show her how he could take care of her for a while. Lay her down across the bed and smooth her skirt up to her waist, kiss her over her panties until she begged him to tear them off. And then the real care would start, until both of them were left breathless and spent, lying in each other's arms.

If she kept kissing him like that, her full lips gliding along his throat, the tip of her tongue tracing little circles and making him rock-hard, he'd have no choice. Especially when she shifted her weight and discovered his erection with a little gasp. Before he lost his mind completely, he needed to talk to her.

She stopped kissing him and looked into his eyes. His heart pounded—did she feel his body go tense and think it was because he didn't want her? "Hey there, Gorgeous. Everything okay?" he asked.

Elena bit her lower lip. "Don't take this the wrong way. I am so, so turned on right now that I can barely think."

"That makes two of us."

She grinned and licked her lips, driving him a little further down the road to crazy. "I know you wanted to talk tonight, and that's probably still a good idea. I think. Maybe." She giggled. "Brain shutting down."

Camden leaned forward and pressed his forehead against hers. "We're on the same page, babe. I'm trying my best to stay a gentleman while I have the loveliest," he kissed her nose, "sexiest," he kissed each cheek, "most desirable woman in the world," he didn't dare kiss her mouth so he pressed his lips to her chin, "who is way better at keeping her mind clear than I am."

"Barely," she answered, her eyes smokey with desire. He didn't miss her hand sneaking up to touch the wedding ring on her necklace and he watched her eyes clear. He had a choice—he could feel sorry for himself and get angry at a ghost, or he could man up, meet her reluctance head-on, and do something about it.

"Do you want to talk about your husband first? About Antonio?" He nodded at her fingers still toying with the ring.

She dropped her hand. "You must think I'm a tease." She looked down at her empty hands. "The truth is, I haven't been with anyone since him." Her cheeks caught fire. "I feel a little pathetic right now."

Camden tipped her chin back up. "Missing Antonio isn't a weakness. Your loyalty tells me exactly what kind of woman you are. You love hard and strong and faithfully. Antonio was damn lucky to have you. So is Tina."

"If you say so."

"Elena. You've got to stop putting yourself down. I don't think you're pathetic or a tease. I'd love to throttle the person who so much as hinted that you're anything less than amazing." He took a chance and touched the wedding ring. "I have a feeling this guy never did that." He held his breath. Was he pushing too hard? Or was he actually being a coward and stalling, not wanting to talk about himself or ask her about Cici?

He breathed in when she smiled, gently took his hand, and kissed it. "No. Antonio always made me feel like I was the center of the universe. Even though I came from nothing."

Camden tilted his head. "What do you mean, nothing?"

Elena sat up and Camden instantly missed the heat from her body. He reflexively tightened his arms to keep her from pulling away, but she was only sitting up, not leaving.

"I grew up in New Mexico," she said. "I never knew my father, just that he was originally from Costa Rica. My mother was a little wild and didn't want to be tied down, I guess, so she took off with me. Why she didn't leave me behind, I'll never know. The first place I remember living was a studio apartment until we got kicked out. Then we stayed in a rented room until we got kicked out of there, too. After that, we lived in my mom's car. One day when I was ten, I walked back from school to the strip mall lot where we'd parked the night before to find the car and my mother gone without a trace."

Camden stroked her face. "I'm sorry that happened to you." Inside, he howled at the thought of a little girl, of his Elena, walking into an empty parking lot all alone and finding herself abandoned by the one person who was supposed to care for her the most in life. No wonder she put herself down all the time. He couldn't believe how calmly she talked about what had to be one of the worst days of her life. Camden fought to match her tone, to keep the rage out of his face and his voice even. "I can't imagine what I would do. Did you find her?"

She shook her head. "Yes and no. That was the last time I saw her. Years later, I tracked her down online. From what I could tell, she'd run off with some guy and they ended up in jail in Florida. Armed robbery. I found her after we had Tina. I guess I was flooded with new-mom hormones and wanted to reconnect. Needless to say, I didn't get in touch."

Jesus Christ. Camden's jaw tightened. "So, what happened after she left?" He couldn't imagine how afraid she must have been.

I got put into the system and sent to a group home in Albuquerque."

Camden couldn't help himself. He pulled Elena in tight against his chest, wishing he could reach back through time and tell that lost little girl how much she had to look forward to, all the love that was in store for her.

To his surprise, Elena's voice perked up. "Hey, it was way better than sleeping in a car. And I ate regularly. That's where I learned to love the kitchen. I loved the warmth and the good smells and the comfort of four solid walls around me. If someone was mean to me, I baked brownies for everyone but that kid. When the bully smelled them and demanded one, the other kids defended me. Eventually, the kid would apologize, I'd hand over a brownie, and then I'd have one more ally. I baked birthday cakes and recreated meals I'd only smelled coming from restaurants. I made the other kids and even the staff my Guinea pigs."

Camden laughed. "Lucky Guinea pigs."

Elena grinned. "It's still how I make friends. Food is love."

Ah. "That's why you brought several dishes to Bette's."

"And it worked. I met Cici."

Camden's stomach plummeted to his toes. "And you met Cici."

Elena lifted her head from his chest. "Who you really don't want me being friends with. That's what you wanted to talk about, isn't it?"

Shit. Dammit. Here we go. Camden considered his options again. He didn't want to play games, so he just came out with it. "The lady does a lot of good work. She's a good person to know in this town. Any other time, I'd cheer your friendship on."

"But not right now. Why?" Elena cocked her head to the side and studied him.

Tread carefully. "Because I'm working security for them. They're already in the spotlight, but they're about to go supernova with Roger's upcoming announcement and fundraiser. That attracts the wrong people sometimes. Perfect example was the Bash. I don't want you caught up in the middle." *Even though you already are,* he desperately wanted to tell her. He hated how she'd stiffened in his arms at his words.

Elena pressed her lips together in the straight line Camden had come to dread. He waited for her to argue with him. Instead, she said something worse. "It...might be a little too late for that."

Fuck. "What makes you say that?" Would she tell him about her lunch now? Did he want her to?

"Well, Cici came to Brant and Phillips today and asked me out to lunch to make up for the scene at the party. She was embarrassed, Camden. What was I supposed to say?" Color rose up her neck and spread across her face, not the embarrassed blush from earlier but one that signaled she was getting upset.

Camden put his hand up. "Hey, I'm not judging or getting mad here. You're the kind of person Cici would want for a friend. Someone who's warm and understanding. I'm not surprised she's seeking you out." *I just wish she wouldn't,* he thought.

Elena relaxed again. She placed her hand on his chest at the top of his shirt. The tip of her finger touched his bare skin just under the hollow of his throat and he fought back shivers. "That's just it. She must know a ton of women she could confide in, but she's choosing me."

That put Camden on high-alert. "Confide in?" He covered her hand with his and wrapped his fingers around hers. "Elena, I'm in a tight spot here. There are a lot of things I can't tell you."

Elena's lips pressed into a straight line again. "She's in trouble, I think, and she doesn't know who to trust, who to confide in. Maybe that's why she's seeking me out. So let me help her by helping you."

Her eyes shown so brightly with the idea of it that Camden blurted out, "I can't let you do that. I can't let you get in the middle of this. I have to protect you and Tina." *I can't fail. Not this time.* The long-ago memories roared back like a visceral gut punch.

Elena laid her hand on his cheek. "Camden?" Her eyes

had gone round and alert. "Where'd you go? I didn't mean to touch a nerve."

He laid his hand over hers. "Nowhere good, baby."

She narrowed her eyes. "But you don't want to talk about that, do you?"

Camden blew out a breath. "Not...yet."

Elena looked away and he hated the sudden distance. More so because he'd caused it.

But when she looked back he saw new determination in her eyes. "So, who protects *you*, while you're being all tough?" She broke into a smile that melted his heart. "Please let me help you. Cici wants to talk to me. She almost told me something before this Lawrence guy came along today. I think it might have been what's bothering her."

Shit. That was probably the worst thing she could have said. Now Camden had to weigh his job against his woman's safety. *Fuck.* "She told you something, or she *almost* told you something?"

"Almost. She said she has regrets, mistakes she's made. I think she's worried that they'll come out on the campaign trail. But I can't imagine what she could've done."

So, it is something from her past, Camden thought, *not something recent that she might be hiding.* But what could it be? "That's the word she used? Regrets?"

Elena nodded. "That's when Lawrence showed up, so she never finished telling me what had her worried."

Damn. He could ask Elena to set up another lunch date, or even better, invite Cici over to her apartment so they'd have privacy. He could set up a wire—

Camden stopped mid-thought, hating the way his training tried to take over, to see Elena as a resource instead of a loved one. And here he went projecting that on to Gina earlier. *I'm an asshole.*

So which would it be—the former SEAL with a job to do, or the lover and protector he wanted to be—who would win? Why did it have to be an either/or? Why did he always have to choose?

The last time he'd chosen the SEAL, he'd lost everything.

So, he'd just find another way.

Camden stroked Elena's hair. "I don't need you getting involved, babe. Besides, it's not your problem. You've got enough to worry about. You don't need some woman dumping on you."

Elena stiffened. *Wrong answer*. "I don't see it that way. She wants to help me get started in the restaurant business. The least I could do is listen to her, even if you don't want to hear about it."

"You want to open a restaurant?" Camden broke into a grin. "That's awesome. You'd be amazing at it."

"I..." Several emotions played across her face—surprise, wonder, happiness. "I think I do. Maybe not one to start. I don't have that kind of money. But, maybe a food truck, or personal chef service, or a catering business. I don't know."

"I think you do know. Babe, I would be one-hundred percent behind you on that. Whatever I can do to help."

Elena's lips curved up into a teasing smile. "You just want free food."

Camden tilted his head. "I'm that transparent, huh?"

She laughed. "Hardly. Unless it comes to food. Then I know just what you want."

A wicked grin appeared on his face. "Only when it comes to food?"

Her eyes widened and her mouth opened in mock-shock. "I have no idea what you're talking about, Camden Bains."

He pulled her in close, framing her face with his hands. "Then let me show you."

FOURTEEN

He started with her mouth, seizing her lower lip and pulling it between his. That sent heat straight between her legs. She moaned and squirmed in his arms, seeking to relieve the growing ache. It had been years since she'd felt this way, this burning need that sent her heart racing and shut down rational thought. Her lips moved to his throat, kissing him just under his ear. Camden leaned his head back, offering his throat up to her. As she kissed along his neck, he made the most delicious noises. *I'm causing that?* she thought in wonder. A thrill ran through her, a subtle feeling of power. It had been so long since she'd desired anyone, or made anyone desire her, she'd come to doubt that it would ever happen again. And yet, here was this amazing man reacting to her every touch.

Camden grabbed her around the waist and shifted her until she was straddling him. That felt incredibly good, incredibly *right*. She looked down into his eyes, hazy and half-lidded with desire, the sexiest smile on his lips. He stroked her back, his hands sliding down to cup her bottom, pulling her in closer until she was pressed tightly against his hard cock straining against his jeans. She couldn't help but rub against him as the pressure against her clit made her wet. His fingers slid under her skirt and found her soaked panties. He chuckled when an involuntary gasp escaped her as he swiped a finger over her swollen bud. God, she wanted him, wanted to satisfy the ache at her core with his body. She reached for his jeans to unbutton them, when he gently moved her hands away.

"I want this to be about you tonight, Elena. You said you wanted to go slowly." His finger stroked her clit through her panties, teasing her.

I did? I do? "But I want to make you feel good, too," she whispered.

"You do, Gorgeous. And you will. But for now, just enjoy." He pulled her panties aside, adding fingers that slid along her lips and pressed on either side of her clit. "So wet for me, Baby."

"All for you." She moaned when he slid a finger inside of her, finding just the right spot to rub. Gasping and panting, she arched against his hand, feeling her orgasm build, her body become weightless. She bit her lower lip to keep from crying out as the first wave hit her, then the next, bigger and brighter and taking her higher than she'd ever gone. When she came back down, Camden was watching her with a look of absolute joy.

"That was beautiful. Utterly beautiful, watching you come for me. Thank you."

Elena laughed quietly, still trying to catch her breath as she climbed back into her body. "Thank *you*, Cam. It's been so long since...well, since *that*." She laid back down against his chest and felt his heart hammering against her cheek. "Are you sure I can't return the favor?"

He growled as he ran his hand through her hair. "Another

night, when we have more time. I want to enjoy you thoroughly, and I want to make you come so many times you can't remember your name."

He lifted her chin and their lips met. She was on the verge of asking him to spend the night when he stopped kissing her and looked deeply into her eyes." As much as I want to keep going, we both have early days tomorrow," he told her. But something in his eyes made her think there was more to it. *He was going to tell me something*, she thought. She wondered if she should press him about it, but after that orgasm, she didn't think she had quite the brain cells to process a deep conversation.

After Camden secured a leash to Toby's collar (Tina would be so disappointed to find the dog gone in the morning) Elena walked him to the door half in a daze. Before letting him leave, she told him, "Next time, I'm not letting you go. There's a lot I still need to learn about you."

His eyes blazed. He answered her with another deep kiss.

Elena woke up the next morning alone in her bed. She reached across the sheets to touch the empty place where she wished Camden were. God, how she wanted to wake up in his arms, to smell his warm skin and run her fingers through his thick, curly hair to wake him up. She wondered how his morning kisses would taste—he had a full buffet of them. The spicy-hot forbidden kisses they'd shared in Bette's library that left her skin tingling and her mouth on fire. The sweet one he'd given her in the kitchen as she was getting Tina ready for bed. And the kisses on the couch last night that made her hungry for more, which he happily gave her.

Elena could have spent the rest of the morning in bed thinking about Camden, but she needed to get Tina to school and herself to work. Luckily, her Pepita was in a cooperative mood and they got out the door way ahead of schedule, which meant Elena got to work early. On her chair was a photocopy of the page from the company manual outlining professional behavior, with a note from Julia asking Elena to please review the guidelines and take them to heart.

So much for small victories. She'd worked overtime the day before to make up for the longer lunch, and there'd been a couple days when she'd skipped lunch entirely. Julia had highlighted in yellow a line about treating clients respectfully. So was that it—she thought Elena wasn't good enough to actually have a friend like Cici, that she was acting like some kind of fangirl? *Ugh.* She put her lunch cooler in her bottom drawer with a little pang—Camden had made it for her—deciding she would go out today after all. Two could play the passive-aggressive game.

Before turning her phone off, she sent a text to Lissa to see if she wanted to go with her to Delia's for lunch. That would give her a chance to ask Delia in person about catering for Cici. Talking to Camden the night before filled her head with ideas about the appetizers she would serve and how she'd go about doing it, if the job was hers. Elena set those thoughts aside with a sigh. She'd taken Camden's warning seriously, but she still wanted to help Cici and Camden both. What could be bothering her new friend? Maybe it was nothing, and Elena could put her at ease. On the other hand, if it was something big, wouldn't it make Camden's job easier and safer if he knew? The dilemma tied Elena's stomach in knots all morning, as if her stomach weren't upset enough from Julia's behavior.

Lissa picked up on Elena's tension on their walk to Delia's. "What's up? You look clucked."

Elena glanced at her friend. "I look what? Like a chicken?"

Lissa giggled. "Sorry. Surfer term. You look like you're facing down some waves you don't like."

Elena grabbed Lissa's arm. "God, am I. I'll tell you over lunch. But first, I need to ask Delia something." By now it had become a habit to walk past the line and go straight in. Pete just gave them a wave as they headed for the kitchen.

"Ladies," Delia said from the prep line. Her tone told them the kitchen was in the weeds—it looked like they were down a person and Delia had hopped on the line to try and get them caught up.

"I have something to ask you when you get a minute," Elena said.

"Girl, does it look like I'm gonna get a minute? You wanna ask me something, grab a knife and hop on."

Elena's heart did a little jig, then sped up the good way it had every time she'd faced down a breakfast or lunch crowd. She grinned, took her blazer off, and draped it over the back of her chair.

"She's kidding, Elena." Lissa pulled out her chair.

"No, I am *not* kidding." Delia bashed a clove of garlic with the side of her knife as if to prove her point.

"Whoa," Lissa half-laughed. "Better get in there, then."

"My pleasure." Elena grabbed a black apron with the logo for Delia's in gold printed on the front. It felt so good to suit up and do something she loved for a change. She washed her hands and joined Delia. Not to be left behind, Lissa was right behind her, scrubbing up and grabbing another apron.

"Is this even legal in California?" Elena asked.

"If a health inspector materializes, you were hired five minutes ago," Delia answered.

Elena's heart did another little flip at that. "Good enough." She took one look at the already-prepped food and figured out the special of the day and what needed to be done. She went to work chopping peppers.

"Damn, you're good," Delia said. "Lunch on the house for life."

"How about you just do me a favor instead?"

Without pausing, the chef gave her the side-eye. "That all depends."

"This is a good one." Elana scooped up the diced pepper and dropped it in a glass bowl, then grabbed another. "Cici Bennett, Roger Bennett's wife, needs a last-minute caterer for Roger's political shindig. She loved lunch yesterday and asked me to ask you if you'd be interested."

"Hmm." Elena wasn't fooled by Delia's lackluster response. The woman paused and pursed her lips before attacking the next garlic clove.

Elena decided to sweeten the pot. "She said the publicity couldn't be beat."

Delia snorted. "You think I need *more* business? Pete, what's it look like out there?" The maître d had just come through the door.

"They're about to eat each other. I'm in hiding."

"My maître d is in hiding." Delia pointed her knife at Pete.

"But without the business crowd, this place is so dead on the weekends you don't even bother with lunch on Saturday and you're closed Sundays. Catering could make up for that."

Delia huffed.

"Please?" Elena asked. "She's kinda desperate. And really nice."

Whoops. Elena wasn't sure about the sudden triumphant look in Delia's eyes. "Okay, okay, you twisted my arm. But on one condition."

"Uh-oh," Lissa chimed in. She bumped shoulders with Elena, but she had an excited smile on her face. "Here it comes."

"Here comes what?" Elena looked back and forth between the two women.

"I will agree to this if you manage the gig for me."

"What, are you joking?" Elena's heart leaped.

"She's offering you a job right now, Elena," Lissa bounced on her toes. "And about time. I've been telling her—"

"I'm offering you a *chance* at a job, if you choose to take it. My kitchen manager just gave me a month's notice, and she was a no-show today, as you can see. She'll be back, but I'll need to replace her pretty quick. What do you say?"

"Yes!" Elena squealed before she could think. "I already have some great ideas."

Lissa gave her a quick hug from behind. "I'll help."

Delia grinned and nodded. "Then I'll need both of you here Saturday morning. We'll have the kitchen to ourselves to try out your ideas before the dinner prep. Be here at eight sharp." She looked around. "I think we're caught up. Go sit and I'll feed you."

Elena and Lissa took their aprons off and sat down to Delia's famous cheese and meat board with warm bread. Lissa looked like the cat who swallowed the canary.

"So, do I have you to thank for this opportunity?" Elena popped a cheese cube in her mouth.

"Do you just love me?" Lissa grinned from ear to ear. "I so wanted to say something on our way over because you looked totally bummed."

"You mean clucked?"

"Yeah! I figured you and Julia were at it again and this is your chance to get the hell outta there. I've been telling Delia how efficient you are at work, how you've got all the agents on track *and* eating out of your hand—"

"I do not."

"Shut up, you do. And Delia's been sizing you up anyway. I could sing your praises all day long, but if she didn't think you'd work hard, that you didn't want this job with your heart and soul—and that you'd be perfect for it—she wouldn't have offered. You're a natural and she knows it."

Elena laughed. "Hardly. I have a background in fast food and greasy spoons."

"Whatevs, that's like everybody else in here. So, what did you want to talk about? Am I right, is it Julia?"

"No. It's..."

Shit. The full implications of what Elena had just agreed to hit her full-force. If she was going to manage the catering job, that would put her right smack dab in the middle of things. Right after she told Camden she'd stay away from Cici. But there was no way in hell she was going to pass up this opportunity. Besides, it was just one gig for just one night. She'd be totally in the background, right? Cici wouldn't exactly be hanging on her caterer at an event where she needed to be the supportive wife of the newly-announced candidate. And, Camden did say he was one-hundred percent behind her aspirations. He'd understand. Right?

"It's what?" Lissa tilted her head, her smile replaced with a frown, her eyebrows drawn down in concern.

Elena waved her off. "Oh, it's nothing. You're right, Julia's getting to me. You're lucky you don't report directly to her." She picked up her water goblet and clinked it against Lissa's. "But now, everything's going to be fine."

They hurried through the rest of lunch. When they

walked back through the dining room, the crowd had thinned. Lissa was talking about her plans to someday get to Maui for some sort of big competition, but Elena didn't catch what it was.

She felt eyes on her, watching her every move.

Predatory, the same feeling she got from her days at the meat-packing plant. No, worse—she hadn't had this prickly feeling of dread since the day she'd gone to pick Tina up from school and was stopped in the parking lot by a man who had her little girl drugged and in the back of his car. His eyes had told her she was helpless prey, taunting her, daring her to fight, to scream, to even say a word, and risk never seeing her daughter alive again.

Elena looked around the dining room until she saw the source of her fear. He sat alone at a corner table, one where he could survey the entire place.

Lawrence Franklin.

And he was looking directly at her. It took everything not to gasp at his cold hard stare. In a blink, it warmed as he lifted his rocks glass and toasted her. He stood and Elena's first impulse was to push Lissa ahead of her so they could run for their lives, when he turned toward another familiar-looking man with white hair and a cane who had approached the table. As they were about to shake hands, the white-haired man burst into a coughing fit. Lawrence's attention left her as if she'd never existed.

She was sure she'd never seen Lawrence at Delia's before yesterday, and now he'd been there two days in a row. *Is it just my imagination that he's stalking me?*

Lissa had gotten a few feet ahead of Elena so she caught up to her. "...but if I do, I'll be going alone because there's no way I'm taking Brice."

"I don't blame you," Elena said, with absolutely no idea

what Lissa was talking about. She glanced back to see Lawrence engaged in an animated conversation with the new guy, Elena completely forgotten, it seemed. She shook off her feelings as paranoia. Lawrence had barely paid attention to her at lunch the day before. In his eyes, she was no one special —a woman to be talked over, dismissed, forgotten. Besides, didn't he say the person he was meeting with yesterday had canceled on him? It made sense they'd reschedule for the next day at the same place. *Get ahold of yourself, Elena—this isn't Ross, Nebraska and that isn't Earnest Deal.*

All the same, she wondered if she should tell Camden. Or rather, how much she should tell him.

FIFTEEN

C amden rubbed the tight spot between his eyebrows when Gina finished giving her report. They were in Watchdog's conference room along with Jake, Costello, and Lachlan, who seemed to be chewing especially hard on his cigarette substitute, the plastic clicking against his teeth and driving Camden to the edge of crazy.

"So, you're telling me that Franklin was back at Delia's today at the same time Elena was there?" Camden asked.

From her usual place against the wall, Gina nodded. She bent down to scratch Fleur's head. Along with Toby and a couple other dogs, Fleur was given free rein in the office. "Franklin came straight from the Bennetts house. Both Roger and Cici were home, so I don't know which one he was visiting. Before yesterday, I would have assumed he was there on campaign business, but now I'm not so sure. I'm glad I decided to follow him instead of sticking with Cici. Lucky for me, he'd make a terrible agent. He never noticed I was there. But he made no secret of watching the room at Delia's, and looked pretty upset when Elena walked out of the kitchen."

"What the hell was she doing in the kitchen?" Lachlan asked, his anything-but-subtle stare piercing Camden.

"She's friends with Delia. She and another mutual friend from B&P eat in there on the regular." Camden turned his attention to Gina. "Did they speak?"

She shook her head. "They didn't communicate directly unless you count the body language. Our girl did not look happy to see him."

Lachlan took the cut-down pen out of his mouth. "He's intimidating her?"

"Sure looked like it, Lach. When he stood up she looked ready to bolt."

Camden fought back his desire to storm from the room and go straight to Elena's office, throw her over his shoulder, and lock her away along with Tina, then stand guard until this all blew over. Or maybe just find Lawrence Franklin and beat the ever-loving shit out of him. Problem solved. Instead, he asked, "What happened after he stood?"

Gina turned to Camden. "Senator Higley showed up."

"'Solid as a Rock' Higley's been mentoring Roger," Camden said. "But I wonder what Franklin wanted to meet with him about."

"I couldn't get close enough to hear. What did Elena tell you last night about her lunch with Cici and Franklin yesterday?"

Camden bit down on the insides of his cheeks before answering, remembering how he'd decided to use kid gloves with her. He was regretting that choice now. "Nothing that we don't already know. Cici started to confide in her, talking about past regrets and bad decisions, when Franklin showed up and took over the conversation. I'm starting to think his interruption was intentional. He's keeping Cici from revealing something from her past. Maybe he showed up today to make sure that if Elena does know something, she'll think twice before talking."

"But she doesn't know anything, right?" Lachlan asked.

Camden didn't like the look in his boss's eyes. He'd seen that calculating gleam before, both on the job and on missions back when they did reconnaissance before storming a suspected stronghold. "She doesn't."

Lachlan rubbed his chin. "They have any plans to get together again?"

"Lach. I see where you're going with this. But, with all due respect, I don't want my woman going anywhere near this situation again."

"She could be our shortcut in. Whatever Cici has on her mind, she's willing to spill for Elena."

Camden's temper flared. "Did you not fucking hear me when I told you I don't want her getting mixed up in this?"

"Camden," Jake started.

Lachlan started to stand, when Gina put a hand on his forearm. "She's a civilian, Lach." Gina looked at Camden. "Camden reminded me of that."

The big, gruff man spared Gina a glance as he sat back down.

Costello raised his hands, palms out. "If I may, of course we don't want to put a civilian in danger, especially one who's been put there before. But if Cici does contact Elena again, anything she tells her could be extremely helpful. And by the sound of it, Camden, Elena is already involved. You're not protecting her by ignoring it, you're creating a blind spot."

Ignoring it. Blind spot. Of all the words to use, Costello couldn't have picked four worse ones. The rest of the man's words were lost in a dull roar filling Camden's head. The drone of the aircraft carrying him back Stateside after the phone call from the sheriff. *To make it worse, they were in his blind spot* the sheriff told him. The roar of his own voice at the news. And now the blood roaring in his ears at the unintentional reminder of his greatest failure.

"...could even bug her phone so she wouldn't have to get near," Costello finished and watched Camden expectantly. "Camden?"

"Brother," Jake said when Camden didn't reply. He laid a hand on Camden's shoulder. "I know where your head's at right now. Get it the hell away from there because that's not going to help anything. Elena's in the here and now."

Camden blew out a breath he didn't know he was holding. *Pull your ever-loving shit together, Bains, for fuck's sake* he chastised himself. *Your boss is sitting right there and you're fucking this up big time.* "For being psychic, Costello, you sure couldn't have said something worse."

"Sorry, man." Costello laced his hands behind his head, elbows out, and leaned back in his chair. "See? Told you, there's no such thing as psychics."

"Obviously. But, you've got a point about the blind spot." It hurt even saying those words but he did it on purpose the same way he once poked at a cavity just to feel the deep ache —part of him couldn't help it, and the other part used the pain to sharpen his attention. "If we bring Elena in, even on a temporary and limited basis—which I'm in favor of—I want to be her personal bodyguard."

Lachlan started to speak, but Camden held his hand up. "Cici obviously knows Elena and I are dating. She'll expect to see us together." Something just at the edge of his awareness flickered and disappeared. He reached for the thought but it eluded him. "Lawrence Franklin probably knows, too. So nobody would be surprised if I spent the night at Elena's place. Or better, if she and Tina came to mine. I could protect them overnight without suspicion."

Lachlan had picked up his chewed-up pen and stuck it back in his mouth. Plastic clicked as his left-side molars clamped down. "I'm wondering if you're too close to this to still be leading the team."

Bam. If Camden didn't go toe-to-toe with Lachlan right now, he'd probably lose this assignment entirely, old teammates or not, and how would that help anyone? "Look, I'm sorry I lost my cool. I can damn well still lead this team. If the chatter is correct about a foreign agent trying to build the next Manchurian candidate from the ground up, we're all fucked, and that includes Elena. I recognize that, and I'm willing to put my personal life aside for the greater good. If she can get intel out of Cici, we'll use it. But we'll bring Elena in only within that scenario, and we'll bring her in and protect her the way I see fit."

"Elena may not even agree to help, seeing as she's been in danger before," Gina said. She pushed off from the wall and approached the table, Fleur following like a caramel-colored shadow. "And if she doesn't, we're back to digging for intel in other ways. Camden, are you still thinking of looking into the Bennetts' medical records with the infertility clinic?" Gina actually took a seat at the table. Fleur plopped down at her feet.

"It's about all we've got after digging through her college years, which were both boring and exemplary. But, HIPAA makes getting medical records difficult, especially in California. A crime hasn't been committed yet that we know of, we aren't trying to identify a victim or perp, we don't have a missing person. No way a court's gonna give us permission to grab Cici's infertility records, especially if we have no idea what we're looking for, if anything."

While he'd been talking, he watched a spark grow in Gina's eyes. "So, Spooky, how *do* we get those records? I'm almost positive there's something there."

Gina templed her fingers and her red-painted nails clicked together. "Research team."

"Research team?"

"A public or private nonprofit educational institution can request medical records for research purposes."

Camden couldn't stop the grin overtaking his lips. "And you just happen to know of an educational institution that would request records from a certain clinic?"

She nodded. "I think a study on the prevalence of twin births after fertility treatments ten years ago *just* got funded."

"How long would this take?"

"You're not going to get the info overnight. HIPAA won't allow a patient's privacy to be violated. The clinic will still have to release the records minus any patient ID markers. That means no names, addresses, or identifying characteristics. We'll have to narrow down the records to the dates Cici was treated and compare what we know about the Bennetts to the patient info they *do* give us."

"I can find the needle in that haystack," Costello said.

"Cici's and Roger's ages are our best bet," Gina told him. "So, the research team will ask for the patients' ages as part of the data specifically required for the study."

She said this so quickly and smoothly that Camden got the feeling Gina had put this idea into play the minute he'd mentioned the fertility issues at their last meeting. *While I'm playing checkers, she's playing chess. So glad she's on the team.*

"Any more chatter? Anything about Bennett being approached?"

"Nothing more yet," Gina said. "That's up to us to figure out."

Camden ended the meeting feeling more lost than he had in years. But he knew one thing for certain—he'd do anything to keep Elena and Tina safe. Starting tonight.

When Camden went to the courtyard to pick up Toby, he was still thinking about the best way to keep everyone safe, including his clients. Kyle was just finishing up an obedience training class with a group of civilians. He held up a hand acknowledging Camden, while his other held Toby's leash. Kyle often used Toby for his demonstrations with the classes or as a dog ambassador when he did a public demo. Toby had been assigned to Camden when he started at Watchdog, and the two immediately started to bond. When Camden sat in on Kyle's second job interview, he'd been surprised to learn that Kyle didn't have his own dog. He continued to be dumbfounded that the Pup hadn't particularly bonded with any of the other dogs, though he obviously enjoyed working with all of them, and they loved him.

"Be sure to practice all week and stay consistent," Kyle told the class as they got ready to leave. "Constant reinforcement does the job."

"That advice works on kids, too," Camden joked. "And new recruits."

Kyle gave him a half-smile. "Next you're gonna tell me there's no difference between the two."

"Aw, you stole my punchline." Camden crouched and gave Toby a vigorous head-scratching.

Kyle handed him the leash. "This good boy makes my job easy."

"That he does. Not that you need it. I've never seen someone handle dogs so well. How come you don't have one of your own?"

This time, Kyle beamed. "I do have a dog, sir, but he's still serving." Like a proud dad, Kyle took out his wallet, removed a bedraggled photograph, and handed it to Camden. In head-to-toe desert fatigues, Kyle knelt next to a dog kitted up in a battle vest, a pair of goggles slung around his furry neck, large pink tongue lolling out the side of his smiling muzzle. "That's my old partner, back when I was the dog handler on my team."

Camden squinted. The dog looked like a Lab, but unlike any he'd ever seen before. Instead of solid black or yellow or chocolate, this dog's coat was mottled black and yellow, like a tortoiseshell cat. "I thought they only used Malinois and German Shepherds."

"Mostly they do. But my boy's special. See his coat? He's a chimera. I don't know all the science, something to do with two sets of DNA, but I understand it's like having two animals in one. All I know is that his sense of smell is twice as good as any other dog I've ever worked with. He's found IEDs other dogs walked right past. And he tracks people better than any Bloodhound. He once found a little boy after a mortar brought down the house around him. Kid wouldn't be alive otherwise. His name's Camo. Short for Camouflage."

Camden chuckled. "Perfect name." He handed the photo back to Kyle.

"I haven't seen him in nearly two years, not since I...left the SEALs." Camden took note of the hesitation. "But, I put in the paperwork to adopt Camo once his duty is done and he's back Stateside."

Camden had never seen Kyle look so excited. He didn't know if that would make what he was about to say easier or harder. "Lach and I have been talking. We're both blown away with how well you're handling the dogs, and the owners, truth be told."

Kyle's enthusiasm faded. "I hear a 'but' in there."

"Not a 'but' so much as a decision. We want to keep you with training and handling the dogs. We think that's where your greatest strength lies. So, we're promoting you to Kennel Master. Congratulations." Camden stuck out his hand. Kyle took it and they shook.

"Thanks. But I think I know what this means. No bodyguard duty."

Camden nodded.

"You don't trust me."

Shit. Not the reaction I wanted. "That's not it at all, man. If we didn't trust you, you think you'd be working here at all? With the dogs, with Lach's sainted pooch, Sam? Hell, no. Lach wants the strongest team possible for Watchdog. We all have our different strengths, and nobody beats your mad skills with the dogs."

Kyle looked toward the obstacle courses. His jaw tightened, then relaxed. He took a deep breath, held it, then exhaled. Finally, he nodded to himself as if he'd come to some internal agreement. "Okay, then." He looked Camden in the eye. "Thanks, boss."

"You earned it, man." Camden tagged Kyle on the shoulder. "Hope you get to adopt Camo soon."

"Me too."

Camden took a deep breath. "Can I ask why it's so important to you to do the bodyguard work when you're so good with the dogs?"

Kyle's mouth tightened. "I just want to prove myself," he finally said.

"Spoken like a true SEAL. But you've got nothing to prove to us. You're solid, man."

"Thanks. I appreciate it." Though Kyle's body language said otherwise. The kid was wound up, fighting some private demon inside.

Aren't we all? Camden thought.

SIXTEEN

Elena couldn't quite shake her uneasiness about seeing Larry at Delia's when Camden called her cell at the end of the day.

"Hey! You must have read my mind. I literally just turned my phone back on."

"You still at work?" Camden's characteristically cheerful voice held the faintest undertone of concern. *What's that about*, Elena wondered.

"Just got to my car, on my way to pick Tina up from after-care. How are you?"

"Great. Get the Mermaid and I'll be by with dinner."

Elena started her car and the phone connected to the radio. "You don't sound great, Cam, you sound a little worried. What's up?"

After a pause, he said, "Damn, you already know me too well. Yeah, okay, something's up. We need to talk tonight, for real." His voice lightened up. "Even if that means I have to wear a blindfold and tie my hands behind my back to keep from getting distracted by you."

Elena laughed. "Um, that sounds more kinky than anything else. *I might get distracted if you do that.*"

"You aren't making this any easier, Gorgeous." His growly voice filled the car. She shifted in her seat, wishing she was already at home, talk over, Tina sound asleep, and Camden...

Do I want him in my bed? After all this time of being alone? She had last night, but it was hard to think straight when his fingers were sending her over the edge. Though, if her racing heart and lightly sweating palms were any indications, then yes, she did want him in her bed.

"Give me an hour because I need to get Tina, then I need to—"

"Old Tobes and I will be waiting in the lobby for you."

Again, the alarm bells went off in Elena's gut. *Dammit.* "Camden? What's going on?"

"Just excited to see you and talk to you, Gorgeous. How long does it take to get Tina and get home?"

"Half an hour, but she'll hurry to get her stuff together if she knows you and Toby are waiting."

"Then I'll see you in half an hour or less. I'm in the takeout line right now and about to pick up my order. Talk to you in a few. Love you."

Love. You? Elena nearly rear-ended the Beemer ahead of her. "Camden? Did you just say...?"

But the line was dead.

Love you. The way Camden said them, the words sounded so natural, something a husband would say to his wife on any given day at the end of a call. Like it was a given, a well-worn but cherished sweater you'd put on to feel cozy. And they sounded like they'd just slipped out of his mouth without hesitation, without a second thought.

Camden loved her. Full-stop.

And I love him.

No use denying it. No use hiding behind shyness or widowhood or momhood or any other excuse that kept her from feeling it. She loved him. She wanted to be with him. She wanted her daughter to know what a good and loving relationship looked and felt like. But even beyond that, Elena wanted to feel loved and cherished and protected by a man again. And there was nothing wrong or selfish about that. It didn't mean she loved Antonio any less, or that she would ever forget him. All she had to do was look at her smart, beautiful, sweet daughter to see that Antonio lived on, in the best way possible.

All this time, I've been afraid that Tina wouldn't remember her father if I fell in love with another man. Maybe I'm the one who's been afraid of forgetting my husband.

But there was an even bigger fear lying under that realization, one that Elena wasn't yet ready to face. She pushed it down deep and tried to focus on picking up her daughter and preparing for whatever Camden wanted to talk about.

And, deciding if she was ready to say out loud that she loved him back.

Tina burst through the glass doors and ran straight to Camden and Toby. Camden stood up from the bench beside the elevators, opened his arms, and swooped the little girl up over his head before tucking her to his side. Toby stood wagging his tail, waiting for his turn to marinate her in love.

"I've got the food," Elena said, grabbing the good-smelling bags on the bench with one hand and reaching for the elevator button with the other.

"Now, now, just wait a minute," Camden said as he took her outstretched hand before she could hit the up button. He turned his head to the side to look Tina in the eye. "With your permission, Mermaid, I would like to kiss your mother hello."

Elena's eyes went wide. She tried to remember if Tina had ever actually seen them kiss beyond a peck on the cheek. She studied her daughter's face for any sign of hesitation. Instead, she found sudden surprise, followed by a brief look of joy that she quickly minimized to nonchalance. Elena felt like she'd just caught a glimpse of the future—Tina as a teenager was going to be a challenge.

Tina shrugged. "Yup. You can kiss her."

Camden turned to Elena, his expression neutral but his eyes dancing with humor. "Now that I have permission from the mermaid, I'm asking you. May I have the honor of kissing you?"

Remembering what she and Camden had done on the couch, Elena stifled a laugh at his mock-chivalry. He certainly did earn his nickname, Joker. "Well, sir, it is a bit bold for you to ask, but I shall grant it."

There was nothing pretend or joking about the smile he gave her. It was warm and serious and grateful and full of love.

He loves me.

She put the food back on the bench as he set Tina down, then took Elena in his arms. He brushed her hair back. "Welcome home, Gorgeous," he whispered, then pressed his lips to hers in a soft, sweet kiss that still managed to get Elena excited for what she hoped would come later.

"You're *blushing*, Mama," Tina said. Elena blinked, realizing it was true.

"Let's get upstairs and get you fed," she said, mentally adding, *and get you to bed a little earlier than normal.*

"Mama and Camden sitting in a tree, K-I-S-S—"

"And that is enough of *that*, young lady," Elena said,

putting her hand on Tina's head as the elevator doors opened. Over her daughter's head, she rolled her eyes at Camden. But his expression had turned serious and distant—almost angry—before he covered it with a smile and mirrored an eyeroll back at her.

She raised her eyebrows with the silent question, *What's wrong?* Her stomach knotted up at the thought that Tina had somehow offended him.

He shook his head and gave her another smile, one he probably thought looked reassuring and was anything but.

Her stomach knotted up more, and she knew, just *knew*, that look had nothing to do with Tina's antics and everything to do with Cici...and Lawrence Franklin.

Her deepest fear gripped her in its sharp, pitiless teeth.

That damned look spoiled Elena's evening, but she didn't want to admit it. Even after she'd changed out of her work clothes, she still felt uneasy. Tina picked up on Elena's mood during dinner, and Elena made the mistake of snapping at her daughter when Tina called her on her grumpiness. That put Tina in a bad mood, which manifested in the girl's behavior. She dug her heels in at every turn, refusing to take her plate to the kitchen sink after she'd been scolded for giving Toby table scraps.

And Camden was no help, taking Tina's plate from the table. "Look, it's no big deal, I was planning on washing the dishes anyway."

"That's not the point. She knows not to feed Toby table scraps and now she's just being defiant."

Camden reminded Elena that Toby had eaten far worse than takeout burgers. Elena ground her teeth and Tina took

Camden's efforts to lighten the mood as carte blanche to continue misbehaving, until Elena ordered her to her room where she could get ready for bed early.

"Camden, tell Mama she's being *mean!*" Tina shrieked the last word.

"Now, Mermaid, there's no need for that," Camden went to one knee in front of the little girl, his voice gentle. Which was not the back-up Elena wanted. Any other time, her heart would have melted the same way it did every other time she watched the big strong SEAL turn into an oversized Teddy bear under Tina's influence. But this just felt like he was undermining her. Especially when Tina gave her a look full of triumph.

Elena pointed at Tina's bedroom door. "That's *it!* You are going to bed right now, no talking back, no whining, and no Toby!"

Tina's triumphant look turned to a mask of tragedy. But Elena stayed firm. She would not let her daughter manipulate her just because Camden was there—*especially* because Camden was there. But oh, God, the look on Camden's face. *Dammit.*

Tina gave one last stomp before marching to her bedroom and slamming the door behind her.

"Elena—" Camden started, but she was in no mood.

"It's easy for you. You spoil her, you do every little thing that she wants while I'm the one who has to lay down the rules all the time to make sure she's safe, to make sure she stays healthy. I'm the one who almost lost her when she was a baby and I had no idea what was wrong, while she was slowly starving to death right the hell in front of me because her tiny helpless body couldn't make insulin. I'm the one who had to be both her mom and dad when my husband died and left us stranded in godforsaken Ross, Nebraska. And then I almost lost her there again because of something that wasn't even my fault."

The apartment blurred as her eyes filled with tears. "I tried so hard to give her the best life I could while everything around us turned to shit. So hard all the time, and all by myself. When there wasn't enough money to feed the both of us, I went hungry, and I never, ever, not even once resented her or thought about leaving her, even when it would have made my life easier."

"I do know, Elena. I know how hard it was for you. I was there for the kidnapping." His face was full of hurt, his eyes anguished. Instead of softening Elena's mood, it spurred her anger. How dare he think he was *there*? That he understood anything about her life?

"You were there for the big rescue. Just doing your job, and then back to sunny California. You would've never seen us again, never given us a second thought, if we hadn't moved out here. You have no idea what it's like, day in and day out, how hard it is to be a parent."

Elena immediately regretted her snotty, ungrateful tone and sentiment when Camden inhaled as if she'd just kicked him square in the balls and gave his dick a punch along with it.

"I'm sorry, that was so out of line. Most single guys don't want to even be bothered with kids, and you go out of your way to make mine feel special."

When she looked at him, Elena flinched. Now Camden looked like he wanted to punch something.

Her heart plummeted into her chest. *Here it is.* She'd gone too far and pushed him away. He had every right to be pissed when he'd been nothing but good to her and Tina. Maybe if she apologized again, she could salvage something, at least get back to a point where she didn't have to avoid him at parties in the future. "Camden—"

"No, stop right there," Camden cut her off and Elena's stomach flipped. "We're going to address this. You have no... no *idea*, how much your words hurt me just now, how they damn near kill me. No fucking clue. So, yes, we're gonna address this, and I'm going to set you straight on a few things. But first," his expression softened as he stood up. "I'm the one who should be saying sorry."

"What? No, you have nothing to apologize about. I'm the one being a fucking bitch."

Camden shook his head. "First, don't you ever let me catch you calling yourself a bitch again. That is not you, and it will never be you, so stop it. I'm mad at you right now, sure, and I'm hurt. But you have every right to be pissed at me, too. Look, I adore Tina, and so it's easy for me to bend to that little girl's will. You're right, I'd do anything for her."

Camden crossed the short distance between them and cupped her face. "Second, I'd do anything—*anything, Elena*— to make you happy. But instead, tonight I put you in a position with Tina where you've got to be the bad cop to my good cop, and that not fair to you. So." He leaned forward and kissed her forehead, then looked into her eyes. "I'm sorry that I've been a complete dumbass, and I promise—from now on, I'll do the heavy lifting with Tina right along with you."

Elena blinked rapidly. *Is this really happening?*

Camden smirked. "You got something in your eyes, Gorgeous?"

"No, I'm just...thank you."

"So, apology accepted?"

"Yes." She placed her hands on his cheeks and brought him in for a kiss. She tried to deepen it, but he stopped her.

"Like I said, we're gonna sort some things before we go too

far down that road, because even though I'm angry, I still want to do this"—he licked the seam of her lips—"until you're begging me for more. Now give me a sec, because I also have to do something else first."

He got up and went to Tina's door. He knocked and Tina yelled something back in an angry voice.

"Open up, it's Camden," he answered, and Tina's tone of voice sounded much sweeter than before. He left the door open after he went in, and Elena had to keep herself from eavesdropping. After a minute of Camden's stern lecturing voice, Tina did not sound as sweet when she answered him. Five minutes later, Camden walked her out to the living room, where she apologized to Elena for her outburst. And not resentfully, either, much to Elena's shock.

"Thank you, Pepita. I accept your apology. It's no fun for anyone when one of us gets upset for no good reason." She glanced up at Camden, who stood smiling behind Tina, then back to her daughter. "I'm sorry I snapped at you when you called me on my grumpiness. I think we're all gonna try harder next time to listen to each other first, before anybody gets wound up. Sound good?"

Tina gave her a solemn nod.

"Group hug?"

That earned Elena a smile, both from her girl and her guy. She folded her daughter in her arms and Camden wrapped his arms around them both and kissed her cheek. Even Toby got in on the act, licking Tina's face until she giggled.

"Now," Elena said, "I see you've already got your jammies on, which, thank you for that. Go brush your teeth and then it's off to bed."

The little girl looked from her mom to Camden and back. "Do I still get a tuck-in and kisses?"

Elena's heart clenched. "Baby, of course you do! Just

because we had a little argument doesn't mean no kisses. We never, ever, hold back affection like that, and especially never ever after we've made up. I love you no matter what forever."

"That goes for me too, Mermaid. Love you no matter what." Camden gave her one more big squeeze. "Now, no stalling. Go brush your teeth and we'll be right in after."

After tucking Tina in—with Toby at his customary place at the foot of her bed—Elena and Camden found themselves back on the couch. Camden sat down at one end and Elena sat down at the other, mortified at her behavior and what lay under it, afraid that despite what he'd said, Camden was about to break things off. Instead, he slid across the couch and scooped her into his lap before she could protest. He kissed her firmly on the lips then looked deeply into her eyes. "Like you said, we never, ever hold back affection just because we had an argument. Especially after we've made up."

"*Have* we made up?" Elena asked in a voice that sounded unbelievably timid to her ears.

Camden grinned. "Are you calling me a liar?"

"What? No."

"Then, yes, we made up the minute we accepted each other's apologies. But, that doesn't mean we're done here. I've been holding back from you, Elena, and that stops tonight. I don't want to leave you feeling like you're walking through a minefield, and that's what you'd be doing if I didn't tell you about my past. I've been avoiding it, because it's ugly and there are parts of it I'm ashamed of. Parts that, I'm afraid once you hear them, you'll think twice about being with me."

Elena brought her fingers to his lips. "There is nothing you could say that would change the fact that I love you."

His amber eyes went wide. "Elena."

"I do. I love you, Camden Bains. When you said it to me

earlier tonight, I realized I've been in love with you for a while now."

Camden looked confused. "I...when did I—"

"That's what I thought." Elena grinned. "It just slipped out, right before you hung up when you were picking up dinner. Love you. Like you'd felt it for so long, it was just...natural."

"It is. I do. I love you, Elena Martinez. I'm sorry it just slipped out like that. I should have said it to you over a fancy dinner, or at the opera, or—"

"Opera? Seriously?"

Camden shrugged. "It's the fanciest thing I can think of."

Elena laughed.

"No, seriously, you deserved to hear it while we were doing something, I don't know, special. God, I fucked that up."

"No, you didn't. It was perfect, the way you did it. Natural. I love that you did it that way. I love *you*."

Camden looked so soft, and so momentarily vulnerable, that it shook her to the core.

"I'm gonna remember that you said that, baby, after I talk to you."

"Then, talk to me. Get whatever it is off your chest so we can move on."

SEVENTEEN

I *love you.*

Fuck, could she be more special? And could I be more unworthy? Camden stroked Elena's cheek. He took a deep breath and prepared to lose her.

"When you said I didn't know what it was like to be a parent, it killed me. You don't know—you had no way of knowing—how much those words hurt. Because I never told you. I pussed out every time I tried."

And there it was, the dawning realization in her eyes.

"I was a parent, Elena. I was a daddy to a little baby girl."

Elena covered her mouth. *"Was?"* she whispered behind her hand.

Camden looked down. "Was. She...Chloe, her name was Chloe...she and my wife, Susan, they died because I fucked up."

Elena dropped her hand. "I can't believe that. There's no way...you just *couldn't.*"

"But I did, Elena. I was still an active SEAL and I was so damned proud of that. Proud in the wrong way. I thought that I was hot shit, that my life, my needs, took priority. I was out saving the fucking world, right? I let things slide at home. I expected Susan to carry the slack. All the slack. I was barely there, barely in my daughter's life. I took time to be there when Chloe was born, then you know what I did? I went on another deployment as soon as I could. Because that little tiny baby, my little Chloe, she scared me more than the entire Taliban put together. I didn't know jack shit about being a dad.

"My parents are great, don't get me wrong. But, my dad was more interested in his grad students and his studies than he was in trying to raise a family. My mom did all the care-taking right from the moment they met when he was studying abroad at Cambridge. After they got married, she followed him back to the US where she did all the childrearing. My aunties pitched in when they were in town or when we visited them in London, but that was it. My mom was pretty much on her own, otherwise. At times, I heard her even refer to my dad as 'her oldest.' He leaned into the absent-minded professor shtick when it was convenient, so she was the one who took care of all the school pick-ups and drop-offs, paid all the bills, and arranged for handymen and all that shit, and she did it without complaint. So I never realized how hard that was. How unfair.

"And when I got married, I assumed—no, I *expected*—that it would be the same for Susan. And she did do all that, my Susan, and she did it well, and she did it without complaining. Always with a smile for me when I came home from my latest deployment. Up until after she had Chloe."

Camden scrubbed his face. *Now comes the hard part.*

"The pregnancy was hard on her. Really hard. Again, I wasn't there for most of it, so I didn't know the full extent. Labor was hard, too. She was anemic and exhausted going in, and I had no fucking clue. I was too full of myself to notice the worried looks the nurses gave her. Because, look at *me*, I'm gonna be a daddy." Camden cringed.

"When we got home with Chloe, Susan was totally cashed. I figured that was normal. Labor looked fucking exhausting. I thought she'd be back to her old self, taking care of everything like a boss in no time. But until then, I had this scary little creature who demanded so much all the time, to help take care of, and it freaked me the fuck out."

"Camden, babies *are* scary, especially when you don't have any experience."

He held up a hand. "Don't make excuses for me, Elena. Hear me out, okay? I'm not saying I didn't love her. I loved the hell out of my baby girl. I lived for the quiet moments in the middle of the night after Susan got her breastfed, and Chloe'd close those big blue eyes and drift off in my arms while I rocked her so that Susan could get some more sleep. Those moments were the best of my life. Even though I was more scared and exhausted than I ever was in the sandbox, I cherished that time with my daughter. I thought how awesome it was gonna be when she was older and I could teach her all the cool dad-shit my old man taught me, the times he was present and not off lecturing or writing a book."

Camden swiped away a tear. "Which makes me an even bigger shit that the rest of the time, all I could think about was getting away. Going back overseas where I didn't have to worry about taking care of this tiny, breakable miracle I'd help make. Nope, I left that all up to my wife. Just one more fucking thing for her to handle all on her own. The biggest fucking thing ever."

"She must have had other people, Cam. Where were *they*?"

Camden laughed bitterly. "Oh, no. No, I took her away from that. She had family, sure, but they resented me. I was some dumb soldier boy she fell for, when they wanted her to marry up, marry a nice golden Harvard boy. Someone, ironically, more like my father."

Camden went silent, ashamed. This was the first time he'd ever talked it all out with another person. He'd held so much back from the shrink they'd sent him to after, and the guy was so overworked, he was more interested in writing a scrip for antidepressants that Camden would never take than in helping him dig out his pain.

"So, once I thought Susan had her strength back, I signed up for the next deployment. And then I re-upped for the next one. And I ignored how each time I came home, she wasn't quite back to her old, efficient self. She was letting things slide. Not with Chloe—never with Chloe—she was a wonderful mom. My baby girl had the best mom who did exactly what I watch you do, which is take care of her daughter to the detriment of her own needs sometimes."

Camden held up his hand before Elena could protest. "I heard what you said earlier, and I'm in no way, shape, or form throwing anything in your face. I respect you, Elena. I'm in awe of you and what you've done to give that sweet girl a life full of love and hope and light, no matter what darkness and full-on shit that went on around you two. That was *hard*. It's still hard. I understand that. *Now*, I understand that." He wiped away more tears and noticed that Elena was crying, too.

"So, Susan was letting things slide. Some bills got missed and paid late. The kitchen wasn't as spotless as it had always been. Laundry piled up. And me, I thought I was being fucking magnanimous by not pointing it out. Yeah, I thought I was being a real big man, when I was actually being a lazy, spoiled ass and not pitching in to help. I did the fun part, playing with my daughter while I ignored the problems. The mess. My wife's needs.

"So, when she finally asked for help, I actually got mad. I got indignant. I hid behind my job, my all-important, world-saving job. It was a cover that kept me from admitting that I wasn't taking care of my woman—and by extension, my daughter—the way I'd promised I would when I asked her to marry me knowing her family would more than likely turn their backs on her. Which, they did."

Elena's face flushed red. "That's on *them*, Camden, not you. They abandoned their daughter, Their *granddaughter*. I never met them, but I know them. And they can go fuck themselves."

God, she was adorable, the fierce way she spit out the word fuck. Fierce, but still adorable. She really did hate them for what they'd done to Susan. To the woman Camden had loved before her. Where other women might be jealous, or want Camden to stop talking about Susan, Elena felt compassion for her, even empathy. *God, she's too good for me.*

"What?" she asked. "Why are you looking at me like that?"

"I'm looking at the most beautiful, big-hearted woman I've ever known and wondering how she can tolerate me right now."

"Because I love you. Even when you're telling me something hard and ugly. *Especially* when you're telling me something hard and ugly, because I know it has to be hell on you, but you're trusting me with it anyway. I just wish you'd told me this before I went off on you. I never would have said the things I did. Never."

Camden closed his eyes and leaned forward to rest his forehead against Elena's. "I think I needed to know that you loved me before I was strong enough to tell you something that might make me lose you."

"Camden," she whispered. "There's nothing you could tell me about your past, about Susan and Chloe, that would make you lose me."

"We'll see," he said, opening his eyes and pulling back from her warmth.

"She asked me to do one thing. One stupid little, absolutely critical thing, and I blew it off. She told me her car was acting weird. I asked her to explain and she couldn't, just that it felt weird when she drove it. It was an older car, she'd had it since college. I thought...fuck me, but I thought she was angling for a new one. I told her we'd go shopping for a new car when I got back, that she could suck it up and drive my truck in the meantime, even though she was a tiny thing and hated driving my truck ever since she misjudged her parking and bumped a light post in a parking lot. Fuck me twice, I'd teased her about it until she wouldn't dream of driving it again.

"And so she smiled. She just fucking smiled and nodded, and I ignored that the smile was a tired one, a defeated one. I was a dick. Instead of taking her seriously, instead of taking the damn car for a drive around the block and realizing that not only was something wrong, but it was bad, I blew her off. And the next day, I kissed my exhausted wife and my tiny helpless baby girl goodbye."

"Oh, no." Elena's voice was barely above a breath.

"I did my job." Camden shook his head. "I did my fucking job, and in the middle of the night, in the middle of the fucking desert, I got the call that military families Stateside dread getting above all others. My wife, the love of my life, and my baby girl, were both dead. It was the brakes. They went out at the worst possible time. She was on a hill and she couldn't stop. She hit a semi, and the driver, that poor son of a bitch, blames himself for not seeing her in time. But it wasn't his fault. The cops who investigated the accident, the witnesses, they all said she was in his blind spot anyway.

"It wasn't his fault. It wasn't even her fault. It was mine. It was mine for being a selfish coward who expected to be taken care of, then ran away from the people who loved and depended on him. I have no other excuse."

He closed his eyes, ashamed to even look at Elena. Long, silent moments passed while he waited for her verdict.

Finally, she spoke. "I have one question."

"What is it?"

"Do you still feel like running away?"

He opened his eyes. "Running away?"

Her face was a blank mask. "Yeah, Camden. Running away from the people who love you. Because my gut says no, you don't. It's telling me that you've learned the hardest lesson there is to learn, and now you're not a man who would run away anymore. That you wouldn't have told me all this if you planned on turning tail right after. That you've learned to trust, not just in the people who love you, but in yourself. Trust that you're strong enough and worthy of forgiveness—from yourself. But, I need to hear that out loud from you. Because I've got my own fears, my own ghosts, that I'm fighting, and if you can't say out loud that you're not going to run again, those fears are going to win."

She took his face in her hands. "And, baby, I'm only fighting them so that I can have you."

Oh, my God, my beauty. My strong, courageous woman. My lady of mercy. "I'm not gonna run from you. I'm not gonna run from Tina, not ever. I was dead serious when I promised that I'm going to help you do the heavy lifting. I'm going to be right by your side, giving you whatever support you need.

Protecting you and Tina from whatever shit life's gonna deal, and it's gonna deal us some, probably sooner rather than later."

He clasped her hands in his. "From the moment I gave Tina back to you in Nebraska, I knew, I fucking *knew*, that it was the two of you I'd been running towards. Because I was ready. I was ready to sort my shit, but I needed someone strong to help me. And you're still the strongest person I know, Elena Martinez. I saw it then, and you've only gotten stronger since."

EIGHTEEN

He called her strong, when she'd been nothing but weak all evening, afraid of facing her own fears. And she still couldn't, not her deepest one. Not the one that had kept her lonely ever since Antonio died. Especially now, with Camden working security for the Bennetts. Elena needed to talk to him about that, and she would, just not right now. First, she needed to show this sweet, strong, vulnerable man how much he meant to her. Not in spite of what he'd just told her, but because of it. She could see the doubt still lingering in his eyes, and all she wanted to do was kill it so that Camden would finally have the room to forgive himself.

"Thank you," she whispered. "Coming from you, calling me strong is high praise."

"It's the truth."

Elena wiggled in Camden's lap and kissed his throat. "Now that we're done talking, I think earlier on the phone we'd discussed something else happening tonight."

Camden's eyes lit up in surprise. "Do you...I mean..."

"I've been thinking about nothing else all day. Now, where were we?"

"Since the last time we were on your couch," he growled as he pulled her in tight. "This seems about right."

"*About* right, yes, I agree. But not quite." Elena grinned.

"Not quite?" His eyes held the question, *what am I doing wrong?*

"Nope, not quite." *Can I do this? Yes,* she answered herself. *It's time. Beyond time.* "*Absolutely* right would be if we continued this in my bedroom."

Camden's eyes went round. "Are you sure? What about Tina? She might...what if she...?" God, his blush was adorable. "What if we accidentally wake her up?"

"The way she was rubbing her eyes, she's probably already conked out. I think she was over-tired and that's part of why she had a meltdown. Besides, the main bathroom and mine are between the bedrooms. They'll help block any, um, sounds we might make."

Camden gave her a wicked grin. "No 'might' about it, Gorgeous." He leaned in to her ear. "I'm gonna enjoy every sigh, every gasp, every moan that comes out of your sweet little mouth. And I'm gonna give as good as I get." Bad enough that his growl soaked her panties, the tug he gave her earlobe with his soft lips did her jeans in, too.

Elena untangled herself from Camden's arms and stood up.

"Wait," she said, walking backwards and holding up one finger. "Don't move a muscle."

Camden actually chuckled. "As if heaven or earth could budge me from your apartment right now."

Once inside her bedroom, Elena went to her nightstand. She knelt down in front of the photograph of her and Antonio holding Tina outside the children's hospital. She sighed as she ran her finger down the side of Antonio's face.

Mi amor, I will always, always love you she thought. *But I'm lonely. I'm ready, because Camden is a good man who loves me and loves our daughter. Please, I hope you understand.*

She removed her necklace with Antonio's ring and opened the drawer. In it went along with the photograph.

She expected guilt. Tears, even. Sadness, of course. But there were no tears. Negligible guilt. And as for sadness, she felt something else—something as bittersweet as caramelized sugar, a hard crust about to give way to something soft and decadent underneath.

Elena took a deep, clean breath. She stood and smoothed down her shirt. Then she turned to invite her new lover into her bedroom, into her arms, into the soft and secret places only one man had known before.

"Camden," she called softly. "I'm ready."

He paused in the doorway only long enough to look her up and down before he broke into a big grin.

"What?"

"I was afraid you were changing into some sort of lingerie, or worse, just getting naked."

Was he being sarcastic? Should she have changed or gotten naked? She didn't own anything even remotely sexy anymore. Now she regretted not taking Elissa up on her offer to go shopping. "I'm going to say it again—what?"

Camden crossed the bedroom and stood in front of her. "What I'm trying to say is, it's been a while for both of us. I want to savor you, slowly. Like this." He placed his hands on her shoulders and she was suddenly aware of how big he was —how his hands enveloped them.

His amber eyes roved over her face, her throat, to the V

neckline of her shirt, and stopped at the bit of cleavage peeking out. He'd never looked at her so deliberately, and it made her skin heat. "I love that little freckle you have right there on your left breast. I've only glimpsed it a couple of times, and I've wondered if there are more. I've lost sleep thinking about all those other freckles and dimples and everything else that might be hiding from me."

Elena felt her nipples tighten into stiff peaks at his words. They immediately drew his gaze and made him smile. He smoothed his hands down her arms until they were even with them, then he brushed her nipples with his thumbs, making her tremble. "I've wondered what color these are. Seashell pink, dusty rose, sandy brown." He stroked them again and Elena mewed. She pressed herself into his hands, wanting more, right now.

"Slowly, Gorgeous. We've got all night and I intend to use every minute of it pleasing you. I need to tell you though, I brought condoms in case we need them. I haven't been with a woman since my wife." He blushed as his voice dropped, absolutely charming Elena. "But I don't know if you're on birth control."

"I am. And you can probably guess that I haven't been with anyone else, either." She bit her lip. "So, I think we can skip the condoms."

"Gotta say, I'm glad about that." He dipped his head to the side of her neck and ran just the tip of his tongue from her ear to the hollow of her throat where he placed a lingering kiss. Elena lifted her chin and closed her eyes in pleasure. She ran her hands across his broad back, fighting the urge to dig her fingers in. If Camden wanted slow and sweet, she'd give it to him. For now. But if he kept kissing her and touching her like this, she was liable to lose control.

She ran her hands into his hair as he lowered his head.

"There it is," he whispered, then kissed her freckle. She realized he was shaking under her hands.

"Are you all right?" she asked.

"I've wanted to do that for so long, Elena. And so much more."

She reached for the hem of her shirt and he covered her hands with his. Together, they pulled her shirt over her head and tossed it aside. Her thoughts went immediately to her not-ready-for-a-bikini body and her hand moved to cover her belly, which had stayed soft and rounded ever since Tina was born.

Camden frowned and carefully moved her hand away. "Told you before, I like a woman with soft curves. I'm going to tell you how gorgeous you are until it sinks in. And if that doesn't work," he moved his hands to her waist and pulled her to him until she could feel the hard length of his erection, "then I'll demonstrate for you at every opportunity how hot you get me."

He slid down until he was kneeling at her feet, then he pressed his cheek against her belly. "Just as I thought, a nice, soft place where I'm gonna love resting my head after we make love." He pulled back and undid her jeans. As he tugged the zipper down, Elena thought she'd lose it. He peeled back her jeans and pulled them down her legs until she stepped out of them. She could tell her panties were soaking when the air hit them. Camden ran his hands back up her legs to the insides of her thighs and stopped just short of where she wanted them. She mewed in frustration.

"What do you need, Gorgeous?" He ran his thumbs along the lacy edges of her panties and she sucked in a breath with a hiss. "Tell me. Tell me everything you want."

"You. I want you."

Camden gave her a rumbling chuckle. "Specifics,

Gorgeous. Do you want this?" He ran his finger straight down the middle of her panties, pressing against her clit and running between her lips. Elena felt her knees go weak as he ran his finger back up the way it came and then plunged it into his mouth. He closed his eyes as he savored her taste. He opened his eyes and smiled up at her. "Well?"

"Yes, I want that."

"What else, Gorgeous? Tell me. Tell me everything you've missed about being with a man. Tell me, so that I can give it back to you."

Elena felt her whole body heat up. Could she do this, could she be this bold? Antonio never talked to her like this, he was way too shy, but damn did it turn her on.

"I've missed...I want...your mouth."

"My mouth?" He chuckled. "Where do you want my mouth? Do you want it here?" He kissed her belly, dipping his tongue into her belly button. "Or here?" He kissed the crease between her right leg and her pussy and ran his tongue along the seam. That made her gasp.

"That's not talking to me, Gorgeous, though your noises are getting me so damn hard right now." He exhaled a long hot breath over her wet panties. "Tell me," he whispered.

She dug her hands into his hair. "There, right there. Right where you blew."

Camden pressed his lips to her swollen clit and hummed, nearly sending her through the ceiling. "Is that the spot?"

"God, yes," she growled.

That made him chuckle harder. "My woman is so damn hungry, isn't she?" He blew against her panties and the cool air contrasted with her heat. She whimpered, silently begging for mercy.

Camden hooked his fingers into the top of her panties and pulled them down. She watched his expression go from playful to something close to awe when he gazed at her pussy. "Elena," he whispered. "Thank you for trusting me."

Then he plunged in and sent Elena soaring.

His tongue—his magnificent tongue—laved her clit, dipped between her lips, searched out every last drop of pleasure. Elena rocked her hips against him until she lost the ability to stand on her own. He slid his hands to her ass and laid her down gently on the bed, her legs still over the edge.

"Keep your legs apart for me, Gorgeous," Camden said, still kneeling on the floor. Elena gripped the coverlet in her fists as he licked and sucked and teased her hard little button. He added his fingers, playing with her lips, teasing her opening until he plunged in and massaged her walls.

"That's...oh, God...that's...." Elena arched her back as he sent her over the edge into ecstasy.

Elena's eyes fluttered open when she felt him lie down at her side. He took her into his arms.

"Wait. You're still dressed?"

Camden laughed. "You haven't undressed me yet."

"I really need to fix that." With a strength she didn't know she still had, Elena pushed Camden onto his back and straddled him. As she started with the top button of his shirt, he reached around her back and undid her bra with one hand. He stopped her hands with his other, then slipped her bra down her arms. He stared at her nipples and a smile broke across his face.

"Sandy golden brown. Perfect." He curled his torso up and flicked his tongue across the left one.

"Come on, you're distracting me." She playfully—and futilely—tried to push him back down. Instead, he sat up and positioned her on his lap. She wrapped her legs around his back while she worked on unbuttoning the rest of his shirt. He played with her breasts, running his thumbs over her nipples.

When she pulled his shirt off—revealing a washboard below his muscular pecs, she returned the favor by licking and sucking his nipples. She was shocked at the level of response she got—he threw his head back, closed his eyes, and blew out a breath.

"Very sensitive," he murmured, which just made her wetter.

As she sucked on one, her hands went to his waist and she undid his jeans. He slid his hands under her and lifted Elena while she helped him shrug out of his jeans. His cock strained against his boxer briefs, a damp circle of pre-come clearly visible at the tip. She ran her hand lightly over his bulge before pulling his boxer briefs off. His cock sprang free, long and thick and irresistible. She cupped the tip and ran her palm back and forth across it until beads of sweat broke out across his forehead. She'd never been so forward in her life, or felt so in control. She liked it.

Elena pulled Camden closer and whispered in his ear how lonely he must have been all this time, how much she wanted him, how handsome he was.

"You're gonna undo me if you go on like this," he said.

So she kissed him instead. His lips were soft and strong. His arms wrapped around her. She felt his hardness pressing against her belly, insistent. Camden stroked her hair, running his fingers through it. Her hands found his cock again and she stroked him faster, harder. It curled into a "C", the tip bending back like a bow that wants to shoot, touching his belly. Pre-come slicked the skin below his navel and he gasped.

"Are you all right?"

"Not used to getting so close so quickly."

God, that's hot. She brushed her belly against his length and he groaned, then clutched her arms and rolled over until she was under him. His amber eyes practically glowed with lust as they searched her face. The tip of his cock pressed against her entrance and he slid it up against her clit. When he saw her reaction, he grinned wickedly and rubbed against her until neither one could stand another moment.

"Tell me what you want, Elena," Camden growled. "Tell me fast, Gorgeous, for both our sakes."

This time, she didn't hesitate. "I want you inside me. So deep inside me."

Camden didn't hesitate, either. He slipped his tip into her and groaned as she gave him a welcoming squeeze.

"Goddamn. Oh, fuck, Elena," he gasped. He pushed in another inch and she squeezed again. Inch by inch, he thrust and she squeezed each time until he was buried up to his tightening balls. He pulled back and glided in, his cock dancing inside her.

"Wanna watch you come, Gorgeous. Wanna see it in your eyes."

Each thrust rubbed her clit, until he sent her back over the brink. He stared down into her eyes and she gazed back, certain she could see forever at the moment he roared out his climax.

NINETEEN

Oh, God, I did not mean to do that.

From under him, Elena quirked her eyebrow at Camden. "What's wrong?"

"If that didn't wake Tina up, I'll eat my boots. Without any of your dipping sauces to go with them."

Elena stifled a laugh. "Get to chewing then, because if she were awake, she'd be calling my name and halfway in here by now."

"You sure?"

"Positive." Then she gave him a squeeze that made him groan. Dear God in heaven, she was the best lover he'd ever had. Warm and generous, bold and not the least bit ashamed of what they did, of what he did to her. "Want to go for round two?"

"Are you trying to kill me, woman?" He chuckled and nuzzled her neck. Truth was, he was still mostly hard and it wouldn't take much to get him going again. That squeeze damn near did it all on its own. But he also wanted to bask in the afterglow—hold her in his arms, taste her skin, smell her vanilla-and-mint scented hair, listen to her heart beating when he pressed his ear against her. If only for tonight, he'd found the peace that had eluded him since that long-ago phone call that had shattered his sleep.

He wanted to drift off in his newfound peace, let it carry him until morning, then he wanted to wake up beside her and begin the rest of their life together at her side. He wanted to sit Tina down at breakfast and explain to her that she could count on him to be there always, for the rest of her life.

But first, he knew they had to get past the Bennetts and any sort of trouble Elena might have inadvertently put herself in. Really, that Cici had dragged her into.

"Okay, now, what's *that* look?" Elena asked, running her hand across the stubble on his cheek.

"Gorgeous, there is nothing I would rather do in the world than make love with you again, even if we risked waking up the Mermaid. But, we aren't done talking. Not about the past this time, but about what's going on right now with the Bennetts. With Cici. With Lawrence Franklin."

She stiffened under him, and he knew he'd hit a nerve. "Yeah, we do need to talk."

Camden shifted them until they were side by side. He propped up on one elbow. "Hey, I'm not angry." Camden stroked her hair. "You didn't ask to be in the middle of this."

Elena looked away. "Well, today, I kinda did put myself in the middle of it."

She's worried about Franklin, Camden thought. He tilted her chin until she was looking at him again. "Babe, we've got an agent on Franklin. That's how I know he was at Delia's today, and so were you. That's also how I know the two of you made eye contact and that it was unpleasant—"

"That's an understatement."

"But, you didn't do anything to draw his interest. He's the one who showed up at the restaurant after you'd gone with Cici. And hell, you're there all the time, and he's a new face, isn't he?"

Elena looked almost relieved. He'd hit again—she was just as confused by Lawrence's presence as they were. "Yeah, exactly, he is new. I'd never seen him there before and it's not like I'm a stranger to Delia's. Then he shows up two days in a row." Elena shook her head. "I was thinking that maybe I was being paranoid, that it made sense if his meeting got canceled that he'd reschedule for the same place the next day. But, do you guys think it's weird, too?" She fixed Camden with a worried look. "I don't like him, Cam. I don't know why I have such a bad feeling about him, beyond that he's just kinda skeevy. I know you can't talk about it, but...should I be worried?"

Camden stroked her hair to reassure her. "Not when you've got me. I still can't tell you all of what's going on, but I can tell you some more. Roger Bennett is possibly being targeted—I see that look in your eyes and it's okay, his life isn't in danger and neither is Cici's or the twins, else we'd be doing things much differently. But, Roger might be more vulnerable to blackmail now that he's in politics. We're just running interference for the moment, trying to assess the threat level, figure out the players."

"You think Lawrence Franklin is a player?"

"Babe, he's one of the top political campaign finance managers in California, of course he's a player. Thing is, we need to determine if he's *our* player, or if he's gone to the other side."

Elena nodded. "Makes sense. *Dónde está el dinero.*"

"Come again?"

"Where's the money. If you're going to find corruption, you follow the money trail."

Camden grinned. "Gina was right, we should hire you."

Elena raised her eyebrows. "Gina your co-worker?"

"One and the same. Actually, she's the one who's on Lawrence."

"Wait, what? I never saw her."

Camden grinned. "Spooky is as Spooky does. She's damn good at her job. So, if you ever get tired of good old Julia, you can always come work for Watchdog," he joked.

Elena bit her lower lip. "Well, about that. I'm looking at a new job opportunity, actually."

Camden propped himself up higher. "Really, that's great! I'm proud of you." Except, Elena didn't look excited or happy, she looked anxious and stressed. "Are you afraid you're not going to get it?"

She gave him a tight-lipped smile. "Oh, I'm pretty much guaranteed to get it, and it's an amazing opportunity. But, there's one thing you're not going to like." She propped herself up. "Please, promise me you're not gonna be mad when I tell you what it is."

Oh, God. She's leaving. For one moment, his world sank. Now that they'd worked out their shit, she was going to leave.

"The job's across the country, isn't it?" *But, if it starts right away, she'll be out of danger.* He wrestled with his conscience —encourage her to take it, or to stay with him.

"No, babe, it's here in town."

Immediate relief.

"But, here's the thing."

Relief turned to concern, then to outright dismay as she told him about the deal she'd made with Delia.

Well, shit, he thought.

"So, you see, I did put myself smack dab in the middle.

I'm sorry. I told you I'd stay away from Cici, and then I went and did the opposite. How mad are you?"

Camden sighed. "I'm...mad isn't the word."

"You're disappointed."

He held up a finger. "Do not put words in my mouth. Am I upset that you're gonna be at the villa, that you're entangled? Yes, I am, because that's gonna put more stress on me. But." He lifted her chin again as she started to look away. "I'm excited for you. This is the big time, this is what you've wanted to do, what you're meant to do as far as I'm concerned. I'm not going to stand between the woman I love and her shot at success. Like you said, it's not like you're going to be on Cici's arm the whole night. You'll be doing your thing behind the scenes. I'm going on recon at the villa on Saturday, figure out the security needs and challenges. Does this mean I'm going to pay more attention to the kitchen than before? Absolutely."

He cupped her cheek. "I'm not mad that my gorgeous lady saw her chance and took it. I'm fucking happy for you, and I'm going to do everything in my power to support and protect you."

Elena looked relieved. Then her eyes brightened with excitement. "I can help you in the meantime and while I'm there. I know Cici's got something big that she's afraid will ruin Roger's chances. And I'm pretty sure that Lawrence has something to do with it. Maybe I can get her to open up to me. I can call her and—"

"Babe. We're on it. This is *my* job, not yours." As tempting as it was to wire Elena up and send off to a three-cocktail lunch with Cici, he just couldn't put her directly in harm's way.

Elena narrowed her eyes at Camden. "I'm not her."

Shit. He furrowed his brow. "Not Cici?"

"Not Susan."

Camden still decided to play dumb. "Not following."

The way she tilted her head, he knew she could see through him. "I see what you're doing, trying to make up for your past mistakes with her through me. I get it. I do. You're telling yourself you're doing it out of love—and you are," she added when she saw him start to protest. "But, you're also doing it out of guilt, and I'm not going to stand for that. You leave that behind as of tonight, or else you're sabotaging us from the start."

Fuck. She'd sent a missile straight to the heart. "Dammit. I'm not... I'm..."

"Camden. I'm not trying to be a bitch."

"Never said that. Never even thought it." He gritted his teeth. "I hate this because you're right. I am treating you like her. No, like I *wish* I'd treated her." He shook his head. "I'm in a shitty position because the truth is, you'd make a perfect asset. Your instincts are good about something being fishy with them. You've got an in with Cici, and I think you could uncover intel that we need faster than what we're doing. But I'll be damned if I put you in danger, if I make you a target— no, *more* of a target—than you already are."

"You aren't *making* me do anything, Cam. I'm volunteering. You aren't trying to deceive me or manipulate me. I'm offering because it's the right thing to do. I'm not naïve. I've been in bad situations before. I..." Her eyes darkened, probably thinking about the kidnapping. "This is bigger than me, than us. If I can help, then I want to help. I've done it before."

Camden sighed again. She was right, of course—his smart, sweet, giving woman was right. "I'm not gonna set something obvious up—"

Excitement sparked in her eyes.

"Cool your jets. I'm not gonna treat you like an operative

because you don't have the training and there's no time to get you up to speed. I'm not sending you in. But, if Cici presents the opportunity, then I want you to take it, but *you call me immediately*, all right? You'll need back-up."

Fuck. What am I doing? Camden just hoped that the fertility clinic would pan out before any of this happened.

"Don't look so worried," Elena said, running her hand through his hair. "I have an idea that will relax you," she added with a wicked grin.

It did.

F irst thing Saturday morning, Camden drove the SUV up the winding road toward the villa where Roger Bennett would make the announcement that he was running for the House of Representatives. Costello rode shotgun, and mercifully didn't commandeer the radio the way Jake always did. But, Nashville sat in the back and fidgeted worse than any kid on a cross-country road trip.

"Seriously, dude, do you mind not kicking the back of my seat?" Camden groused.

"Sorry." Nash uncrossed his leg and the kicking stopped for about a minute, until he crossed the other leg and it started again.

"That's it. I'm overruling the rock, paper, scissors fight you toddlers had over riding shotgun. Nash, you're riding up front on the way back."

"Shit. Sorry." Nash rolled down the window as far as he could. Camden wouldn't have been surprised to see him stick his head out like Toby did. The man hated to be indoors.

The top of the villa came into view above the palm trees and cedars—pale stucco walls with a red-tiled roof. It was impossible to gauge the true size of the place from the road, but Camden and his team had studied the schematics and he knew the place was huge. But you can only get some much info from a piece of paper, so Camden wanted to get boots on the ground to check the place out ahead of time. He'd arranged to meet Cici at the villa, telling her he needed to go over details of the night's agenda so that he could have security in all the right places.

Luckily, the crowd would be herded out to the massive courtyard and discouraged from wandering the mansion-turned-museum. The only exceptions were that Elena and her crew would be allowed access to the kitchen, and another room was set aside for childcare. Roger intended to be the 'Families' Candidate' so everyone attending was encouraged to bring their kids along for a big photo op at the end. He reassured himself that the adults were the real issue here, but just thinking about security for all those kids made his head pound.

Camden had gotten a guest list from Roger, which included thirty-eight kids under thirteen years old, the cutoff age for the kids' room. He'd station two armed guards outside the door who would check the IDs of everyone who came and went. The adults numbered two-hundred. No foreigners were on the list, and everyone's background check came back fine. Jake checked up on fifty-two guests who had traveled outside the country over the past year on the chance they'd met with any foreign operatives. Camden had plans to put Jake, Costello, Gina, and now Nashville on the guests who'd visited Eastern Europe, Russia, or the Middle East. They'd follow them closely but discreetly through the evening, keeping an eye on who they talked to, especially if and when they spoke to Roger, Cici, or Larry Franklin. Camden would stick close to the Bennett family. His team would be wired and in constant communication.

Camden pulled into the lot and parked next to Cici's champagne-colored Mercedes. There was no sign of her so the three men walked to the entrance. She was just inside chatting with a woman who introduced herself as the director for the villa. Cici actually took Camden's arm and stood on her tiptoes to kiss him on the cheek as if they were old friends.

"I'm so delighted to have Delia's restaurant handling the refreshments, all thanks to Elena." She looked behind Camden as if expecting someone. "She isn't with you?"

Interesting, Camden thought. *There are eyes on us.*

He thought back to the beginning of the week, how after making love a second time, he'd told Elena that since she was involved in the case, he would be staying with her, or she and Tina would be moving in with him. She argued, of course—that was his Elena—saying that she didn't want to put him out, but he stood firm. He would've preferred they stay with him in his well-secured house, but she made the case that it was too far out of the way for her to get Tina to and from school and aftercare, and herself to work without spending half her life in traffic. Plus, she wanted to keep Tina's life as chaos-free as possible, and that meant staying in their apartment. He relented, and she had to smile—he'd brought a duffel with several changes of clothes and his dap bag. *You knew I'd win* she'd said, and she hadn't been entirely wrong.

Tina took it all in stride when she saw Camden in the kitchen the next morning. There was precedent—they'd all stayed together in the safe house—but she didn't seem worried or afraid. Her biggest concern was that Toby be allowed to continue sleeping in her room.

They'd spent the week together, and it was one of the

happiest of Camden's life. He'd even picked the Mermaid up from aftercare a couple of times and brought her home to Elena's amazing cooking, which she'd insisted on doing, even though Camden had offered to take them out to dinner every night. One thing they did do every evening no matter what, was to go to the beach, where Camden did the 'sunset trick' as Tina called it. She still wanted to see a sunrise and a sunset at the same time on a monitor, and Camden promised her it would happen. He had a trick up his sleeve for that, too, but it had to wait for the right time.

So, they were living together, but Camden made a point of telling Elena not to let Cici know that when she talked to her—just on a hunch. And now, that hunch paid off. Cici slipped, expecting Elena to be with Camden because she knew he'd moved in with her. But, was Elena being watched, or was it him? *Now, to play this right.*

"Elena?" he asked, feigning surprise.

"Oh, I just figured you two would come together. I texted her just a little bit ago to come up here to see the kitchen. It only just occurred to me we were already scheduled for today and she'd want to see it. I've been so busy and a little scatter-brained." Cici laughed it off, but the nervousness stayed in her eyes.

Just then, the front door opened and Elena came in, breathless. "Sorry, I got here as soon as I could after I got your text. I had to drop Tina off at Bette's." Her voice hesitated on Bette's name, and he realized she was still awed by the woman.

She looked so gorgeous—fresh-faced, with her hair up in a messy bun. To Camden's eye, Cici couldn't compare even though she was a knock-out, because her look was artificial and carefully groomed. Never a hair out of place or an outfit that wouldn't have cost Camden a week's pay. With Nash's mad hacking skills, they'd learned Cici dipped into her trust fund pretty regularly when it came to Rodeo Drive.

Cici brightened when she saw Elena and walked to her. "You're right on time, don't worry." She gave Elena a hug and kissed her cheek. "Why don't I let Patricia show you to the kitchen while I take everyone else out to the courtyard to show them how we're going to set up?" She looked at the director, who nodded and led Elena away as they chatted about the villa.

Cici gestured to an archway leading outside. For the next two hours, Camden, Costello, and Nash walked around the villa and its courtyard and extensive gardens, talking with Cici about her plans and with the director and the villa's own head of security about logistics. Camden loved this part of the job—scoping out a site and deciding how best to secure it. Costello proved invaluable—Psychic could spot a trouble zone like no one else. Nash wasn't too shabby, either.

They ended their tour with a walk through the gardens. Camden had plans to rope off most of it. Too much to watch. He did take note of a statue that Tina would love. *It must have been sculpted just for her*, he couldn't help thinking.

A weathered copper mermaid, waist-high, emerging from a wave and holding a crescent moon with a sundial on it. He thought about going home—home! —and telling her about it over dinner. Along with photos of the villa, he took a couple of pics to show her.

The other place he paid special attention to was the kitchen. It had two entrances, but the one leading deeper in to the villa would be locked. He didn't think it would present too much of a challenge. And, Elena personally knew all of the staff and trusted them. They were fiercely loyal to Delia and had become fond of her, too.

He couldn't help but smile and wink at his gorgeous lady

as she politely listened to the director going on and on about the history of the kitchen. She looked like a queen surveying her new queendom. Proud, competent, happy. His heart leaped and bounded. How had he gotten so damn lucky? He'd do anything to keep her happy and safe.

TWENTY

Late Saturday morning in Delia's restaurant kitchen—
sun streamed through the window and coated a wire
bowl full of oranges and lemons. A blue glass pitcher
of cold water beaded with condensation chimed as the ice
tapped against the sides. Freshly-sharpened knives gleamed
beside three thick wooden cutting boards lined up on the
metal prep table. And now that she was done touring the
kitchen at the villa, Elena had the entire day in front of her to
spend with her two new friends as they prepared for her first
catering gig.

"Okay, ladies," Delia clapped her hands once and rubbed
her palms together. "We're going to run through a few test
recipes. Cici will be by later for a tasting and we'll decide
which ones are gonna work best. Elena, thanks again for
opening this door."

"Thank you for taking a chance on me." Elena chose the
cutting board at the end of the row. Delia took up her station
in the middle so she could supervise Elena and Lissa.

"This is gonna be fun," Elissa said as she grabbed one of
the knives.

"Let's start with one of the sides. Lissa, you mince up some mint and Thai basil. Elena, grab a cucumber and slice it in half lengthwise."

Elena grabbed one from a container and sliced it in half while Lissa chopped the herbs, filling the kitchen with a fresh green smell.

Delia watched and nodded. "Okay, next you're gonna wanna bash the cucumber—"

Lissa snorted.

"What?" Elena asked, grinning at Lissa's infectious good mood.

"Bash the cucumber? Seriously, that sounds naughty."

"Naughty? That sounds painful, at least for the dude," Elena said.

"I wouldn't know," Delia said, mixing sesame oil with rice vinegar.

"Why are there so many euphemisms for sex that involve food?"

Lissa put her hands on her hips. "You're right, there really are. Like, hide the sausage."

"Plant the carrot. Butter the biscuit," Elena added.

"Putting a bun in the oven. Tossing the salad." Lissa giggled.

"Oh, I know a weird one," Elena said, pointing her knife at the cutting board. "Squatting in the cucumber patch." That threw Lissa into hysterics.

Delia looked up from adding crushed Aleppo pepper to the oil. "I know a weirder one. When I was in culinary school, one of my instructors was fond of telling us that during Victorian times in France, they said that a bachelor had to grind his own chocolate."

"What? Who the hell grinds chocolate?" Lissa asked.

"Victorian French wives and bachelors, I guess," Delia said.

Lissa grabbed her stomach. "Now I've got this image of some dude feeding a chocolate bar into a meat grinder." She swayed her hips like she had a hula hoop circling them. "Grind that chocolate, baby!"

"Ew! Chica, you are *crazy!*" Elena collapsed with laughter. When she could speak again, she asked, "So, what was the term for when a single Victorian woman, um, got off."

"I don't think they had one. Ladies simply didn't do that," Lissa said in a mock-prudish voice.

Delia rolled her eyes. "Bullshit they didn't. It's not like the clit suddenly appeared in 1967."

"I bet there are a bunch of old terms relating to women's sex lives, we just don't recognize them," Elena said.

Delia nodded. "Oh yeah there are. Like, if I were living in Victorian England, I'd be going home to my 'bosom friend' every night, not my wife."

Elena raised her eyebrows. "Oh, wow. That puts a different spin on a few old novels I've read."

"Thank God times have changed and we can actually talk about sex," Lissa said.

"More like laugh our asses off about it." Elena picked up her butcher's knife. "Now let me bash this cucumber."

"Yikes!" Lissa said. "What would Camden have to say, about that, poor guy." She went back to mincing the herbs. "Now that you're hiding the sausage on the regular."

Elena dropped her knife. "Oh my god, what is wrong with you?"

"What? Any other woman would have done a number of 'euphemisms' to Camden within thirty seconds of meeting him. I'm happy for you that you finally, um, squatted in the cucumber patch."

She felt her cheeks redden.

"You're blushing! That's adorable."

"Guess I'm a Victorian."

"Oh, you are not."

"Ladies," Delia cut in, grinning, "less talk, more chop and bash. Cici'll be here at four o'clock, and I know that sounds like a lot of time, but it's gonna fly, so I'd better see your hands flying, too."

Elena pressed down on the back of the cucumbers with the side of her knife, grateful for the reprieve.

Delia was right—the time flew by. Pete came in to help prep for Cici's arrival—the restaurant was closed for a 'private party' so she could do the tasting in peace. He complained that it was too quiet so he turned on the radio and the air filled with happy salsa music—which of course, Lissa had to joke about how appropriate it was for a kitchen. The kitchen became a dance hall as they all worked around each other. But the time Cici arrived, they'd gone through eleven recipes, discarded three as too time-consuming and complicated, and had whittled the others down to the six best-tasting ones. Elena was proud that two of them were entirely her own creations. She'd never cooked for Delia; she'd only brought her desserts like cookies and brownies.

They sat at one of the tables in the dining room while Pete brought out each sample.

"I'm so glad you're including that dip you brought to Bette's party. It's perfect in the wonton skins," Cici said after her second one. "And the mini street tacos are incredible."

"Those are *both* Elena's," Delia said. "I have plans to add them to our regular rotation."

Elena stared at her new boss. This was news to her. She couldn't help the smile that accompanied the proud warmth in her chest. If she wasn't careful, she'd start crying right in front of everyone. *These are the days when my heart sings like Rachael*, she thought.

In the end, Cici selected four appetizers—both of Elena's and two of Delia's specialties.

"Well," Cici said, dabbing her mouth with a napkin. "This has been so much fun; I'll get out of your way so you can get home. Take the rest of the night off, ladies, you've done an excellent job."

"I'll walk you to the door," Elena said, standing up. It was true her heart was still singing at this minor triumph, but part of that song was also a warning. She'd never told Cici that Camden had moved in, but according to the text he'd sent after their visit to the villa, she somehow knew. Maybe Cici was speculating, but maybe not. She decided to find out what else Cici might be hiding.

She laid a hand on Cici's arm when they got to the front door. "I don't want to keep you, because I know you must be insanely busy, but I just want to let you know I'm here for you, not just for the catering, but...if you ever want to talk."

Cici glanced at Elena and gave her a quick smile. "That's kind of you."

"It's just that, at our last lunch, you seemed upset about something. And at Bette's party."

Cici glanced back at the table. Delia and Elissa had already returned to the kitchen. "Will you walk me to my car? I—" She blinked back tears.

"Of course, let's go." Elena held the door open.

By the time they got to Cici's Mercedes, she had pulled her face back into a mask of calm, but Elena watched the woman's hand tremble as she opened the passenger car door for her. By the time Cici had walked around the car and gotten in, she was back to being teary-eyed.

"Cici." Elena reached over and took her hand.

She shook her head and smiled at Elena. "I'm happy for you, Elena. It looks like you're making your way already."

"Thanks to you, Cici. I really am grateful. That's why I'd like to help with anything I can."

"You're too...you're very sweet." Cici pulled her hand away and gripped the steering wheel but didn't start the car. Elena glanced through the windshield, realizing that it was probably not the best idea to have gotten into the car with her. She looked for anyone who might be watching them. Especially Lawrence. "Cici, is anyone threatening you or Roger or the twins?"

"No, no, nothing like that."

Elena relaxed, but only a fraction.

Cici continued. "L.A. probably seems like a huge city to you. But, it's not. It's a bunch of small towns, really. Small towns that gossip. You know what that's like?"

Elena nodded.

"Of course you do." Cici sniffed and wiped her eyes, then grabbed a tissue from her purse. "I think that's why I feel like I can talk to you. You're not part of this scene. You're new. And," she turned to face Elena, "you're dating the guy who's going to keep my family safe. I can trust you, right?"

"Of course," Elena said. "I don't want anything bad to happen to you or Roger or the kids. What's going on?"

Cici's face crumpled. "I was so stupid. We do such stupid things when we're young and then try to justify them. I don't know if I was wrong or right, but I didn't have any real choice at the time, not if I didn't want to ruin my life."

"What, Cici? I can't imagine you ever doing anything bad."

She wiped away more tears. "I was in college. Roger and I went to different universities after high school, but we were still dating, and then we weren't." She waved her hand in dismissal. "We were young, and I don't even remember what we fought about. But we broke up for a while. And I... I did something really, really dumb and it got me in trouble."

"In college?" *Did she have a secret boyfriend?* Elena wondered. *Why would that matter now? She obviously got back together with Roger, and they were broken up at the time.*

Cici looked Elena over. "Things were different then. I hid what I did from Roger. I hid it from everyone. Almost everyone. I had one person I could turn to, who helped me through all of it. I'm still thankful to this day."

"Whatever this is, is it still a secret from Roger? Are you worried he'll find out and be angry?" *Or that it'll ruin his political aspirations* she added silently to herself.

Cici shook her head. "Oh, no, Roger found out. I told him, years later. I had no choice at that point. But, we talked through it, and he's stayed with me." Cici had to stop talking while her sobs overtook her. "He's such a good man. I love him so much. I love our family."

Any lingering doubt Elena had about Cici possibly seeing Lawrence Franklin on the side evaporated. No one, not even in Hollywood, was that talented of an actress. Not even Bette. Cici truly adored her husband.

Elena leaned across the console and hugged Cici. "Of course he's a good man, and he loves you. It's so obvious." She pulled back and looked Cici in the eyes. "Why are you so worried? How bad was that mistake?"

"It could have been worse. I could have..." Cici pulled herself together and nodded. "But, now we're under a microscope, and I don't want my past mistakes to ruin Roger's chances. You know how people sling mud. Or worse."

Elena nodded. "Oh, I'm intimately familiar with people who abuse their power." Now, Elena found she was the one fighting back her tears. Ross, Nebraska had had its secrets, many of them deadly. And the authorities were still digging them all up, both figuratively and literally. Elena shivered.

Cici smiled, dug in her purse for another tissue, and handed it to Elena. "I can see that. I'm so glad we're friends. I'm trying to protect my kids, and I know you understand what that's like. So, you'll understand when I ask you to please ask Camden for a favor."

Elena's heart lurched. Cici *was* using her, Lawrence *was* watching her, and it all had to do with Camden.

"Anything, you know that," Elena said, trying to keep her voice even.

Cici sniffed. "There will be rumors flying, and there will be truth mixed in, and neither will be pretty. That photographer who got into Bette's party, I know he was filming my kids. I saw him staring at them with those glasses on. Who paid him to do that? Who else close to us will they pay? People know Camden is doing security for Roger, and they might try and get some private information from him. Please, if anyone approaches him, could you ask Camden to maybe look the other way on a couple of things? Or even, I hate to say it, deny something?"

"Deny what, Cici? I still don't know what you're talking about."

"My twins. They don't know, and I don't know how they'd feel, if they'd hate me. I was planning on telling them when they were older, maybe." She shook her head. "They have a seventeen-year-old half-brother who I gave up for adoption. I had one year left in college and my parents would have disowned me. My life would have been ruined, not to mention the baby's. I took a semester off, had a baby boy, and gave him up. No one knows but Roger and the father. The records are sealed. I don't know where the boy is, and he doesn't know who I am. But I'm so afraid of the story coming out and getting used against us."

Elena breathed a sigh of relief. *Was that all?* Elena thought. *And here I was just saying how great it is we can talk openly about sex these days. But there's still so much shame and blame. At least in some people's eyes.*

"Cici, I can't imagine why anyone would care. Like you said, times have changed—"

Cici only cried harder.

"Look, if you want my advice, I would sit the twins down and tell them tonight. Mitigate the damage. Like you said, if they hear it from someone else, they might be angry and hurt that you didn't tell them."

"I can't. I just can't. They can't find out, Elena. I have to be perfect." The wild look in Cici's eyes almost scared her.

We really do come from two different worlds Elena thought. Cici seemed so strong, and yet she was acting like a scared little girl. Was it because she hadn't been protected enough, or had she been protected too well, never having to face the hard consequences of her decisions until now?

She waited until Cici had composed herself enough to drive safely. "I can tell you that Camden is so far above bribery that you never have to worry about him spilling anything about you or your family to the wrong people." She put up her hand when it looked like Cici was about to protest. "I swear, he and everyone at Watchdog is dedicated to protecting all of you. From *every* threat. But, I can also tell you that it would be for the best if you come clean now—to your kids, and maybe even to the world. You didn't do anything wrong. You did what was best for the baby."

Cici nodded, her lips pressed tightly together. Elena

doubted the woman would follow her advice, but at least she'd tried. "Are you okay to drive?"

Cici nodded again as she gave her a tight-lipped smile. "I'll be fine. Thank you." Her voice was cooler than before. Not hostile, but certainly not overflowing with friendship. "And thank you for reassuring me about Mr. Bains."

Okay. The distance was growing. "You take care, and I'll see you at the villa. It will be a wonderful night for Roger."

Cici seemed to warm a bit. "Yes. Oh, and please be sure to bring your daughter. The twins think she's adorable, and we'd all love to see her again. The more children, the merrier."

And the more for your husband's photo op. Elena smiled and left Cici to drive away through the L.A. streets, back to her big house behind its guarded walls.

E lena thanked Pete for all his help as he was leaving out the front door. Then she returned to the kitchen where Delia and Elissa waited, hoping to fake a happier mood for her friends. But she didn't have to fake anything. Delia pulled out three brown, unlabeled bottles dappled with condensation and set them on the table.

"Ladies, this is elixir. Homemade ginger ale brewed by my wife. I'm going to make it into *gin*–ger ale and we are going to celebrate."

Delia popped the bottles open, sliced, zested and juiced several limes in the blink of an eye, and added them to the ginger ale with a generous pour of Bombay Sapphire. The results were spectacular—sweet and bite-y and sour and quenching. After two (or maybe three, but who was counting?) she announced, "It's time for pasta!" She pulled out the biggest stock pot she had and filled it with boiling water and a ton of salt. Fifteen minutes later, they were digging into pasta with sautéed garlic, capers, sundried tomatoes, olives, cheese, and roasted chicken—and loving life.

"Drunk pasta," Delia called it. "Different every single time you make it." So Elena didn't bother asking for the recipe, but she never forgot the richness, the savory notes, and the hysterical conversation that floated above the plates and the glasses of alcohol. The laughter, the camaraderie. She finally felt like L.A. was hers. That she'd definitely made the right decision for herself and her daughter. She loved her apartment, the beach, and she loved the two women currently sharing the kitchen with her.

And she loved Camden. He was such a good man, with her and Tina's best interests at heart, always. Even now, he was swinging by Bette's house to pick up Tina, then he'd get her and they'd all go home—together. The way it should be. The way she wanted it to be for the foreseeable future, she realized. Elena decided she would ask Camden's thoughts on living together, but she had her suspicions that he would be all for it.

Elena was surprised when her phone rang and Bette's number came up. Still a little tipsy, she answered, careful not to slur any words. Bette asked if Tina could spend the night, suggesting that perhaps Elena and Camden would enjoy a little 'adult time.' She happily took Bette up on her offer and thanked her profusely, while trying to ignore the absolutely surreal feeling of having one of Hollywood's biggest stars for a babysitter.

Camden came by later to pick her up, and Delia and Elissa begged him to stay. They physically pulled Camden into the kitchen, shoved spoonfuls of drunk pasta into his mouth—which he didn't appear to mind—finally grabbing a bowl off an open shelf and filling it with the amazing stuff. As for the *gin*-ger ale, he turned it down, since he was the designated driver.

By the time they got out of there, he was practically carrying Elena to his truck. She'd long-since sobered, but she was drunk on happiness, on contentment, on all things good.

"Are you okay?" Camden asked from the driver's seat.

"I've never been better," she answered, and meant it. She rolled down the window, stuck her arm out, and let the air carry her hand in the breeze. "I have friends here, Camden. I mean, I love Rachael to pieces, but I was afraid she'd leave me behind. That we'd drift apart. We haven't," she said, holding up her hand to reassure him, "but she's so busy, and I don't want to hold her back. I want to make my own way, you know? And I think I am. I finally am."

She reached over and grabbed Camden's hand. "And I'm glad you're here with me now." She took a deep breath. "I'm... also glad that Tina is gone for the night."

Camden chuckled. "Babe. I'm not the kind of man who would take advantage of a woman." He brought her hand to his lips and kissed her fingers.

"No, I stopped drinking over an hour ago, so I'm not drunk, I promise. At least not on alcohol. I might, however, be drunk on happiness."

"Well," he drawled, and gave her an appreciative look, "only if you promise you're of sound mind and capable of making responsible decisions."

She slipped her hand over his thigh, fingers exploring until they found the eager bulge in his jeans. His throaty groan shot heat straight to her core.

"Driver faster," she purred.

TWENTY-ONE

Camden drove faster, straight to his house. He wanted the privacy—even though Tina was at Bette's for the night, he still felt like Elena's apartment walls were too thin. And he had to admit, part of him wanted to show off his home to Elena, to prove that he could provide a good life for her and the Mermaid.

While it wasn't a mansion, Camden had done well for himself, buying his house when the market was down and doing home improvements through the years. It helped that the entire neighborhood had gone through a renaissance, while maintaining its original character. He was happy to see Elena's face light up when he pulled into the drive. Security lights lit the front yard and house, so she could see the brick façade and the careful landscaping.

"This is your place? It's lovely. The SEALs must have paid well." She slapped her hand over her mouth and turned Camden's second-favorite shade of blush—the first being whenever he had her under him. "I'm sorry, that was crass," she added from behind her fingers.

"Crass? You just sent my ego through the stratosphere,

Gorgeous." He parked in the garage and went around the SUV to open her door and help her down, then led her inside. "I was worried that after seeing where Jake grew up, you'd be less than impressed."

Elena tilted her head and squinted her eyes. "No offense to the Collins family, but I have different tastes. I'd just get lost in their house all the time if I lived there. Though," she looked up at him through her thick, dark lashes, "I do have a certain fondness for their library."

God, she was killing him. He couldn't get her to his bedroom fast enough. "Do you really? I wonder why."

She pretended to pout. "Maybe I can remind you." She turned and ran her hands up his chest. Her fingers glided deliciously along either side of his neck and tangled in his hair.

They stood in the mudroom leading to the kitchen. He swooped her up and quickly carried her through the house. "Let me give you the grand tour. This is the kitchen. It's where I keep my food. This is the TV room where I kick Jake's ass at video games. That's Toby's bed, where you can see he's crashed out instead of defending his master's castle. Good boy. This is the hallway, there's the guest bathroom with the fancy soap my mom bought me and told me never to use. To the right is a guest bedroom where you'll never stay. And this," he swept into his bedroom and plopped her on the bed while she laughed hysterically, "is the most important room in the entire house and the only one you need to see in detail right now."

He lay down beside her, waiting for her to stop laughing. *Fuck it*, he thought, and caught her mouth with his, mid-laugh. As much as he loved to hear his woman's mirth, he wanted to hear her moaning even more. His cock pleaded for it. He rolled her on top of him. Her shiny brown hair fell like a curtain around their faces, it's heady vanilla-mint fragrance feeding his desire as he looked up into her eyes.

"Oh my God, Gorgeous. I want to devour you." He captured her full lips and tasted strawberries. Her tongue swept into his mouth, unafraid to explore as she ground her hips against him. He was in serious danger of shooting off before he even got undressed. Camden grabbed the hem of her shirt and pulled up. He needed to see her breasts *now*. She sat up, straddling him, and he hated losing the full-body contact even for a second, but knew it would be worth it. He slid her shirt over her head, revealing the sexy lacy bra beneath it.

When his eyes widened, she laughed. "Remember when I told you I had to work a little late this week? I snuck out to a little boutique with Lissa and bought a couple of things. Forgive me for fibbing?"

"Only if I can expect something matching on the bottom." Camden reached for her waistband and tugged down until she'd taken off her pants. When he saw the tiny scrap of lace not so much covering her as teasing him, he growled, "I forgive you immediately and in the future in case you ever want to do that again."

Elena grinned. "Your turn." She scooted back from Camden and he sat up. She knelt on the bed and unbuttoned his shirt, then pulled it off. When she started on his jeans, he told her, "I'm afraid my underwear isn't nearly as lacy and exciting as yours."

She laughed. "I guess I can forgive you this time." She pulled his jeans down and blatantly admired him in his boxer briefs. "Oh, yes, I think you did just fine." When she ran her palm over his bulge, balls to tip, he shuddered.

"Oh, God, Elena," he hissed as she ran the tips of her fingers back down.

She reached behind her back and undid her bra. He hooked his thumbs under the straps and slid them down her arms. The lace peeled away from her breasts, revealing her nipples which pebbled the moment they hit the air. He took them in his hands and ran his thumbs over them as she arched her neck back and closed her eyes. Camden bent forward and took her right nipple into his mouth. He licked her areola until it stiffened even more. He did the same with the other as Elena moaned under his administrations. He teased her cleavage with his cheek stubble until she grabbed his boxer briefs and tugged them off.

"Fair's fair," Camden said as he slipped the lace panties down her thighs.

Elena scooted back and stepped off the bed. She motioned for him to sit on the edge.

Then she dropped to her knees between his legs and looked up at him, her eyes glazed with desire.

Susan had been a generous lover, but once Camden realized she wasn't big on giving head, he'd never asked her to do it again. She'd left him with the impression that most women weren't crazy about it. So he said, "Elena, you don't have to."

"But I want to. You made me feel so good with your mouth. I want to return the favor before we..." She turned her attention back to his cock. She ran her thumb over the tip and smiled at the resulting drop of pre-come.

Camden shuddered and gripped the comforter. "Really, it's okay—"

All rational thought ceased as she leaned forward and licked the drop off. She caressed his tip with her tongue, swirling it around and around until she wrapped her lips around the head of his cock and sucked him in. She ran her tongue tip along the flair, tracing the curves with her lips and tongue. He sank his fingers deep into her long, thick hair.

His eyes closed and he arched backwards. "Elena. Christ, Baby."

She released his head and ran her lips up and down his shaft. "I love doing this to you," she murmured against his skin, the vibrations and her husky voice full of lust driving him crazy. She cupped his balls and fingered the skin gently. He shook under her touch and knew he couldn't take much more.

Before she could plunge his entire length into her mouth, he pulled her to her feet. "No one's ever done that for me, Gorgeous, not like that."

"I'd love to keep going. All the way until you come in my mouth."

Camden took a deep, shuddering breath. "Next time. Now it's my turn again."

He pulled her back on the bed until she straddled him. The head of his cock brushed against her clit, and he felt her swell against him. He gripped her ass, moving her slowly up and down over his shaft. Elena clung to him, glassy-eyed as she told him she was his now, safe in his arms. They moved together, or rather, he moved her, and her juices ran down her legs.

"I'm aching inside," she moaned.

"Tell me what you want, Baby."

"I need you inside me, now. I want to be filled with your cock."

He kissed her throat again, then moved to her ear, tracing it with just his tongue tip, sending her into a near-frenzy as she gasped and gripped his shoulders. She sank her nails into his arms and he moaned at her rough touch. He stopped moving and held her tightly, looking into her eyes. "Now?"

"God, yes."

The need in her eyes, her parted lips, the way she

clutched him, all of it made him light-headed. He lifted her hips and positioned her swollen opening over his cock. Then he slid her down quickly, drawing a gasp out of her as he groaned. So tight, and soft, and wet. He made sure to caress her clit with every stroke, until he felt her walls pulsing around him. They both found ecstasy at the same moment.

Elena went limp in his arms and he laid her down carefully. Camden pulled the comforter over them both and held her, their legs tangled together. Her eyes were closed and her breathing slowed from panting to smooth and even. He nuzzled in her hair and she kissed his throat.

"I love you, Camden," she whispered.

"I love you too, Gorgeous."

"I never thought I'd find someone I could love again."

"Me neither." He ran his hand through her glossy hair.

The tears against his neck surprised him. He tilted her chin up. "What's wrong, Elena?" His chest tightened at the thought that he might have hurt her. "Are you okay? Did I hurt—"

"No, no, you didn't hurt me, Baby." She stroked his cheek. "You couldn't, you'd never hurt me, not like that."

"Then why the tears?" He brushed the newest one away.

"I know what I'm holding in my arms. I'm so fortunate to have you, to have a second chance." She looked down.

"Elena, look at me. What else is going on?"

"I'm...I've been afraid to face something, but if I don't I'll be the one sabotaging our chances." She looked back up and gazed into his eyes. "It's selfish, considering what you do for a living. But, I'm afraid of losing you. Like I did Antonio."

He pulled her in for a tight hug. "There is not a selfish bone in your sweet little body, Elena. I understand how you could feel that way."

"No, you don't. Not entirely. Even though you lost your wife, she wasn't...." Elena shook her head. "It's different."

"Talk to me, Baby. Why is it different?"

"After I married Antonio, I thought, this is my happily ever after. He was a fourth-generation cowboy. We had a home at the ranch. Friends who were like family. Then things changed. The economy went south. There was a drought. And the ranch owner sold out to a developer. It broke our hearts."

"Your life was so different than it is today."

"Very different. After the sale, Antonio couldn't find work on another ranch, so we literally followed the herd along the highway north to Deal's meatpacking plant in Nebraska. He got on there and I took a job at the local diner at first, then at the plant too after Tina was born."

Elena took a deep breath. "That job...that *man*." Elena shuddered in his arms and he held her tighter. "They took my husband's life."

"He died in an accident there, you'd said. I'm so sorry. That must have been devastating." Camden came to a realization. "You're worried you're going to lose me to my job, too, aren't you?"

Elena nodded silently and buried her face in his neck.

"Baby, I'm not going to insult you by telling you that you have nothing to worry about. Damn straight, what I do is sometimes dangerous. But I'm trained for it. I'm a former SEAL who served his country in some of the most dangerous places on earth. You've seen my scars. Thing is, I made it through all that. Nothing I face here is nearly as deadly."

Her voice cracked and her eyes watered. "There's more you don't know. That I didn't know until recently. About Antonio's death."

"What is it, Baby?"

"It...wasn't an accident. Antonio learned some things about Deal, things he didn't even tell me, and Deal had him killed to keep him quiet. It all came out during the trial."

"Oh, Baby. I'm so sorry."

"Rachael was just as devastated as me when we found out. She was afraid I'd hate her, or even blame her just because she's his daughter."

"Of course you wouldn't."

"Never. She's the sister of my heart. And I made sure she knows that. But, Camden, do you see why I'm afraid? The first man I ever loved was taken from me by violent men. I'm so, so afraid I'll lose you the same way." Her tears fell. "I don't know if I can survive that a second time."

Please, I can't lose her now. I want to spend the rest of my life with her. Camden sat them up and cradled her. "Like I said, I've been trained to anticipate and fight damn near anything. Life is full of risk, Gorgeous. What it's not as full of is love. Unless you get really, really lucky. So, when you find real love, it's worth every risk to hold on to it. I know you, Elena Martinez. I know how brave and strong you are. Don't let this last thing scare you away from me. Because love's too rare and important for the 'what-ifs' to kill it off."

He took her face in his hands. "As long as I know you and Tina are in the world and waiting for me back home, do you think I'm gonna let anyone or anything stop me from coming back to you?"

Elena shook her head. "Looking into those eyes, I know you mean every word you say."

"Hell yes, I do. If you have faith in me, then I've got this. You let me protect you and Tina. You let me worry about taking out the bad guys. Besides," he gave her a wicked grin, "in SEAL school, they taught me how to blow shit up."

That got him a giggle.

"You think any asshole stands a chance against me and a little C_4?"

"Oh, heavens no." Wiping her eyes, she laughed. "The C_4 is just window dressing."

"Damn straight, woman," Camden said, shoulders shaking until he couldn't hold back his laughter anymore. He squeezed her tight and kissed the top of her head. "Now, funny girl, there are roughly fifty-eight more positions I'd like us to try."

Her eyebrows raised. "How many do you think we can through tonight?"

He gave her a wicked grin. "What do you mean? I was *only* talking about tonight."

The next morning, Camden sat at his kitchen island—at Elena's insistence—while she made pancakes. And bacon. And sausage. And eggs. And toast. And fresh-squeezed orange juice.

As she flipped a pancake, she said, "You were right last night, the kitchen *is* where you keep your food."

"And I see your objective is to cook every last scrap of it."

She glanced over her shoulder and grinned. "Something like that, considering everyone's coming over."

"Don't remind me." Camden rolled his shoulders, trying to ease the tension in them. Lachlan had called at oh-dark-thirty saying that Gina had some interesting news about the fertility clinic data. He wanted everyone at Watchdog ASAP. But Elena wouldn't hear of it and told Camden to tell Lach that breakfast was at Camden's and she was cooking. His boss had eaten her cookies and was no fool, so now the team was headed their way.

"What?" Elena put a fist on her hip. "You love your job."

"I do. But, it means I don't get to see you wearing my shirt for as long as I want to." And damn, did she wear it well. As a matter of fact, he wanted to run his hands over her while she was wearing it, so he stood up and crossed to the stove.

"This old thing?" She grinned and spun. "I've had it for ages. No, wait, I'm planning to keep it for ages."

"You are?" Camden wrapped his arms around her from behind and nuzzled into her neck.

"Mmm. I am. And its owner, too."

"You'd better, because he's planning on keeping you. Even if he never gets to wear this shirt again." He patted her bottom. "They should be here any minute. I'll finish up here while you go get dressed." He smacked his lips together and frowned as if he'd just tasted something bad. "Man, I did not like saying those last words."

Elena laughed, turned, and stood up on tiptoe to kiss Camden. "Better?"

"Mmm. Much."

As he plated up the last of the food, he thought about how much he loved to hear her laugh, and how he loved being the guy who made that happen.

———

Lachlan arrived first, just as Elena came back out of the bedroom. Gina showed up a couple minutes later with Fleur, who made a beeline for Toby and the backyard. Gina was followed by Jake, then Nash. Costello, as usual, was running behind.

"Sorry," he said as he grabbed a plate and joined everyone else around the island. "Not a morning person."

"Wet dreams just too good to get out of bed?" Nash asked.

Costello's eyes went wide.

"Dude! Seriously?" Camden said. "You mind? My woman's right here."

"Also a woman," Gina said as she lifted her finger in the air. "Either way, not interested in hearing about Costello's nocturnal emiss—"

"Damn, you're worse than the rest." Costello cut her off while red crept up his throat, as if Nash's comment hit a little too close to home. From everything Camden had seen, the man hated to look anything less than distinguished. Mr. Proper. Which was why he was so much fun to tease.

Gina winked at Elena as she popped a bite of pancake in her mouth. To her credit, Elena didn't laugh out loud, but Camden could feel her shaking with suppressed laughter.

"So, what sort of news do you have for us, Gina?" Camden asked.

The kitchen went dead-still. Jake appeared the most uncomfortable. Gina looked at Elena, then back at Camden.

"She's on the team now," Camden answered her—and everyone else's—unasked question.

Lachlan nodded. "Good to hear. And we're gonna do everything to keep you safe. We appreciate it, ma'am, along with this incredible breakfast." He chomped down on the pen stub that he'd shoved into his mouth immediately after he finished eating.

"Hey, I made the coffee," Camden said.

Jake golf-clapped. "Congrats, brother, you get a participation ribbon."

Elena laughed. "Thank you, Mr. Campbell. I hope I can be of some help. I did talk to Cici yesterday."

What? Camden tried not to give away his surprise, but he couldn't stop his body from tensing up. Why hadn't she said anything until now?

Elena motioned for Gina to keep talking. "You first."

Gina set her fork down. "After narrowing the patient information down to the Bennetts, which was much easier than I'd anticipated, I discovered something interesting."

"Patient information?" Elena asked, then looked around. "Is she sick? Sorry, late to the party."

"That's okay," Gina said. "She's not ill. On Camden's recommendation, we decided to look into the Bennetts' past visits to a fertility clinic twelve years ago." Camden felt Elena tense up. "And the record was pretty surprising. It said that she'd had one pregnancy already, resulting in one live birth."

"Whoa," Camden said. "One live birth? But they only have the twins."

"In college," Elena said. Now Camden was really confused, but Gina only nodded.

"She told you," Gina said.

"She did. Yesterday evening." Elena filled them in on her conversation with Cici, and as she did, Camden's admiration for his woman grew. "Now I know she was telling the truth— not that I doubted, but there's the proof. So, Cici's biggest concern was that you all would dig into her past and find out, and that you might leak the information to the media, or maybe a political rival. She wasn't clear on that," Elena finished.

"Well, Cici was half-right, we did dig it up," Lach said as he leaned back and crossed his arms. "But I have to say, I'm a little insulted that she'd think we'd turn around and sell her out."

"I don't think you should take it personally." Elena reached out and laid her hand on the big man's arm, quick to soothe him. "She doesn't trust anyone much."

Lachlan belted out a laugh and patted her hand. "You really think my feelings are hurt?" He looked at Camden.

"Your lady is a sweetheart, trying to make me feel better like that."

Camden put an arm around her. "And not a half-bad operative."

"She's hired," Lach added.

Elea put her hands up. "Oh, no, I'm already looking at a new, less-exciting job at Delia's restaurant, but thanks."

"That's right," Jake said. "Rachael told me about that. Congrats. We're both happy for you."

"Thanks! I'll be at the villa in the kitchen. I can keep an ear open. I could even ask the servers to look for anything suspicious."

This time, Nash laughed. "Look out, Lach. I think she's secretly after *your* job."

Lach grinned. Normally wound tightly, Elena had managed to get him to smile twice and even laugh—*damn near a miracle*, Camden thought. "Again, my lady, that's very generous, but we've got this. Truth is, I'm gonna have to ask you to not talk about it to anyone, to play it like there's nothing going on at all but a big ol' party."

"I wouldn't say a word, but I just thought I could help."

"Already have, thanks. Now, she say who the baby daddy was?"

Elena shook her head. "But she did say he knew."

"And he didn't keep the kid, either." Lachlan looked at Gina. "What're our chances of getting into sealed adoption records?"

"Slim to none within our timeframe, Lach. I'm tapped out. California keeps those records sealed tighter than a drum."

Costello raised a finger. "I think I can make an educated guess as to the father."

"I think we all can, without being psychic," Camden said. "Lawrence Franklin."

"But that's crazy," Elena said. "Cici said Roger knows, that he found out later. Now we know that's obviously because they went to the clinic. I imagine she came totally clean then. So, why would Roger work with a guy who got his future wife pregnant in college?"

"Because Franklin is the very best in the business. Politics makes for some strange bedfellows," Jake said.

"Well, this one takes the cake," Camden said. "Hell, it takes the wedding cake, the Jordan almonds, *and* the beer cans tied to the back of the 'just married' car."

Lach nodded. "We need to figure out how this info can be used against the Bennetts and stop it."

Camden's top concern went unspoken because he didn't want to spook Elena. Did Lawrence target Elena? And if so, how much more danger was she in now?

TWENTY-TWO

"Tina, sweetie, time to go to the kids' room." Elena had kept her daughter with her through setting up the catering at the villa—not an easy feat, since the little girl was the definition of curious, and Camden had shown her pictures of a beautiful mermaid sundial in the garden, promising that if she was good, they could go see it after the party.

"I don't really want to go to the kids' room. I won't know any of them."

"You'll know the Bennett twins. They'll be there and they love playing with you."

Elena watched her daughter consider that. She was flattered that a couple of older kids—twice her age, she loved to point out—played with her.

"Okay. But you promise we can see the sundial after?"

"Promise, Pepita."

"I want to see if the moon works on the gnomon like the sun does."

One of the servers, Claudia, looked at the little girl. "Smart, that one," she said.

"Sure is," Elissa chimed in as she passed by with the first platter loaded with small plates of mini street tacos.

Tina beamed.

The little stinker dropped the word Camden taught her just to show off, Elena thought. She laughed to herself as she shook her head. "*Vamos,* Pepita. I need to get back here quickly."

"She *is* a smart one." Elena cringed when she recognized the man's voice behind her.

"Lawrence," she said, turning. "Did you need anything?" *Or can I just tell you to kiss off?*

"I'm just making sure everything is going to plan."

"Well, we're good in here." Elena put her hand on the small of Tina's back to encourage her to go.

"Aren't you going to introduce me to this smart and charming young lady?" Lawrence bent his knees until he was face to face with Tina, who clearly didn't like the attention she'd been trying to get a minute before. But Elena had raised a polite daughter. Tina extended her hand and said, "I'm Tina Martinez and it's a pleasure."

"Pleasure's all mine." Lawrence shook her hand then stood.

"We were just on our way to the kids' room, so if you'll excuse us." She pushed past Lawrence, Tina in tow.

Elena smiled at the two Watchdog security guards and one dog flanking the door to the kid's room. She didn't recognize one of the guards, but the other was Kyle, who had helped her move in. He gave her and Tina a brief but warm smile as he did some sort of hand signal that probably told the dog that they were friends, not foes.

Cici was just inside the door talking to another woman. Elena assumed she must be one of the sitters, since she wasn't dressed to the nines. Cici saw Elena and Tina and smiled.

"It's a little Lord of the Butterflies in here, isn't it?" Cici said as a little girl in a poufy white party dress ran by shrieking.

Elena laughed as Tina moved closer to her. By the way Tina grabbed her hand after she smoothed down her daughter's hair, she'd just realized the same thing Elena had—the twins were nowhere in sight. *Crap.*

Cici waved and walked away while the sitter told Elena about the movies they were going to watch, and that a magician would be by later. Elena looked down at Tina and was relieved to see her smile back at her. *Must have been the magician*, she thought.

"Have fun, Pepita. I'll see you after." She turned to hurry back to the kitchen.

But before she could get far, Tina stamped her foot.

Elena turned again, trying to hold back her temper. One of the sitters was already coming toward Tina. She took her by the arm to lead her in. But Tina shouted, "No!"

"Tina." Elena headed back to the door. Another woman laid a reassuring hand on her arm. "It's probably best if you leave right now. We've got everything under control. Your daughter will be just fine."

"We've got her covered, Elena," Kyle stage-whispered. Elena smiled at him.

"Oh, will you be in there?"

He shook his head, looking annoyed. "Mrs. Bennett wants us staying out here. She's afraid we'll scare the kids."

"I doubt they'd even notice you, but whatever." Elena took another look at her daughter, nodded, and jogged back to the kitchen. Tina would be fine. This was a good lesson in patience and getting along with other kids her age.

By the time she got back to the kitchen, nearly everything had been plated up and servers were coming back in with empty trays already. "What'd I miss?" she asked Claudia.

"Not a thing, boss. You got us into a good routine and things are going smooth." She held her hand up for a high-five. Elena grinned, tied an extra apron back on, and dove back in, feeling like the queen of the castle.

Elissa came back in to refill her tray. "Don't look now, but Julia is here. She's in a mood, fair warning."

Elena rolled her eyes. The big news over the past week at B&P was their newest client, Roger Bennett, and the event on Saturday night. "I'm not surprised. Did she see you?" Elena took Elissa's empty tray and passed her a full one.

"She looked right through me. I don't think she was expecting someone from IT passing around appetizers, so she didn't recognize me." Elissa laughed. "That, and she's too busy shoving her nose up every potential client's ass." She lifted the tray. "Are you going to stay in here or go out there?"

Elena blew out a breath. Now that she knew the night was going to plan and the job at Delia's was ninety-nine percent hers, she planned on giving B&P her two weeks' notice on Monday. She should have known Julia would be here, though she'd counted on someone higher up who probably wouldn't recognize her. Her boss would probably chew her out for taking yesterday off, now that she could guess why. Julia would probably see her no matter what later during the kids' photoshoot, but maybe not.

"I think I'll just stay in here for now. It'll be easier that way."

"Elena, you have no reason to hide. Julia owes you for bringing the Bennetts on."

"I didn't. We just happened to be friends, and Brant and Phillips is one of the biggest firms in town. They were considering it long before I came along."

Elissa shook her head. "Modest to a fault, girl." She winked and headed back out to the party.

Toward the end of the evening, Elena felt a tap on her shoulder and turned, expecting to see Claudia or one of the other servers.

"What do you need...oh."

"I wondered if I'd find you in here when I saw your friend from IT." Julia had a look of absolute disgust on her face.

"Julia. I—"

"You're fired." She crossed her arms as her expression went from disgusted to triumphant. "Not only did you skip work on Friday, but you're breaking the rules about professional conduct with our clients *again*. As our receptionist, you're the frontline face of B&P, and right now, you're making us look unprofessional, moonlighting as a *waitress*." She spat the word out like it was rotten food. "I took a chance on your low-class butt when I hired you, and I should have known better. You'll amount to nothing."

Elena stood up as tall and straight as she could. "First of all, I arranged for Friday off over a week ago and you approved it. Second," she pulled out her cell phone, unlocked it, and hit a button. "Check your email. You can't fire me, because I quit. I just sent you my letter of resignation which I also typed up over a week ago. Third, as for amounting to nothing, I was not hired as a waitress, which, by the way, is a tough job and not to be looked down on, *ever*. No, I'm in charge of food service tonight, and it's been perfect down to the last detail. I'm just getting started here."

"Oh, really?"

"Yes, really. When you're still stuck in your little power-vacuum of a job, my name is gonna be in lights as one of L.A.'s top restaurateurs, count on it. Now, get the hell out of my kitchen because you're a walking health code violation."

Elena waited only long enough to watch Julia turn fire-engine red, then pale as a ghost before she turned on her stiletto and marched out.

That's when the clapping and cheering started behind her. Delia's voice carried over the sound, "Girl, that was poetry."

Elena turned to see Delia, Claudia, Elissa, Pete...and Camden. They were all clapping, with huge smiles on their faces, but Camden's was the biggest. Delia stepped forward, black cloth folded in a neat square in her hands. She unfolded the cloth, revealing a chef's apron with *Delia's Restaurant* emblazoned on the front.

"Welcome to the family," Delia said.

"So...I've got the job?" Elena asked, her eyes wet.

"You even have to ask?" Delia laughed. "Now turn around so I can get this on you."

Elena took off her own apron from home, turned, and lifted her hair. But instead of Delia helping her, Camden's hands draped the apron over her head, tied the straps around her waist, and then pulled her in close for a hug. He turned her, tipped her chin up, and kissed her deeply to whistles and catcalls.

"Congratulations, Gorgeous. Knew you'd kick ass at the gig, but didn't realize you'd also kick Julia's ass. Just glad I got to watch."

Elena pushed playfully against his shoulder. "Don't you have a job to do?"

He tapped his ear, where earlier, Elena had watched him insert the tiniest earbud ever. "Doin' it right now. But I do need to get back out there before the kids' photoshoot."

By the smile on his face, Elena knew the night had gone well for Camden so far, but she asked anyway. "All good?"

"We'll talk at home, Babe." He kissed her again. "Proud of you. Love you."

"Love you, too."

He snagged a couple dumplings off a platter and stuffed them into his mouth as he went to get Roger.

Elena and her crew cleaned and packed up the remaining food while sounds of the clapping and cheering crowd drifted in from the courtyard. She thought the night must have gone well for Camden and thanked God for that. Maybe nothing would come of all this after all.

"Elena," Claudia said as she came in after collecting the last platter full of dirty wine glasses from the crowd. "Some guy wants to talk to you. Says it's photo time for the kids?"

"Oh yeah. Be right there." Elena wiped her hands on a towel and headed for the courtyard.

Ugh. Lawrence was waiting right there. But at least Senator Rock Higley stood next to him, so maybe he wouldn't try anything. Both men smiled at Elena as if she were an actual human being and not a window to look through. She glanced around, hoping to see Camden, or any other Watchdog employee for that matter.

"There she is, the unsung champion of the evening," Lawrence said, extending his arms as if to hug Elena. She folded her across her chest. He went on as if nothing was wrong, taking Senator Higley by the upper arm. "This is the lady you asked to see, Senator. I'd like to introduce Elena Martinez. Ms. Martinez, this is Senator Rock Higley. He's been raving about your food and asked to see the chef."

"Ms. Martinez, it's a pleasure. Not a lot of food agrees with me these days, but yours was top-notch." *What an odd statement.* He held out his hand and she shook it. His grip wasn't as strong as she expected. Up close, he looked pale, too. Was he ill?

"Thank you, Senator, but it was really a group effort."

"Don't let her fool you, she was in charge of every step," Camden's voice sounded from behind her.

Oh, sweet relief. Camden put a protective hand on her shoulder. Lawrence's smile faltered before he snapped it back into place.

"I'm sure she was," the senator responded, smiling. "Elena, if you can give me a business card, I'll pass it on to my assistant for our next event."

Her eyes widened, and she patted her apron pockets despite knowing she didn't have any cards. "Oh, that's wonderful! I'm afraid I don't have any with me, but you can reach me at Delia's." She pointed to the restaurant's name on her apron.

He laughed. "Perfect."

Lawrence cleared his throat. "They're lining up the kids for the photos and I wanted to make sure you were right up front." He glanced from Elena to Camden and back. "Both of you, I suppose."

"Great, thanks." *Though I think I'd rather stick chopsticks in my eyes than stand anywhere near you.* The four of them navigated through the crowd as a line of kids made their way onto the lighted stage. Lawrence stopped them at the corner edge of the stage where they had a good view. Elena breathed a sigh of relief when the man continued on to the very middle of the front row. At least he was away from her so her skin could stop crawling. She heard Camden murmur something and turned to look back at him. He subtly tapped his ear—oh, he was talking to a teammate, not her. She smiled and turned back to the stage.

Tina was right in front, and she looked downright upset.

Great, she had a crappy time and she and Camden would hear about it.

Rock put an arm around her shoulders, taking her by surprise. She glanced back to see what Camden thought about that, but he'd disappeared. Senator Higley leaned in and asked, "Is that your daughter?"

"Yes, that's Tina."

"The two of you look so much alike. Such a pretty girl."

"Thanks." She tried to smile at the compliment, but she hated this false familiarity. When Tina looked her direction though, she gave her daughter a genuinely encouraging smile. Pepita looked so uncomfortable up there in the lights with the other kids. Maybe if they went to find this mermaid sundial right away after the photo, they could soften her mood before she had a tantrum.

"Smile, everyone! Smile!" Lawrence encouraged the kids from the front row.

To Elena's relief, Tina's smile was the biggest one as the cameras flashed.

TWENTY-THREE

At the end of the night, Camden followed Elena's car back to her apartment, his mind turning over a million things. The event had gone well in some ways, and completely sideways in others. Camden had stuck closely to Roger, keeping his ears open for anything amiss. But the newly-christened political hopeful stuck to the typical script of 'thank you for your support' and Camden didn't notice anything out of the ordinary from the guests who approached him. Gina reported that Cici was pretty much a carbon copy of her husband, thanking guests and accepting compliments for the party.

Jake reported the same about Lawrence Franklin. The man was keeping back, letting Roger take the spotlight. He directed his campaign staff members and talked to Senator Higley who was actually offering pointers, Jake said, which appeared to ruffle Franklin's feathers. Good on Higley.

Then Jake lost them briefly as Higley pulled Franklin away from the crowd to talk privately. They wondered what that was about, until Senator Higley took the stage at his appointed time—the man needed an escort up the stairs and

Camden wondered if the rumors of his illness were true—and instead of giving his support for Roger Bennett's bid for the House of Representatives, he dropped jaws by announcing that he would be stepping down from his Senate seat and was endorsing Bennett as his replacement.

So, that's what these meetings have been about Camden thought as the crowd broke into surprised cheers. He asked Roger about it as soon as he had the chance, irritated that the man hadn't let him in on the change in plans. Roger shrugged and told him that Higley had sprung it on him as well, but Roger would've been a fool if he didn't accept the senator's offer. Camden couldn't argue. The man had just been handed twice the power he'd been gunning for.

Still, Camden hated surprises on the job, and this was a big one. Jake agreed.

The rest of the night went pretty quickly after the big announcement. Camden sneaked into the kitchen in time to see his badass woman put her former boss in her place, then accept her dream job. That made everything worth it.

Then, his hackles went back up the second he saw Franklin talking to Elena. The skeevy guy at least had the sense to back off the second he saw Camden. Apparently, he was kissing Higley's ass, introducing him to Elena. Camden's guard wasn't about to drop though, and he stuck by her in the crowd, until Franklin got the hint and moved away from them to the front of the crowd.

Kyle spoke to him through his earbud right before the photos. "Camden. We need to do a quick headcount of all the kids."

Fuck. His stomach turned sour as he scanned the faces on the stage. Tina was right there in front with the rest of the younger kids, and the Bennett twins stood right behind her in a row of taller kids.

"What's up?" He stepped away from Elena and walked toward one of the women who had herded the kids in, hoping she had a list of names.

"Just making sure. We did a headcount as they left the room and came up with the correct count, but when Mac and I went in, someone had opened one of the windows, so I'm double-checking."

"Fuck. I was told the windows were locked, and the babysitters were under orders not to open them anyway." He cursed Cici for insisting that his guards stay outside the room in order not to disturb the kids. "Jake, you hear that?"

"Copy. I'm already counting, brother."

Nash and Costello confirmed they were counting as well.

"Excuse me," Camden said to the lady who had been at the head of the line. "I need to see your attendance list." Before she could protest, Camden swiped the piece of paper out of her hands. There was a checkmark beside each name, showing they were all accounted for. Camden quickly counted the kids on stage while they smiled for the photographer. Adding in the number of teens who were allowed to mingle with the other guests, the count on stage matched the number of names. He counted again, and then a third time. Same totals.

"Everything go okay in the kids' room tonight?" he asked the woman.

"Just fine, why?"

"It's my job to make sure."

Jake, Costello, and Nash reported their counts. Their numbers matched. *Crisis averted.* But his gut stayed sour over the close call and nothing felt right about it. Tina had been in that room. He didn't know what he would have done if something had happened to her.

"Sorry to scare you, boss," Kyle said. He sounded like a dog about to get kicked for no damn good reason. *Poor Pup*.

"Not at all. Good work. We got lucky this time is all."

The guests departed after the photoshoot. Camden's team made sure the stragglers got to their cars and rides, and that no one lingered behind. He wouldn't breathe easy though until the Bennetts were safe and sound back in their home and he could follow Elena and Tina back to their apartment in his SUV.

Now that he was doing that very thing, he should've been at ease. But the Mermaid had him worried. Ever since he'd shown her the photos of the sundial in the garden and explained all the parts and how it worked, she wouldn't talk about anything else. He figured they'd have to show it to her as soon as things wound down and then they'd have to drag her away with a promise to come back during the daytime. Sure enough, the minute the photoshoot was over, she practically leaped off the stage to get to Elena.

"Can we go now?" Camden heard the little girl ask as he walked back over to them. She tugged Elena's hand.

"Hang on, Pepita. Camden's still working. We'll see it when he's done."

"No. I want to go *now*."

Time to shut this down. "Hey, Mermaid, I'm gonna give you two choices. Either you wait for me to finish, or you let your mama show you now, and then I'll either catch up or we'll go home if you're done looking at it."

Tina looked up at him like he'd just slapped her. The level of betrayal he saw in her eyes turned his soul to ice. "Take me home," she whispered. She turned to Elena. "Mama, take me home right now." Her voice grew louder with every word.

"Tina. You are being so disrespectful right now," Elena said as she dropped to her knees. "You will apologize... honey, are you okay? You're all sweaty." She touched Tina's fore-head. "Clammy."

"What's wrong?" Camden felt like he'd taken a shot to the heart with a syringe full of adrenaline. He dropped down beside them.

Elena was already checking Tina's pump. "Dammit, she gets cranky like this when her blood sugar's low. Plus the sweating...yup." Elena shook her head. "I need to get some glucose into you, Pepita, and then some food."

"Camden's hands shook as he reached for his phone. "I'm calling nine-one-one."

"No, no, she's okay, it's not off by much. I promise, we've had much worse. She'll be fine before they'd even get through the traffic and get here."

"Just wanna go home," Tina whimpered.

Elena was already picking her up. "We will, baby. I need to get my purse with your glucose in it from the kitchen, and then...oh. Tina? Did you have an accident?" Elena looked over Tina's head at him, confusion in her eyes and her brows drawn down as she mouthed *I think she wet herself.*

"Does that happen with low blood sugar?" *You'd know if you'd taken the time to look up diabetes in kids, you jackass* he berated himself.

She shook her head. Tina burst into tears and cried against Elena's neck. The pump beeped a warning. The sound might as well have been a gunshot to Camden.

"I've gotta get that glucose." She started toward the doors.

"Elena—"

"She's okay, I promise. We caught the drop early, even before the pump. Don't call."

Fuck, fuck, fuck. He fought an internal battle between trusting her and calling an ambulance. No. Elena wouldn't ever risk Tina's health. She knew what she was doing. The best way to help her was to get everything buttoned up here and then get them home.

But damn. Is this what he was in for? How often did Tina's sugar drop like that? Would he be able to recognize the signs if Elena wasn't around? Doubt crept into his heart with sharp, needling fingers.

"Jake, you there?"

"Copy, brother." Jake's voice came through loud and clear in his earbud.

"Costello."

"Copy."

"Jake, need you to turn your post over to Psychic and check on Elena and Tina in the kitchen, stat."

"Copy," was all Jake said though the tone in his voice added *what the hell is wrong and I'm hurrying the fuck to find out.*

As Camden gave the rest of his team orders and walked the perimeter of the courtyard and garden, he made a to-do list. Item numero uno was reading every damn thing about diabetes he could lay his hands on. Item number two required a shopping trip.

Once he was satisfied that everyone was out, the Bennetts were home, and the job was done for the night, he headed for the kitchen. Jake had given him regular updates, saying that Tina's blood sugar was slowly rising, though she still wasn't the sweet little girl or commanding general they were all used to. By the time he got to the kitchen, she was mostly asleep in Elena's arms as she sat in a rocking chair Jake had found somewhere.

He knelt next to the chair and kissed his gorgeous woman on the lips and his girl on the top of her head. "Is she okay?"

Elena nodded. "She'll be fine. I just need to get her home and into clean clothes. I want to keep her with me tonight."

He answered the hesitation in her voice with, "You have a comfy couch, Gorgeous, no worries. Ready to go?"

"Absolutely."

Camden reached out for Tina, and the Mermaid slipped into his arms and curled herself into his body, sending warmth straight to his heart. She seemed to have forgiven him, but he'd never forget the look she gave him earlier. Elena took his arm as they made their way to her car.

He worried the entire way home. At the apartment, he tucked them both in to Elena's bed along with some of Tina's stuffed animals and dolls. Toby stayed with them at the foot of the bed. Camden kissed Elena one more time before heading for the couch. "Love you, Gorgeous."

"I love you, too."

Camden settled in on the couch. Tina would be okay. Elena had the job of her dreams. He'd successfully guarded the Bennetts through a huge and surprising political event. Everything was good. So what was wrong, and why did it worry him?

After tossing and turning, he gave up and grabbed his phone. After a quick search, Camden found a website on raising a child with type-one diabetes and dug in.

TWENTY-FOUR

Elena kept a close eye on Tina's blood sugar all night. If she drifted off to sleep at all, she didn't remember it. Maybe Tina was getting a cold, or the excitement of the night sucked up her energy. But Tina didn't have a fever or the sniffles, and she'd been much more excited about other things without going hypoglycemic. Sometimes, diabetes just didn't make sense and they'd both learned to live with that. From the fear in Camden's eyes, Elena realized he had a lot of catching up to do. But the fact that he was on her couch right now, that he hadn't run from the fear, reaffirmed what she already knew. He loved them and he would be there through both the fun times and the hard times.

By morning, Tina was stable, but Elena was groggy. She finally slipped into a light doze and woke to the smell of breakfast cooking. She left Tina sleeping—snuggled up with her stuffed horse and Toby at her feet—and went to the kitchen where Camden was cooking eggs.

"What's all this?" she asked as she wrapped her arms around his waist from behind. She breathed in the warm, salty scent of his skin beneath his cotton t-shirt, with just the faintest hint of his citrusy aftershave.

"I was doing some reading about what a kiddo with diabetes needs to eat after a crash. I hope I'm getting it right."

That sent her heart into orbit. "Baby, you're getting it absolutely right." She kissed the spot between his shoulder blades and he grunted. "Thank you."

Camden slid the eggs onto a plate and set the pan aside. He turned and pulled her to his chest. He nuzzled deep into her hair, then down to the side of her neck, and laid a kiss on the sensitive skin just below her ear. "Did she do okay over night?"

"She did just fine."

"Shall we go wake the Mermaid and get some more food into her?"

"Sounds like a plan. But first." Elena took his face in her hands and gazed into his eyes. "I love you, Camden. I love who you've become. I love that you're in our lives."

His eyes turned misty. "I love you too, Gorgeous. So much it hurts. I am so proud to be holding you in my arms. You amaze me every single day."

He dipped his head to kiss her, a soft, sweet landing on her lips followed by another. He ran his tongue along her lips until she parted them and took him in.

They heard Tina's voice in the bedroom and broke off the kiss. It sounded like she was playing with her dolls—a wonderful, reassuring sound if ever there was one. They smiled and touched foreheads before Camden patted her bottom. She turned and he draped his arm around her shoulders as they walked to the bedroom. Camden smiled and she felt his body shake with suppressed laughter, hearing Tina play. Elena didn't blame him. She sometimes stood silently outside her door and just listened to her daughter's imagination run wild. The things she came up with often left her trying not to laugh at the sheer cuteness.

Elena stopped Camden just before they got to the door and put her finger to her lips. She wanted him to have a chance to listen like she sometimes did.

"Would you like to come and feed the horses, Emily? They're at our racetrack." Elena grinned up at Camden. Emily was Tina's favorite doll. The voice she used sounded like a man's. Maybe she was imitating Camden and the way he was always showing her the world. Camden kept his hand over his mouth, trying not to laugh.

"Sure! I love horses," Tina answered herself in Emily's high-pitched voice.

"There they are. They're running on the track. But I don't like the way they're running." She pitched the man's voice deeper. Angry. This didn't sound right. It wasn't the usual way she played.

"I like the horses. I think they're running fine."

"Well, I don't. So I'm going to kill them."

Elena's eyes went wide. Camden's mirrored her alarm. She started to step in the room to tell Tina this wasn't an appropriate way to play when Camden stopped her. This time he put a finger to his lips.

"No! Please don't kill the horses!"

"I can do anything I want. Bang! Bang!"

Elena covered her mouth. Camden squeezed her tight as she shook. What the hell? Tina never played like this.

"I'm going to tell on you! I'm going to run to the beach and get the seals to beat you up. I know their king and his name is Camden and he's going to get you."

"Ha ha ha!" Tina's laugh sounded all the more evil for her

innocence. "Too late. I've already killed him and the rest of the seals and your mother too because you are a bad little girl who told!"

Elena's knees went out from under her. Camden held her up. This couldn't be happening.

Tina stopped talking. Sniffles filled the room.

Camden nodded at Elena and they entered the bedroom. Tina sat in the middle of the bed holding Emily. Her stuffed horse lay sprawled out on his back. Toby let out a whine as he whipped his head to look at them, his expression saying what do I do?

"Tina? Pepita, what...what are you playing?"

Tina's eyes went wide at the sight of Elena and Camden. "Nothing." She wiped her tear-stained face.

Elena rushed to her and sat down. She pulled Tina into her arms. Camden went to the other side of the bed and climbed in, then wrapped his arm around both of them.

"Pepita. Tell me. What happened that made you play like this?"

"I can't. I can't tell!"

"Mermaid. We're right here. We're safe. Everyone is safe and sound. You can tell us anything." Camden kissed the top of Tina's head.

"No. They'll kill the horses if I do." She sobbed, then whispered, "They'll kill you, Mama."

Elena felt like someone had just cut her chest open and ripped out her heart. Camden looked like he wanted to do that very thing to whoever had threatened her baby girl.

"Tina, look at me," Camden said. When she tipped her head up to meet his gaze, he continued. "Do you remember when we met?"

She nodded.

"What did I do the whole time when we were at the safe-house? What did Jake and I do?"

She sniffed. "You kept us safe."

Camden smiled and it felt like the sun coming out. "That's right, baby girl. I kept you safe."

"And Toby."

"Toby?"

"Toby kept us safe." The dog thumped his tail at his name.

"That's right, Toby kept you real safe. Look at this good boy. He's not going to let anyone or anything bad come near you, or your mama, or me, or anyone." The dog crawled forward and laid his muzzle on Tina's lap.

She scratched Toby's ears. "But what about the horses? Can you keep them safe?"

Elena stroked Tina's hair. "Baby, tell us what you mean about the horses. What horses?"

Tina sniffled and swiped a hand across her eyes. She took a deep breath. Within the protective circle of her mother's arms and surrounded by Camden's loving embrace, she began her story. It started with the burning desire to see a mermaid and a sundial.

"It's a little bit lord of the butterflies in here, isn't it?" Cici said to Mama, and Tina had no idea what the lady meant. But she had that kind of smile that always made Tina feel like she'd better be quiet and small around whoever wore it, because that type of smile could turn to tears at any second for no clear reason.

Mama laughed like she got the joke and put a hand on Tina's head, brushing her hair down. Tina grabbed her mama's hand as she watched the other kids. She didn't know any of them—Mama had said the twins would be here, but the last time Tina saw them, they were standing with their daddy and didn't look like they were going anywhere soon. As for the other kids, Tina took one look and didn't want anything to do with them. The ones who were younger were all being crybabies and the middle ones were laughing at them with mean faces, and the oldest ones were off together ignoring the rest and Tina couldn't blame them. There were several grown-ups in the room—all women—and they mostly sat with the crybabies trying to get them to stop.

Tina gripped Mama's hand tighter, trying to let her know that she didn't want to stay. Maybe Mama would get the message and take her out of here and let her play with the twins, who looked kinda bored anyway.

Oh! Tina had a great idea. She could tell the twins about the mermaid sundial and the three of them could go looking for it. That way, the twins wouldn't be so bored, and Mama and Camden could work all night and not have to worry about showing it to her. Best of all, Tina could avoid all these other weird kids. Exactly what her teacher called a win-win, only it would be a win-win-win-win-win if you counted everybody who won.

Tina smiled at her great idea and looked up at Mama. Mama looked worried until she saw Tina's smile. She smiled back and Tina was certain that it was a 'message received loud and clear' smile and that they were about to blow this pop stand. She started to say the words out loud to make her mom laugh, when Mama did the worst thing ever by letting go of her hand and saying, "Have fun, Pepita. I'll see you after." Followed by the *very* worst thing ever—she turned to walk away.

That's when Tina stamped her foot. And Mama looked

mad. And one of the crybaby women got up and took Tina by the arm like she was one of the crybabies. And all the other kids either stared or laughed at her or did both.

All Tina wanted to do was make it all stop. So she shouted, "No!"

And made it worse. Before she knew what was happening, another woman was telling Mama it was best if she left right now, that they had everything under control and Tina would be just fine. The crybaby lady still had her by the arm, and as soon as Mama was out of sight, she gave Tina's arm a really mean squeeze and dragged her to the corner by the windows.

The crybaby lady crouched and looked Tina in the eye. "Sweetheart, you're too big to be throwing a tantrum. Why don't you stay here until you're ready to play nice with the other kids?"

Tina nodded and the woman sprang up and went back to another woman who was watching two of the crybabies across the room. Each woman picked up a kid and sat down, then started talking as they rocked the crybabies.

Tina fought back her tears of frustration and anger. Looking out the nearest window helped. She noticed it was open—just the teeniest, tiniest crack—so she gave it a push and it swung out like a door. The cooler air coming in from the garden smelled fresh and good. The mermaid sundial was out there somewhere. As the sun set, Tina only grew more frustrated. She knew exactly how this was gonna go. Mama and Camden would be too tired to take her to see it and blame it on nighttime, or try to tell her that she was the one who was too tired when she was wide awake.

Tina decided there was only one thing to do, and she'd better do it before it got too dark to see. She looked around the room. None of the grownups were paying her any attention, but a few kids were still looking over her way, whispering with each other, and laughing. She kept herself from sticking her tongue out at them because that would just make one of them tell on her, or worse—come over and tease her some more.

She got her chance a few minutes later when a woman dressed as a clown came in and started doing magic. That kept everyone's attention long enough for Tina to sit on the window ledge, swing her legs over, and drop the short distance to the ground. The window was so low, she'd have no trouble climbing back in if she needed to, though she figured after she found the sundial she'd just follow the party sounds back to where all the grownups were. She'd find Camden or Miss Elissa or even Mama at the end of the night, and go home.

Allons-y, she thought to herself. Then she followed a crushed stone path through the garden, looking for the sundial.

Tina tried to find an open space like Camden had described, but it was hard because all the plants were so tall. Plus, she had to dodge a few of the grownups who'd wandered away from the party. Grownups who caught little kids on their own had a tendency to think they were lost and always wanted to take them straight to their parents or a teacher or police officer or someone in charge. Not to mention, she'd just learned about stranger-danger, and even though there weren't any strangers here because everyone was a friend of the twins' mommy and daddy, she thought it was best to always be careful, like Camden said.

Tina walked quietly down a narrow path that fed into a wider one. The sun had set a while ago and the sky was darkening. The full moon was rising so Tina hurried. Maybe sundials worked with the moon, too, but she'd never know if she didn't find it soon. Then she smiled. The path widened into a round, grass-covered clearing just ahead, ringed by tall hedges. Tina noticed gaps in some of them, leading off to other paths. She'd have to be careful to remember which path was hers. Now that it was darker, she could easily get lost.

There, in the center of the clearing, stood the beautiful little mermaid holding up a crescent moon. A sun-shaped sundial spanned the crescent. Sure enough, one of the horns of the moon served as the gnomon, just like Camden told her. Tina approached the statue in awe. It was even more beautiful than the photos.

The sound of crunching gravel made Tina look up quickly. Footsteps came from the path she'd taken. She quickly ran to a different path and ducked down in the shadows of a tall hedge. Whoever it was, she hoped they would turn around and go back to the party.

Two men appeared. Tina recognized one of them, Mr. Franklin. The other was a really old man with white hair that glowed in the darkening light. He walked with a cane. Both were dressed in penguin suits like all the rest. They walked right up to the sundial and stopped. Tina crouched lower— they were facing her path. All they needed to do was look closely and they'd see her.

The man with the cane started coughing like he had a really bad cold. He spit a giant loogy on the ground and Tina gagged back a little bit of throw-up. When he finished coughing, he spoke.

"Look, this is how it has to go. I've been asked to set aside my plans, and I don't do that lightly. When I got the diagnosis a year ago, I already had someone else in mind to step into my shoes. I'd been grooming her for a while. But, they believe Bennett's got the best chance to go all the way to the White House with their help, and they need my seat in the senate to do it right now."

Mr. Franklin nodded. "Tonight's announcement that Roger's going for *your* seat—with your blessing—is going to be all over the media a hot minute later. I can't believe you aren't going to topple face-first out of that seat and onto the senate floor with your last breath. That's what everyone expects."

"Well, I'm being compensated handsomely." The man burst into another coughing fit. "And I have other reasons."

Mr. Franklin chuckled. "Kompromat. They've got it on you, too, don't they?"

"That's none of your fucking business, is it?"

Mr. Franklin laughed in the way that grownups laugh when something isn't actually funny. "Fine. So, what do you need from me?"

"We need to move carefully. Roger's either so naïve or so egotistical that he thinks I'm doing this because I believe in him. Nobody's *that* naïve—"

"Roger is."

"Really? I would have thought egotistical. It's a trait of Hollywood types. Either way, he can't know who's really behind this. If he's naïve like you say, he won't play ball if he knows, will he?"

Mr. Franklin shook his head. "No way."

"So here's where you come in—"

Mr. Franklin cut him off again. "I told your people already, Cici's...past...stays out of this, understand?"

The white-haired man laughed again, which made him cough more. He spit another loogy and Tina had to cover her mouth to keep the puke in.

The old man finally straightened, and his voice sounded rough. "They're going to manufacture dirt on him. They have a team right now that's hacking into his opponent's servers. They'll lift emails, campaign strategies, anything they can get their hands on that pertains to the race, and copy it to a server that links back to Roger. So here's where you come in. They want the server and everything else financed through a phony account you set up filled with funds embezzled from his own campaign. Make it just sloppy enough that it can be traced with some effort, but not too much."

Now Mr. Franklin looked sick. "What's the blowback going to be on Cici? And the kids?"

"Oh, Larry, they don't need to use Cici." Even Tina could see Mr. Franklin visibly relax. "Well, at least not against *Roger*." He smiled the scariest smile Tina had ever seen. His teeth made her think of a row of Halloween tombstones. Mr. Franklin went right back to being nervous-looking, then straight to really mad.

The old man chuckled. "They cover *all* the bases, Larry, including yours if you back out. And you'd better believe the truth will come out if you get cold feet." The white-haired man leaned on his cane and moved his face closer to Mr. Franklin's, like he was studying him. "You can't help yourself, can you? Even after all these years, you'll do anything to protect her." The white-haired man slugged Mr. Franklin's arm. "Larry, she'll be fine. You certainly aren't going back on your part of the deal—you've got more to win than to lose. You're all set up to swoop in and rescue Cici if Roger decides not to play. But he'll play, especially once he gets closer to the White House. He'll have no choice by then."

"And if he still doesn't?"

"Don't you get it yet? I'm sure my counterpart's talked to our opponent's campaign manager already. Our friends are backing both horses in this race, Larry. They *own* the race-track. And if they don't like how one of the horses is running, hell, they'll shoot it. *They don't lose.*"

Tina shivered. Why would anyone want to shoot horses? *I*

don't care if Mr. Franklin is a friend of the twins' mommy. These men are mean. I hate them.

That's when the white-haired man's face darkened. He looked like he was trying to breathe but couldn't. Even Mr. Franklin, who looked like he hated the white-haired man as much as Tina did right now, grabbed the man's arm and pounded on his back to help him. "You okay, Rock?"

The man nodded and wheezed, "Nothing bourbon and one more damn cigar won't cure. Fuck my doctor. Worthless."

"Then let's get you back, get some bourbon into you at least. Clear the pipes before you speak."

They were leaving. Relief swept through Tina—until Rock held up his hand, signaling Mr. Franklin to stop and wait. He made a fist, then brought it to his mouth and started coughing harder than Tina had ever seen anyone cough. She felt her stomach clench and her mouth got very dry while her forehead felt cold and sweaty. When the man bent and spat out a huge ball of brown and red goop, Tina couldn't help it. Mimicking him, she bent forward and lost everything in her tummy.

"The hell was that?" Mr. Franklin and the man named Rock looked her way. As long as she lived, Tina would never forget the cold dead look in Rock's bloodshot eyes when they locked on hers.

Mr. Franklin's eyes narrowed. "Tina?"

The older man looked at Mr. Franklin. "You know her?"

Mr. Franklin nodded. "Her mom is the help." Then he crouched down like she was a toddler and tried to smile sweetly at Tina. "Well, look at you, sweetheart. You lost, honey? Let Uncle Larry help you get back to your mama, huh?"

Tina wasn't some stupid baby and she sure wasn't gonna

fall for that. She stood up and got ready to run, to scream, to do anything to get herself away from these two big...*jerks.*

But those cold, bloodshot eyes held her in place. "Don't you dare run or make a sound, little girl. Tina, is it?" Suddenly, the old man didn't seem as sick as he had before. He seemed big and powerful as he approached her, his cane stabbing into the ground as he walked. Mr. Franklin (Tina would never, *ever* think of him as Uncle Larry) walked a few steps behind him, that fake smile never leaving his face.

They loomed over her. Tina's fearful gaze darted from one man to the other. The old man's lips were pale and speckled with brown and red. "What are *you* doing here, Tina, daughter of the help?"

"She's just a little girl, Rock. She doesn't care what a couple of boring old men talk about, do you, honey?"

At that moment, Tina thought of Bette. She wasn't allowed to see any of the actress's movies, but that didn't stop her from typing in her name on the internet and finding clips when Mama wasn't looking. Bette was so nice in person, but she could be scary when she had to play a part. Tina realized if she was going to get away from these two, she needed to pretend, just like Bette did. Only, she didn't think she could pretend to be mean enough to scare these two off. She decided to try something else. Mr. Franklin thought she was a dumb little kid, so when he asked her if she cared, Tina shook her head no and tried to look as young and innocent as she could.

"You see, Rock? She has no clue."

The old man ignored him. "What did you hear us say, Tina?"

Tina looked down, shrugged, and pushed some crushed rocks around with the toe of her shoe.

His cold, bony hand clutched her chin and tilted it up. He

looked hard into her eyes, and he gave her an even faker smile than Mr. Franklin's. "You're a very naughty little girl, out here all on your own. You could get into big trouble. Your mommy could get into even bigger trouble if someone finds out she let you run around loose. Do you know what I'm telling you?"

Tina nodded once. Her heart felt like it was about to beat right out of her chest. She felt light-headed, as if her insulin levels weren't right. And now she needed to pee really bad.

"Rock." Mr. Franklin laid a hand on the man's shoulder but he shrugged it off.

"Your mommy could get into so much trouble, you might never see her again. Sometimes, they take troublemaking little girls like you away from irresponsible mothers like her. And sometimes, irresponsible mothers simply go missing. So if I were you, Tina—" he looked at Mr. Franklin— "what's her last name?"

"Martinez." Tina watched his Adam's apple bob up and down when he said it.

Rock looked back at her. "Tina Martinez, I would never tell anyone a single word, or that you even saw us out here tonight. I would suggest that you find your way back to the party all by yourself and keep quiet as a mouse."

Tina glanced at Mr. Franklin just long enough to see him nod the way some teachers did when they wanted you to go along with something. So she nodded back to both of them.

The old man finally let go of her chin. She pushed past them and ran back down the path she'd taken. As she ran, she felt warm pee running down her legs. The second she was out of sight, she squatted and finished, horribly embarrassed that she'd wet herself—no better than one of the crybabies.

By the time Tina sneaked back through the window, it was full-dark. It was dark in the room, too—a movie was playing and had everyone's attention, so no one noticed her.

Tina didn't dare sit down. Scared, angry, embarrassed, and ashamed, she spent the rest of that horrible night standing at the back of the room as far from the window and the other kids as she could get. As the hours dragged by, she thought of the poor horses who might run the wrong way and what would happen to them.

Tina thought again about Bette, and how she'd once been scared of a man who tried to hurt her. Who *did* hurt her—who put her in a wheeling chair. *Would Rock come back and do that to me if I told? Would he do that to Mama? But what about the poor horses?*

No. Camden would stop them. He wouldn't let anything bad happen to Tina or Mama. If someone came near them, he would ask what the H-E-double-hockey-sticks was going on and even punch Rock right in his stupid face. He'd tell the Twins' mommy that Mr. Franklin might not be a stranger, but that he was dangerous anyway. Anybody who was friends with people who'd shoot horses if they didn't like the way they ran was a big jerk, no matter how friendly he pretended to be.

That made up Tina's mind. She would tell Mama and Camden about the horses. They would fix everything, and the horses would be safe, and Bette would tell Tina how brave she was.

Tina watched the silhouette of a woman come to the door. She hoped it was her mama, and was disappointed when the woman flipped on the light switch next to the door, then clapped her hands and announced it was time for the photos. The grownups corralled the kids into a line. Tina shook her head—no way was she going anywhere—and the mean crybaby lady again took her by the arm and pulled her into the line. Then, they marched through the mansion to the stage outside. All the grownups made "awww-ing" noises and clapped as the kids went up the steps and got into rows with the tallest kids in the back and the smallest in front. Tina hated that she was in the front. Now that the lights were shining on her, she could see her white socks were stained yellow. Just to make it worse, the boy next to her whispered, "You smell like pee," and scooted closer to the girl next to him, who shoved him back into Tina.

With the lights in her face, Tina couldn't make out any of the grownups past the first row, but that was bad enough. Mr. Franklin stood right at the center and stared at her.

The woman who came and got them clapped her hands again to get everyone's attention. "Big smiles, kids! We're going to take some photos and do a little filming."

The last thing Tina wanted to do was smile. Just because she couldn't see Mama or Camden it didn't mean they couldn't see her. If she frowned, they would know something was wrong. They'd come up and ask her and she'd tell them about the horses right there in front of everybody. So she gave the biggest frown she could, just to show everyone how upset she was.

"Smile, Tina," Mr. Franklin said. "Everyone likes pretty little girls who smile!" He pushed the corners of his mouth up with his pointer fingers into a fake smile.

And then he pointed in front of his chest toward the side of the stage. She glanced that way—and saw her mama standing next to the old man. He had his arm draped around her shoulders. They were both smiling at her, but their smiles were totally different. Mama's looked happy and real, while Rock's looked mean.

That's when Tina put it together. If these men's friends would shoot horses—they'd shoot her mama, and Camden, and Tina, and anyone else who they didn't like. That's what Mr. Franklin was trying to tell her with his pointing and fake smile. And it's what Rock said too, with his arm around

Mama's shoulders. They could tell their horse-hating friends, and there was nothing Tina could do to stop them.

"Smile, everyone! Smile!" Mr. Franklin shouted.

Except stay quiet. And smile.

So, she did.

Until the next day, when she couldn't smile anymore.

TWENTY-FIVE

I *t's my fault. My Goddammed fault.* Camden wanted to find both Rock Higley and Larry Franklin and tear them apart for hurting his little girl. And it was on him for allowing her to be in harm's way. *If I hadn't told her about the damn sundial. If I hadn't allowed Elena to get involved in the case. If I hadn't met them in the first place.*

Elena has every reason to hate me. When he looked into her eyes over Tina's head, he saw nothing but anguish.

"I tried to be brave like Bette, Mama. I tried to protect you and Camden. But the horses." The little girl dissolved into sobs.

"Sweet baby. Oh, my Pepita. It is not on you to be that brave, or to protect me or Camden or anyone else. That's our job, to protect you and keep you safe and happy."

Camden got up and knelt on the floor in front of Tina. He took her face in his hands.

"You *are* brave, Mermaid. You are the bravest person I know. Braver than any SEAL. Braver than Bette, and we both know that's saying a lot. Nobody's gonna get hurt, not you, not me, not your sweet Mama, nobody. There are no horses, sweetheart. Those bast—*men*—were talking about something else, something you don't need to worry about. But you know what, Mermaid? A lot of people who were in danger are going to be safe now because of you."

He kissed her forehead. "I'm gonna have to do my job now, and you helped with that. So much, when you never should have..." Camden squeezed his eyes shut against the guilt. When he opened them again, he said, "I made you some breakfast and you need to eat. That bad scare you had made you sick, and so we've gotta make sure you're okay. You and Mama are gonna go in the kitchen and eat, but I'm not taking my eyes off you. We're gonna figure it out, okay, brave girl? My Mermaid. I love you."

He looked into Elena's eyes. "I love both of you. So, so much."

Elena took his hand and squeezed it. Tears coursed down her cheeks, but she nodded and mouthed the words, *I love you.*

They went to the kitchen where Elena encouraged Tina to do more than pick at her food. Camden sat on the couch in the living room in the meantime, keeping an eye on them via the kitchen passthrough while talking quietly on the phone with Lachlan. Then they conferenced in Jake, Gina, Nash, and Costello.

"I can't believe Higley is involved in this," Lachlan said. "And the son of a bitch is untouchable."

"He slipped right under our radar," Jake said. "Jesus Christ, the man's been waving an American flag longer than I've been alive."

"Career politician, and yet he seemed to keep himself out of scandals. Too good to be true. When do you think they approached him?" Costello asked.

"I don't fucking care when they did," Camden said,

fighting to keep his voice low and even so as not to scare his woman and his girl. "All I care about is getting Elena and Tina into a safehouse fucking yesterday until we figure out the level of danger they're in and where it's coming from."

"Already done," Lachlan said. "I'm texting you the address now."

"Thanks, boss. I have an idea about how I want this to go down, to keep Elena and Tina as safe as possible and still fulfill the objective of flushing out the operatives," Camden said. "How many people can I get on security for the job?"

"I can't speak for anyone else in this room, but you've got me, brother," Jake said.

"I'm in," Gina said.

"We all are," Lachlan added.

Camden closed his eyes and gripped his phone in gratitude. "Thank you. You have no idea."

"I do, brother," Jake said. "You know I do."

"Yeah, I do know." Camden took a deep breath. "I want you to get Kyle in on this for sure. Pup's got good instincts. The rest of the personnel, I'll let you decide who's best for it, Lach. Here's my plan."

When Camden finished his call, he called Elena and Tina into the family room to join him on the couch. The little girl scratched Toby's ears. The dog was halfway on the couch, his head in Tina's lap. Both Elena and Tina looked exhausted. No, Elena looked downright devastated. *Gonna have to fix that.* But first, he had to get them to safety.

He wrapped his arm around Elena. She laid her head on his shoulder, never letting go of Tina.

"We're gonna talk about this, Gorgeous, I promise. But first—"

"You're taking us to a safehouse, aren't you?"

Camden's heart clenched at the resigned tone in Elena's

voice. This wasn't her first rodeo, or Tina's. "Yeah," he said, and kissed the top of her head. She turned her face to his neck.

"Do you trust me, Gorgeous?"

She looked up into his eyes and answered him in a strong and sure voice.

"With my life. With my daughter's life."

Her words burned into his heart. *I can't fail them. I will die before failing them.*

"Okay. I'm going to ask you to do some hard things. First up, you have five minutes to pack a bag. Don't worry about shampoo and all that crap, it'll be there like last time. Just pack important documents and the stuff you can't live without. You're gonna give me your cell phone, your e-reader, anything electronic that can be tracked." Elena started to speak and he held up a hand. "You'll have a burner phone to use. Mermaid, I'll help you while your mama gets her things together. Okay, let's go."

Camden stood and picked Tina up off Elena's lap. The little girl wrapped her arms around him and buried her face in his neck as if she'd done it her whole life. "I love you, too, Camden."

Camden fought back his own tears as his heart broke open. "Always and forever, Mermaid. That's how long I'll love you. Always and forever."

They pulled into the small Watchdog underground parking garage less than an hour later. Jake and Rachael met them there, Rachael fighting back tears. She took Tina from Elena's arms and they headed for the courtyard with Toby, while Camden led Elena to the conference room for a full briefing with Gina, Lachlan, Jake, Nash, Costello, and Kyle.

Elena related Tina's experience. When her voice hitched and she couldn't continue, Camden picked up the story as he tried to keep the rage out of his voice for Elena's sake.

When he finished speaking, Gina paced while she filled everyone in on the latest chatter. "The foreign operatives are excited about Bennett's big announcement last night and its reception. He's a shoo-in to the senate, and from there, the presidency. If it weren't for Tina overhearing that conversation, we wouldn't have a clue that Higley's in on it, or how they're planning on trapping Bennett. I can tell you that we've now got a guy handling the hacking side of things, but I can't tell you his identity for security reasons. We're also watching for Franklin to set up the phony accounts, and once he does, his ass is ours. The downside to all this is that it won't be long until they know that we know."

Gina stopped pacing in front of Elena, dropped down, and took her hands. "Elena, words are not enough to express both how grateful we are, and how devastated I am that your daughter had to witness that." Gina squeezed her eyes shut. "And that she's in danger for it. Because they're already talking about a possible loose end, and that can only mean one person."

"Oh my God." Elena turned paler than she already was as Camden wrapped her in his arms. Then his strong woman took a deep breath and pulled herself together. She smiled at him, her eyes full of gratitude and steel that made his heart pound.

She turned to the group. "What do I need to do to fix this?"

Lachlan took the pen stub out of his mouth. "Camden has a plan, and it involves you. Camden, you want to lay it out?"

This is it. This is where I might lose her. Camden swallowed his fear. "Babe, are you sure you want to be a part of this? It's gonna mean you're doing things you might not want to. We can work out something else."

She gripped his hand, strong and steady. "Oh, I'm sure."

Camden outlined his plan, including Elena's part in it.

When Camden was finished, Lachlan asked Elena, "Can you do this?"

"Absolutely. What's happening is wrong, not just because of what they did—what they *want* to do—to my daughter, but because this is an attack on all of us."

Camden squeezed her hand, his heart pounding with a crazy mix of pride and love and trepidation. But he knew no matter what, he would keep Tina and Elena out of harm's way. He would keep his family safe.

After dark, Camden's SUV pulled out of Watchdog's garage and drove to the safehouse, to watch and wait.

TWENTY-SIX

Elena made a nest for herself and Tina on the unfamiliar couch in the safehouse that night. Wrapped in blankets, propped up by pillows, and surrounded by all the stuffed animals Camden help Tina pack, Elena read Tina her favorite bedtime story, *The Wind in the Willows*. Camden was in the shower with a promise to join them as soon as he was done.

They were on chapter seven, "The Piper at the Gates of Dawn" about an adventurous young otter named Portly who goes missing one night. Elena almost skipped that chapter, thinking it was a little too close to home right now and afraid that it might upset Tina. Okay, the truth was, she was afraid she'd get too choked up to read it. But as always, the book pulled them right out of their world and into its story of the river and the friendly animals who lived there and went in search of little Portly. By the time Rat and Mole found the little otter as the sun rose—protected by the great Friend and Helper, the Piper—and brought him home to his family, Elena had almost forgotten her own troubles. Almost. Tina seemed much calmer too, and thoughtful.

She touched the illustration of the Piper. "I like him, Mama. I like how he kept Portly safe."

"I do, too, Baby."

"Mama?" Tina looked up at Elena, her sweet brown eyes filled with curiosity.

"Yes, Pepita?"

"In the story, when the sun rises, why does the Piper make Rat and Mole forget him?"

Damn, how do I answer that one? "Well, if he didn't, then he's all that Rat and Mole would ever think about, because he's so powerful and they love him. They wouldn't be able to let go of their image of him. Instead, he makes them forget so that they can go on with their lives on the river."

Tina scrunched up her forehead. "I still think it's sad that he makes them forget." She looked back down at the illustration. "Camden makes me feel safe, Mama. Just like the Piper." She looked back up at Elena. "Just like Papa used to."

Elena's heart cracked in half. She touched her shirt and felt Antonio's wedding ring under the fabric. She'd put the necklace back on before rushing from their apartment. "You still remember him, Pepita?"

Her daughter tilted her head and fixed Elena with a look that said, *duh.*

Elena tapped the tip of Tina's nose. "What do you remember about your Papa?"

"I remember how he used to pick me up and carry me around when he got home. When Camden carries me like that, I think of Papa. He helps me remember how it felt. So I feel double-happy."

Elena couldn't stop the tears coursing down her cheeks. *She remembers. My God, Camden isn't making her forget. Just the opposite.*

Tina wiped one of Elena's cheeks. "I'm sorry, Mama."

"Baby, no, these are happy tears. I am so, so, happy that you told me that." Elena pulled Tina to her and hugged her tightly.

"I love Camden, Mama. Do you?"

"I love Camden very much, Pepita."

"You should ask him to marry you."

Elena laughed and looked down at her daughter. "You think so, huh?"

Tina nodded. "I asked Robert from school to marry me."

Elena's eyes went round. "Robert who?"

"Robert Brogan. But he said he'd have to think about it. He said maybe when we're older."

Elena laughed again. "I like his style."

"Like, in second grade."

Oh, boy.

"But I think you should ask Camden to marry you tonight." Tina looked serious as she pulled at Elena's necklace until Antonio's wedding ring slipped out from the top of her shirt. "You could even give him Papa's ring. Then it wouldn't keep hiding in your shirt. You could see it all the time on Camden's finger, and it would remind you of Papa, and it would make you double-happy too."

Elena inhaled quickly and bit her bottom lip. Her heart skipped a beat. How could her daughter be so wrong and yet so right at the same time? Elena was hiding the ring—from Camden or from herself, she didn't know. Maybe both. What she did know was that as long as she hid it, she'd never be able to let Antonio go, or let Camden fully into her heart.

"I have an even better idea, Mermaid." Elena slipped the necklace over her head and put it in Tina's hand. She closed her daughter's fingers over it. "I'm going to give it to you to keep. We're going to find a safe place to keep it for every day, but you can wear it on special occasions." Elena stuck her finger up. "And don't let me catch you giving it to Robert Brogan, now or in second grade. Deal?"

Tina looked at the golden ring and chain in her hand, then grinned up at Elena. "Deal."

"Then let's think of a good place for you to keep it," Elena said, when movement caught her eye.

Camden stood in the doorway watching them. His expression unreadable, she wondered how much he'd overheard.

Tina jumped off the couch and ran to Camden. Like a reflex, he bent and picked her up.

"Mama and I were just talking about you."

He cupped the back of Tina's head and cradled her against him. He looked at Elena through a glaze of unshed tears. "All good things?" he asked, his voice rough.

"All good things," Tina replied.

"Is it okay if I talk to your mama for a minute? You could go get Toby a treat. The box is on the kitchen counter."

Tina nodded and he set her down. His gaze had stayed locked on Elena's the entire time. The minute Tina was out of the room, he strode to Elena and pulled her up into his arms. His lips crashed down onto hers—wanting, needing, devouring. Her moan escaped straight into his mouth while his fingers tangled in her hair. She brushed a thumb across his cheek and felt wetness there. Elena broke the kiss to look at her man. Sure enough, another tear escaped down his cheek, and yet he gave her the goofiest smile. *That's my Joker.*

"So, I guess you heard me talking to Tina."

"You called her Mermaid."

"Did I?" She hadn't even realized. The name just slipped out.

Camden read her puzzled expression. "Yes, you did. That's the first time I've heard you use my nickname for her."

"I think it's the first time I've said it." Elena thought back. "But, I've never heard you call her Pepita."

"I haven't because that was Antonio's name for her." He held up a hand. "Don't think for a second that I don't use it because I'm jealous or any stupid shit like that. That's the name her daddy gave her. It's special...sacred, in a way. I decided the moment that I knew the origin behind it that I wouldn't call her that. Not my place to. Instead, she's my Mermaid."

Elena grinned. "That she is."

Camden rubbed his thumb over Elena's cheekbone. "So, while I'm beside myself with pride and happiness that you called her that, too, because that means..."—he blinked back more tears—"it means...I can't put it into the right words. The words aren't big enough to describe it, how good it feels to hear you say my nickname for her."

"Oh, Camden." Elena blinked back her own tears.

"But I never want you to stop calling her Pepita. That's her name, too. Her legacy, her heritage from her father." He slipped his hands into hers and sat her back on the couch. Instead of sitting next to her, he knelt on the floor in front of Elena.

Still holding her hands, he said, "Just like I would never make you give up your last name, or insist Tina change hers to mine. That's her daddy's name, and he was a good man who shouldn't be forgotten. But I'd be honored if one day you'd add my name to yours and hers. After I've proven myself."

Elena stopped fighting back her happy tears. "You've already proven yourself, God, so many times over." She swallowed hard. "So, is this your way of asking me if I'll marry you?"

Camden's goofy smile returned and he shrugged. "Well, I

heard a rumor that the Martinez girls like to ask their men to marry them, and I'd hate to deprive you of that opportunity."

Elena laughed. "I'm a bit more old-fashioned than my daughter."

"In that case," he brought her hands to his lips and kissed her fingers, "Elena Martinez, I love you and your daughter more than life itself. I would do anything for both of you. Would you do me the incredible honor of being my wife? Of letting me help you raise the sweetest, spunkiest mermaid girl who ever graced the earth? I promise to always be faithful, to cherish you, to protect you, and to make you happy every single day."

Elena didn't hesitate. "I love you. *We* love you. And we'd both be honored to carry your name, too."

Camden's amber eyes shone. He pulled her in tight and squeezed her tightly, in that way that made her feel safe and loved and cherished. "I love you so much, Elena. So damned much. You brought my heart back to life. It's yours."

M onday afternoon, Elena's heart weighed heavy as she explored the safehouse. Technically, it had every-thing they needed—a fully-stocked kitchen, three bedrooms, two bathrooms, cable, a fenced-in backyard surrounded by tall trees and shrubs that gave them plenty of privacy, and a top-notch security system—augmented by Watchdog security guards hiding outside. But it could have been a cardboard box or a ten-bedroom mansion for all that Elena cared. She'd spent so much of her life in precarious circumstances, if not outright danger. The only time she'd ever had a safe and happy home was during the first years of her marriage, spent on the ranch with Antonio. She thought she'd found that again with Camden in her little apartment in L.A. *Just an illusion.*

When would she and Tina be safe, if ever? She prayed it would be soon.

Her phone pinged, a text from Rachael. She'd insisted on going into hiding with them, and only Elena could convince her not to, so now she was blowing up Elena's phone practically every five minutes with a new text or photo, just to say she was there and that she loved her.

L ove you too, Chica! BFFs always, sister of my heart

S miling, Elena added a string of heart emojis and an angel. Rachael had the kindest heart of anyone Elena knew, a miracle considering her dark upbringing. She could have become a monster like her father, but she chose the path of goodness instead. So different from Cici, it turned out. The more Elena thought of the woman who claimed to be her friend, the more her anger threatened to spill out. *Deep breaths.* Memories of Cici crying now infuriated her. The woman was directly responsible for putting Tina in danger, all because she wanted to influence Elena, even use her to try and get information about what Watchdog knew of her past. And for what? To save her reputation? To spare her from being honest and upfront about her choices?

Infuriating. *Enough of this.*

Now that she'd worked herself up sufficiently, Elena dialed Cici's number. Walking to the nearest bedroom, she looked over her shoulder to make sure Camden was still with Tina in the living room. He glanced up at her. With his laptop open on the coffee table, he pointed the remote at the TV, scrolling for something appropriate for Tina to watch while he worked.

"Elena," Cici answered, her voice bubbly. "You must have read my mind; I was just about to call you. Hey, I was at Brant and Phillips this morning and I was surprised to see you'd moved on. Everything all right?"

"Yeah, Cici. Everything is just fine. I've taken a new position with Delia's, thanks to the catering job, actually." Her voice wavered.

"That's terrific! I am so glad I could help." A little of the bubbly left Cici's voice, replaced with doubt.

"Oh, you've helped all right. See the thing is, I can't start at Delia's right away because I'm here at Camden's house making sure my daughter is okay."

"You're at Camden's house with Tina? What's wrong? Is it the diabetes?" If Elena didn't know any better, she'd think the woman's concern was genuine. Instead, it felt like she was tipping someone off.

"Indirectly. You see, her blood sugar crashed Saturday night after the event. It can do that sometimes during an illness or under stress. Or when someone has a bad scare."

Cici paused. "Goodness, is she coming down with something? I'd bring some chicken soup by Camden's, except you know I don't cook." Her tinkling laughter sounded hollow.

"Cut the crap, Cici. I think you know exactly why my daughter's blood sugar crashed. I think it's also why you stopped by Brant and Phillips today." By now, Elena's voice was shaking with rage. "I'm going to say this once, from one mother to another. Leave my daughter alone. She's just a little girl, she doesn't know anything."

Cici drew in a breath. "*Really*. What did she tell you?" All pretense of warmth had left Cici's voice.

"Not a word. She's too scared. She says she heard two men talking by accident and they threatened her, but she won't tell me who they were or what they said. I suspect one of them was Lawrence, just from what I know about you."

"What do you mean by that?" Pure ice.

"I told you to cut the shit and instead you double-down on it. I'm not stupid. Lawrence is the father of your first son, isn't he? He's protecting you, like he always has.

Cici's breath hitched. "Yes, he is. I don't know how they found out, but the boy's parents know I'm the mother. Larry told me about them today. They threatened to go public, to tell everyone how the wife of the candidate who puts families first had a baby out of wedlock and put it up for adoption. They want money, lots of it. They even threatened to say he had cocaine in his system when he was born. They're lying, but that doesn't matter, people will believe what they want to hear. Roger's opponents will run with it. And my twins will always doubt me, if not hate me outright."

"And now you're threatening *my* daughter to keep you safe. How do you think *my* daughter feels right now? How do you think *I* feel?"

"It's not me! I'm not threatening anyone. I never wanted to hurt anybody. You know that. I'm a good person, Elena. You know how it is when you're a mom. You have to make the tough choices for your family. I'm a good person. I've helped a lot of women who didn't have the same choices I did. I helped *you*."

"*Helped* me? You've condemned me and Tina to a life of hiding."

"Hiding? What do you mean? You just told me you're at Camden's." Cici's voice changed.

"I didn't...that's, yeah, I'm at Camden's," Elena lied. She heard Camden's footsteps approaching the bedroom.

"Elena, it doesn't have to be like this. I can still help you. I'm headed to Larry's. We can figure this out."

"Elena? Who the hell are you talking to?" Camden's voice boomed. "You know you aren't supposed to...get off the damn phone!"

Sounding panicked, Elena said, "Bye Rachael, thanks for calling and checking up. I'll tell Camden you said hi." Elena hit end. She turned and went straight into Camden's waiting arms.

"Did it work?" She looked up into his eyes.

He was all-smiles. "Yeah, Gorgeous, it worked like a charm. I watched the app on the laptop the minute you made the call. I came in as soon as Gina's techie guy pinged that your call had been traced to the safehouse. I imagine if they hadn't finished tracing it, Cici would be giving you a call back until they could pinpoint you."

Elena shook her head. "She's desperate. I think she honestly didn't mean to ever hurt anyone."

"But by hiding her truth and letting Larry fight her battles in the meantime, she's come to this place, and she's ready to sacrifice you and Tina to keep herself safe."

Elena hated asking the next question. "Now what?"

He brushed his hand down her hair. "We wait, but I don't think it'll be long. I'm thinking they'll hit the house tonight, before we have a chance to relocate you."

Elena blew out a breath and laid her cheek against his chest. "I'm scared, Camden."

"Hey." He tilted her chin up. "As I said, I'm keeping you guys safe."

She touched his cheek. "I know you are. But I'm worried about *you*. Who will keep you safe?"

"My brothers and sisters at Watchdog." He kissed her. "Time to go to work."

"Mama, can we read about the Piper again?" Tina asked that night. Elena had moved their nest to the bedroom. She hadn't let her daughter out of her sight for the rest of the day.

"Of course, Pepita. Then it's lights out, okay? Been a long day."

"Why can't Camden be in here with us too?" Tina snuggled up to Elena. "He hasn't heard the story yet. Neither have the people in the front room."

"Baby, Camden's out there protecting us right now and so are they. We can read him the story after he stops the bad guys." *Please, God let him stop the bad guys.*

"Tonight?"

"Tonight."

"Then we can all go home?"

"Yes, we can, Pepita."

"And you'll marry Camden?"

Elena tousled Tina's hair. "Yes, I'll marry Camden."

Tina was fast asleep when Elena turned off the bedside lamp. She lay awake in the dark, waiting for a sound—any sound—that would tell her what the morning would bring.

She didn't have to wait nearly as long as she thought.

TWENTY-SEVEN

C amden waited in the shadows outside the safehouse. Lachlan had picked this one carefully, making sure there were plenty of trees and places to hide, that it was just isolated enough to keep innocent bystanders safe in case of trouble. And tonight, there would be plenty of trouble.

He put on his night-vision goggles and tried to picture the scene as an intruder would: two lights on at the back of the house, one in the living room that flickered from the television, and one in the bedroom. He's up playing a video game, she's in bed looking at her phone, and the kid's probably with her. He wondered if they'd watched the house all evening, watched their silhouettes passing in front of the windows, waiting for Elena and Tina to finally go to bed, hoping Camden wasn't with them. The easier to take them down.

The bedroom light went out.

He imagined Elena lying wide awake in bed, heart pounding, Tina curled up at her side. *This is gonna all be over tonight, Gorgeous. Tomorrow's a new day when I go to buy you an engagement ring. Just hang tight, Baby.*

An hour went by and then, "Joker, we have movement," Jake said over the communicator. He was in the back yard with Camden.

"Copy that, Crooner." Camden caught sight of them a moment later.

"Copy," Costello said from behind the bushes beside the front door.

"Copy. On the move." That was Kyle inside the house getting into position for a breach. Camden heard an excited whine and the click of a leash unhooked.

"Copy," Gina said, also inside. "In position."

Camden and Jake waited for the figures to get closer to the house before closing in behind them.

"Two unfriendlies," Jake said.

"Two more coming for the door," Costello reported.

Two shadowy figures approached the house through the yard. They split off, target one going for the back door and target two toward the bedroom window. Camden motioned for Jake to take target two, who was looking in the bedroom window. Was he just confirming Elena and Tina's presence inside or would he try to get in that way? Either way, Jake would neutralize him.

Camden had his own target to worry about. The guy made quick work of the back door then made a beeline down the hall straight for the bedroom. As Camden pursued, Jake reported that he'd neutralized his target while Costello reported that his two targets had breached the front door.

Where they faced Kyle and an extremely pissed-off and protective Toby. Given the choice, Camden would have rather taken his chances with a dozen SEALs than one well-trained military dog, especially one who was protecting his favorite girl. Camden heard Toby lunging for one of the targets, then the man's screams coming through his earbuds and filling the house.

Camden sprinted down the hallway after the last target who already had his own gun out and aimed at the woman on the bed. Camden grabbed him and shoved his Glock 19 into the guy's neck just as he fired off three rounds.

But Gina was ready for it. She'd already rolled off the bed and charged him while Camden pulled the trigger. They'd wanted to bring the targets in alive for questioning, but he wouldn't do it at the expense of one of his teammates.

"You okay?" he asked Gina. She nodded and pointed back down the hall. They made their way back to the living room in the decoy safehouse, miles from where Elena and Tina waited, guarded by Lachlan and Nashville who reported no activity. Camden wished he could ask Gina for the identity of the tech genius who managed to bounce the phone signals from Elena's new phone to her old one in the decoy house. He owed the man a bottle of Pappy Van Winkle.

"What the fuck?" Jake's voice came over the system. "Joker, we have a situation."

"Copy, Crooner."

Gina kept on going to the living room while Camden veered off to the back to give Jake support. Glock drawn, he thought they had more incoming, and was surprised to hear Jake suddenly counting rapidly. *That's...he's doing CPR.*

Sure enough, when Camden looked out the back door, he saw Jake doing compressions on the target's chest.

"What the hell, brother?"

"Think...the asshole...had a heart attack...." Jake answered as he continued compressions. "Thirty. Give him a breath and we'll switch."

"Fuck." The last thing Camden wanted to do was lip-lock with the son of a bitch sent to kill his family, but they needed him alive. He took a breath and bent toward the asshole's face when Gina tore out the back door.

"Stop!" she yelled. "Don't go anywhere near his mouth!"

"The fuck, Spooky?"

She'd reached them and examined the target. "Same as the one inside. Jesus. It was a suicide mission." She looked at Camden. "Cyanide capsules or some such. One bite, done." She blew out a long breath. "You would have been next if you'd tried to resuscitate him."

"No shit?" Camden and Jake both jumped up and backed away at the same time.

Gina actually snorted. "What, the guy's not gonna explode. I don't think. Doesn't look wired." She looked up at her teammates. "They never gave you SEALs kill pills on a mission?"

"Fuck no," Camden answered. "They didn't generally send us on suicide missions. We cost too much to replace."

Gina considered that. "I guess I didn't cost as much."

Back inside, Kyle and Costello filled them in on their situation. After Toby had lunged for the third target, who went down screaming, the fourth target turned to escape and ran straight into Costello. They fought until Costello had him pinned. He suddenly convulsed just as Gina got to them. If it weren't for her, the team might have lost both Camden and Costello, ironically as they were trying to save their targets' lives. Target three was currently unconscious and bleeding, the kill pill removed from his mouth. Kyle was tending his wounds. Toby was off in the corner enjoying a well-earned Kong, his favorite toy in the whole world.

Jake laid a hand on Camden's shoulder. "One out of four ain't bad, brother."

"If they can even get him to talk. The guy was ready to die. They all were."

Gina approached them. "Not your problem anymore. His ride should be here in five. They'll take it from there. Clean-up crew, too."

Camden watched Kyle administer a sedative as target three started to groan and rouse himself. "Will we ever know their identities?"

Gina gave him a whiplash grin. "I can neither confirm nor deny that you'll be informed."

"That's our Spooky little girl," Jake said.

She rolled her eyes and went to the front window.

"Such a way with the women, brother. It's still a shock to me that you landed Rachael."

"Birds of a feather. Speaking of, have you called Elena to let her know?"

"Not yet. Lach's told her the mission's complete, no causalities on our side. I want to talk to her in person, not over a damn phone. I want to hold her and make sure she's okay."

"I hear you."

"I don't suppose you know of any all-night jewelry stores?" Camden joked.

Jake's face practically split in half with his smile. "You're gonna ask her."

"Already did, but being the impulsive dumbass I am, I didn't have a ring."

"So? Neither did I."

"Yeah, I knew that already. Just proves what a dumbass I am."

"I could call my mom, have her pull some strings," Jake said.

Camden frowned. "Ms. C. doesn't do that prima donna shit. Besides, I don't want to wake her up."

"No, brother, she and Dad are night owls. And she'd be thrilled to do this for you." Jake pulled out his cell.

"Fuck. Really? No."

Jake held up a finger. "Mom, yeah, hi, no, everything's fine. No, it is. Yeah, I promise. But Camden needs a favor."

"No, I don't, Ms. C.," Camden said loudly.

"He does, and you'll love it."

Two hours later, Camden found himself browsing rings with the sleepy owner of a jewelry store and a wide-awake movie star who did absolutely love it.

TWENTY-EIGHT

As she watched the sky grow lighter through the bedroom window curtains, Elena heard the front door open and a dog's leash and collar clinking. She jumped out of bed and ran down the hall, straight into Camden's waiting arms. He picked her up and swung her.

"It's over, Gorgeous. You're both safe."

"We'll let you two take it from here," Lach said, nudging Nashville. Both men stood up from the couch, which Toby took over, chewing on a new toy.

"Thank you guys, so much," Elena said as they let themselves out.

"Our pleasure, sweetheart." Lach smiled at her and gave Camden a chin-lift. "Take the morning off, but the team needs to debrief this afternoon. Gina'll have more information then. And she might even share."

"Thanks, boss. Just so you know, Pup did good tonight. He handled Toby like a champ, kept his cool, and because of him, we still have someone to question."

Lachlan nodded. "Good call, including him. He's finding his place." He closed the door behind him.

Elena started to ask Camden about the night when he kissed her, and all rational thought melted.

When he let her up for air, she asked, "Are you sure? Won't they come after us again?"

He shook his head and led her to the couch in front of the TV. It looked like Lach and Nash had been watching the early morning news with the sound muted. On the screen was a photo of Senator Bigley in younger, healthier days. Camden hit the unmute button.

"...passed away peacefully in his sleep late last night. The cause of death has not been released, but the senator had been quietly fighting lung cancer for a year. Senator Bigley surprised the nation with his announcement just last Saturday that he wouldn't be seeking another term, and instead endorsed Hollywood actor and political hopeful for the House, Roger Bennett for his senatorial seat. Now that..."

The announcer's voice faded from Elena's awareness as she looked at Camden. "That's not a coincidence, is it?"

"No, it is not, Gorgeous. Not after what I saw last night. I don't think the senator passed away peacefully at all, and I'll be damned if it was from natural causes." He glanced at the screen then back to her. "Don't be surprised if they call it a heart attack."

"What's going to happen with Roger and Lawrence? And Cici?"

"I'll know more after the debriefing this afternoon. Maybe. Depends on what Gina can tell us. But, my guess is that Lawrence will be quietly removed from Bennett's campaign. Probably take a trip out of the country. Roger might even be at the debriefing, and he'll have some choices to make after that. Or, our side will treat him like a mushroom."

"A mushroom?"

"Yeah, babe. Keep him in the dark and feed him shit."

Camden shrugged. "It's why I hate politics. Love my country, hate the game-playing." He smiled down at her. "But, you and Tina are safe, and that is the most important thing right now." He grinned and his cheeks flushed red. "Well, that and this." He dropped to one knee.

What the heck? Elna giggled. "Um, did you hit your head tonight? We did this already."

Camden pursed his lips and tilted his head. "Yes and no. I did ask you to marry me already because I want to be in your life and Tina's life. But I did it wrong because I was so damn happy. Time to fix that." He reached into his pocket as Elena's heart skipped a half-dozen beats.

"What? When did you..." Her voice trailed off when he opened the little box and revealed the most beautiful engagement ring she'd ever seen. On either side of the diamond was a deep blue sapphire. Camden pointed to the one on the left.

"That stone represents our little Mermaid." Then he touched the other one and looked up at her, his eyes shining. "And, I'm hoping that this stone will one day mean we've got another little one running around."

Elena covered her mouth as Camden's face blurred. She couldn't speak. Of course she wanted more children, the more the better. And Camden would make the perfect father. He already was, for Tina.

"So, Elena, will you accept this ring and marry me?"

"Yes, on one condition. You'd better be ready to add more gems to that ring."

His face glowed with happiness. He stood and took her in his arms. "All the gems you want. I am so honored that you want me to be the father of your next child. You have me, heart and soul."

"You have me, too, Camden. I never thought, never *dreamed*, that I'd find someone as good and loving as Antonio again. Someone who also loves my daughter, who only has her best interests at heart. From the very first moment I saw you carrying her, there was love in your eyes. Love and worry that she was hurt. But she wasn't hurt, she was fine because you saved her. You saved her life, Camden, and you saved me. You still make both of us feel loved and protected. Cherished." She stroked his cheek, running her thumb over his stubble. "I love you."

She watched Camden swallow the lump in his throat before he pulled her in close and tight. "Then I'm damn lucky, too. I love you, Elena. I will spend every day making sure you feel that love all the way down to your soul." He pressed his lips against her ear. "And I'll spend my nights making sure you feel it everywhere else."

Behind her, she heard the bedroom door open and tiny feet pad down the hall. "Mom? Mama?"

"Here, Pepita, here in the TV room. Guess who's back?"

But Tina didn't have to guess, because Toby was up and headed her way at the very first sound.

"Toby! Is Daddy here, too? Is he, boy?"

If Elena thought she was happy a moment ago, she was wrong—*this* was happiness, her daughter calling the man Elena loved, Daddy. A good, loving man who deserved the name.

The sun took that moment to shine through the window over Elena and Camden's shoulders and into Tina's face as she approached them. She shielded her eyes with her hand and smiled. Camden scooped her up and the three of them hugged.

"Good morning, Friend and Helper," Tina said, then kissed his cheek.

"Friend and helper?" Camden looked at Tina, puzzled.

"*The Wind in The Willows*," Elena said. "We'll read it together tonight. At home."

O*ne week later*
       They got to Santa Monica Beach a little before sunset. Camden had a new magic trick for Tina, one he'd promised her weeks before.

"It won't be exact-exact, Mermaid, but pretty close this time of year." He took the book bag holding his thin laptop from Elena and opened it. After a few clicks, a window popped up and a man's face appeared on the screen. Camden knelt in the sand so Tina could see.

"Say hi to my buddy, Hatch."

"Hi, Hatch."

"Hi, Tina." The man in desert fatigues waved.

"I told him about what you wanted to do and he agreed that it was an awesome idea. So, he's all set up, ready to catch the sunrise while we're watching the sunset. Can't tell you exactly where though, that's classified."

Tina's mouth became a perfect O. "Thanks, Mr. Hatch."

Hatch grinned at the little girl. "My pleasure, miss. Here we go." He turned the camera away to face the brightening horizon. Elena stood behind Camden, her hands on his shoulders as he sat in the sand next to Tina. He held the laptop in one hand and reached for hers with the other.

Together, her family watched the sunset over the Pacific at the end of one day even as they watched it rise to begin the next.

TWENTY-NINE

Two months later, December

Kyle McGuire

"No! No no no *no!*" Kyle slammed his fists on his office desk hard enough to make the cell phone jump. "This can't be possible."

"Sorry, man," Kyle's old teammate said over the phone's speaker. "Just found out today. He's been out of the service for a month and Stateside three weeks now. They moved him to Colorado."

"I was supposed to get a call. *Fuck!* They promised." Kyle rubbed his temples to keep himself from throwing the phone at the wall. *Deep breaths. In, hold, and out.*

"It's all there in the email I sent. I'm sorry, man."

"No, man, it's cool. Thanks for telling me. You're taking a risk, and I appreciate you having my six."

"You always had mine, brother. That's the truth."

That stung, but it was an old pain, familiar, and he didn't have time to think about it now. "I'm gonna figure this out. They can't do this to him." *Or me.* "They promised."

"Here's hoping for the best, McGuire."

"Thanks. You stay safe, Flint."

Kyle hung up. He looked around his office at Watchdog. The building was quiet, he'd gotten in extra-early. With the holidays coming up, all he wanted was to keep busy. He'd work straight through them, even take other people's shifts if they wanted. He had nothing better to do, and no intention of spending the holidays with his parents. It was hard enough to be a failure on his own, let alone in front of them.

He would've felt differently about Christmas, wouldn't have to spend it alone, if things had gone as they were supposed to. As he'd been promised they'd go.

But that was the military for you. They promised you the world, then used you until you broke, then tossed you aside. Like they did to him. Like they'd just done to Camo.

Deep breaths. In, hold, out.

He opened the email Flint sent him. Sure enough, there was the order. Camo had been decommissioned, brought Stateside, and then adopted out to a woman living on a ranch in Colorado. Who the fuck was she? Camo didn't even know her, and she'd had him for three whole goddamned weeks.

Goddammit. Camo was *his* partner. The dog was supposed to go to him, not some stranger. He'd put in the paperwork. He'd called and emailed until they told him that if he contacted them one more time, they'd lose his paperwork.

Looks like it didn't take one more time. *Fucking bastards.*

He had to get to Colorado, ASAP.

Kyle put his head in his hands. He was still the FNG at Watchdog, didn't have vacation hours saved up. And it was Christmas. He'd already told people he'd work for them. And, there was the ongoing case with the Bennetts. Jesus, what a shitshow *that* turned out to be. The one enemy combatant who didn't get a chance to off himself wouldn't talk, no surprise there. But they'd traced his identity along with the others, and that's where things got weird. Gina wasn't at liberty to tell them who any of them were, but she could tell the team their nationalities. One Russian. *Two* Americans, Christ.

And a Kiwi. Freekin' New Zealand? What the hell?

None of it made sense to Kyle, though it sure put Gina on edge. Lachlan, too. Well, the bennies that went along with being the FNG meant it was above his paygrade to figure that part out. He'd done his job that night, he kept Toby from getting hurt and from killing the combatant. Even patched the guy up. It paid to know how to keep a dog alive and well in the field—sometimes humans weren't all that far from dogs.

Just nowhere near as loyal and compassionate.

But Kyle was loyal. To a fault, his buddies told him. And maybe he'd lost some of his compassion along the way, but he'd find it again with Camo, if only for the dog's sake.

The ranch's address was right there in the email. Kyle already had it committed to memory.

Fuck it. He'd just have to tell Lachlan he needed the time off. Family emergency. It wasn't a lie, not really. Sometimes, you had family by blood, sometimes you found your family. And Camo was family. So, he'd wait until Lachlan got in, then ask—no, demand—time off, or else he'd quit. Simple as that. *Important* as that.

He prayed to God Lachlan would understand and give him the time off. He needed this job. It was the only thing that gave him a purpose, the only place where he'd found any semblance of brotherhood since the service. So, he'd ask for the time off and hope.

Then he'd fly to Colorado, find the ranch, find Camo. Bring him home.

And whoever this woman, this Arden Volker was, she didn't stand a chance.

―――――

Kyle and Arden's story continues in More Than Puppy Love, A Watchdog Security Christmas Novel

Olivia's Lovelies

Never miss a release from Olivia Michaels by signing up for the Olivia Michaels Romance Newsletter. Be the first to read advance excerpts, see cover previews, and enter giveaways at https://oliviamichaelsromance.com/

Want more? Come be one of Olivia's Lovelies on Facebook and talk to the author!
https://www.facebook.com/groups/639545290309740/

ALSO BY OLIVIA MICHAELS

Romantic Suspense

Watchdog Security Series

More Than Love

More Than Family

More Than Puppy Love: A Christmas Novel

More Than Paradise (Coming Soon)

More Than Thrills (Coming Soon)

More Than Words Can Say (Coming Soon)

More Than Beauty (Coming Soon)

More Than Secrets (Coming Soon)

More Than Life (Coming Soon)

ACKNOWLEDGMENTS

As always, thank you, Reader, for giving me chance. 2020 has been a roller coaster for all of us and I hope that my books have given you a fun break from reality. Stay safe out there.

I hope to see you around on Facebook, or join the newsletter at oliviamichaelsromance.com so I can thank you personally!

A special thanks to Caitlyn O'Leary, Riley Edwards, Trinity Wilde, Ophelia Bell, and my amazing ARC readers who keep me going.

ABOUT THE AUTHOR

Olivia Michaels is a life-long reader, dog-lover, gardener, and a certified beachaholic. When she's not throwing a Frisbee for her fur-baby, harvesting tomatoes, or writing, you can find her playing in the surf, kayaking, or kicking back on the sand and cracking open a romantic beach read.

Made in the USA
Columbia, SC
11 May 2021